MALEVOLENCE
AND
MUD

A Mystery Where Murder Solves
More Problems Than It Causes

JOHN FARNELL

Published by Sorviodunum Books of London

First published 2025

ISBN: 978-1-7396394-8-8 Paperback

Copyright © John A. Farnell, 2025
All rights reserved

For Sam and the boys

Chapter 1

Evening, Third Day of Gorst
Year 549 of The Brastmere

Some nights, I have regrets. Other nights I have pigeon. Tonight? Both.
I retrieve supper from the desk drawer. Pigeon pie—squashed and leaking gravy like an open wound. "Almost warm," I tell myself with a crooked grin. I tear off a chunk of crust, toss it into my mouth and chew loudly. Morsels land on my tunic and the desk, forming a small, pathetic constellation of neglect.
Outside my window, a pigeon. Nature's little street prophet huddles in a corner, looking in. Both of us scavengers on the margins. Both one wrong move away from ending up in someone else's dinner plans.
There's a creak out on the stairs, then silence. I wait, listening. Nothing, just the building settling, shifting like an old man in his sleep. I take a sip of mead and let it go.
In a world of chainmail and tunics, my coat, my hat, the way I talk, the way I think—aren't quirks; they're tools of the trade, keeping me one step ahead. Some call me a private eye, others a detective. Names shift, but the job stays the same: finding what's lost, uncovering what's buried, and making sure the right people regret it.
What matters is my way with words—they're my weapon, my lockpick—quick enough to tangle, ruthless enough to rip the

truth from people who'd rather choke on it. People learn quick that I'm not here to fit in. I'm here to find the truth and maybe a little trouble along the way.

Tracing the rim of an empty tankard, my aching bones ponder the dubious comfort of my chair versus the honest hardness of the floor. The detective game's a fickle mistress. Most jobs barely cover costs, let alone a decent meal and a bed. Some days, you're chasing wayward pets and marital indiscretions. Others, you stumble onto conspiracies that are best left alone—but getting paid? That's where the real mystery lies.

The stack of unpaid debts in my corner has become a tower with its own shadow. Perhaps my luck will change tomorrow, but tonight it's just me, the pigeon, and the ghosts of every questionable decision that's led to this.

A wax sealed litterae clausae slips under my door like a blade between friends. I snatch a dagger from my desk and let it fly, pinning the letter before it can skitter away. Outside, quick footsteps betray the messenger's retreat. No knocking, no pleasantries—just the sound of someone eager to be elsewhere.

I rise and step to the window. Below, a figure steps into the street. Stocky, purposeful, his shoulders hunched against the night, he moves like a man with no interest in being followed. I catch the flash of thick, curly ginger hair, wild and unmistakable beneath his hood. His beard matches—dense and rust-hued, bristling like a thicket around his jaw.

I return to the knife on the floor and pry it free with a grunt. There's an unbroken wax seal, deep and red. My fingers read its texture like a blind man reading fate. I turn it over, my thumb tracing the fine strokes of the name written on the front. Detective Noel MacAllister.

The main text unfolds in precise, measured handwriting. *Concerning the inheritance of your late aunt's estate.* Formal provisions drone on, but then something catches me. The Mayor, Ellington Crumley, wants MacAllister Hall. It's signed Darius Drummond, Bailiff.

The letter joins the other junk on my desk. Lost among unpaid debts, unanswered questions, and empty flagons that promised solace—but only deliver silence.

I light a pipe and watch the smoke curl like a bad omen. The past is a dog with a scent—it never lets go, just circles back, jaws snapping when you least expect it. And now it's found me—fresh meat.

Ah... Murder's Vale. You don't leave that place so much as slip through its fingers. But I did—just a scrap of a boy with an itch to see what the world looked like without a noose around its neck. That's how I ended up in the big smoke—the city devoured me whole, bones and all. Is it any better than the Vale? Sure. But in some ways, it's the same—if you want to survive. Here, we sleep in our armour, ready to engage. But that's nothing compared to the Vale.

I swore I'd never go back. But here's the truth, the one that always gets you in the end: I need the money. And regrets? I've got room for more.

Damn. Looks like I'm heading back. The thought tastes like prophecy and poison.

Trouble is—this hard-boiled city drawl won't do me any favours. Too sharp, too self-assured. City folk weave their words like a shell game—smooth, shadowed, every syllable implying something just out of reach. But the Vale? Words aren't currency there. They're more like cattle: slow, stubborn, and only useful in the right hands. Best to blend in, walk like I belong, talk like I never left. Swap my clipped speech for something looser. Grunts and shrugs should do it.

I gather my essentials and lock up. The streets are dark and quiet on the way to my transport, the silence thick with questions about what kind of welcome Murder's Vale has in store. But my plan is simple—handle the inheritance, sell the property, and slip the trap.

Will I survive? Not sure.

Chapter 2

People used to call me clever—yeah, the kind of clever that gets you killed in interesting ways. A rat who knows every trap yet still takes the bait. So, what's my latest stroke of genius? Crawling back to my childhood home, that dank little corner of purgatory where hope goes to drown.

I'm wedged inside the only transport headed that way—a merchant's wagon; stuck between crates of pickled trotters and an angry old lady.

Our driver, stooped and weathered as a gravestone, has the personality of a boot. He maintains a constant watch beneath a battered cap. The horses plod along muck-churned roads, following the twisted path through villages and, eventually, to my home village in Murder's Vale. Each jolt sends me lurching against the crates, their edges marking me like a child's torture device.

We crawl through a landscape that's all mist choked fields and sodden hedgerows, painted in shades of grey and brown. Even the road feels reluctant, as if apologising for every turn that brings us closer.

The old lady leans toward me, her eyes glinting. "You're a MacAllister, aren't you? I'd recognise that weasel look anywhere. Why hasn't someone murdered you yet?" she mutters, eyes narrowing, as if poking me might undo whatever miracle—or mistake—has kept me alive.

I kick her leg. "What about you?"

She squints at me, eyes mean and measuring, then clicks her tongue. "Yer a wrong 'un."

As the hours pass, her curses tick away like a demented clock.

Leaning back against the crates, my mind drifts to my youth—growing up in a village called *Murder*, the only village in the Vale. Not that anyone living in Murder wants a neighbouring village. We just call the village Murder's Vale for simplicity. Easier to say. Easier to stomach. Less confusing.

Chapter 3

Late Afternoon, Tenth Day of Gorst

The wagon jerks to a halt after what feels like an eternity. Our driver dismounts with all the grace of a hanged man.

"Murder! All off!"

The Stopping Post clings to the outer reaches of Murder—sorry, Murder's Vale—like a survivor inching away from infection. It's sits below the village on a path that ambles up towards the centre, through woods and past stables. I step out, my boots sinking into mud, as evening's sullen sky broods like a corrupt judge, its grey palette suggesting verdicts already decided, sentences waiting to be carried out.

A boy helps with the luggage, his hands already out for payment.

"How many people live here these days?" I ask, dropping a silver coin into his waiting palm.

"Too many now. With you two, and one away in the city, the dial is probably now plus-one. Thanks a lot," he sneers.

"Dial?"

"The Blood Balance Dial," he says.

"What?"

The driver shouts for the boy to get a move on. He looks at me and says, "Get your arse up to the Square and check the bloody noticeboard. Someone comes; someone goes. Someone goes; someone comes."

"A dial? Sounds more like bookkeeping than butchery."

"Nah—more like the other way round. Blood's gotta balance."

I raise a brow. "And if it doesn't?"

The driver smirks. "That's when the fun starts—ask the Innkeeper."

"What's plus-one mean?" I ask.

"One too many. Minus is too few. It's simple. What are you, the village idiot?"

"They better deduct one," I say, tossing the old crone a wink. "With a tongue that sharp, she'll be lucky to survive 'till morning."

She spits on my boot and kicks the boy in the shin to get out of her way.

He staggers back.

A knife flashes from under his sleeve, small fingers clenching tight around the handle. The old crone's stick slaps against his wrist. The blade tumbles free, spinning before she plucks it from the air.

"I'll add that to my collection!" She cackles.

The boy rubs his wrist, glowering. "That's MINE!"

"Was," she says, tucking it into the folds of her cloak.

I rock back on my heels, watching the exchange. The boy scowls, watching her like a hawk sizing up its prey.

As she heads toward the Stopping Post, she turns to me and says, "Don't worry, you'll get your turn soon enough."

Chapter 4

Evening, Tenth Day of Gorst

I follow the track up to the village, dragging my weathered case along, each step sounding like my soul being surrendered.

"REJOICE—it's Nibblenudge!" comes a shout from above. The voice slices through the air, dripping with mockery.

That damned name. A relic from school, spat out by a tutor who once described my handwriting—a drunken spider's crawl—and declared it 'nibble…nudgery!' It stuck, of course. Like a leech with a sense of humour.

I look up. Twin embers of malicious delight peer from a narrow window. Against the weak glow of a solitary candle, an old man's wiry frame looms, his overly tall hat brushing the rafters like it had a mind to escape. He drawls, voice thick with amusement and something sharper beneath it. "Well, well. I remember you leaving as a lad. You wasn't worth a puddle of piss then, nor a river of piss now."

A pause, pregnant with satisfaction. "Guess the big city thought the same." He cackles.

"Good to see nothing changes," I say.

I turn and walk on before he can sharpen his next barb. With each step, memories surface unbidden. I fled this place once. It felt like slipping a hangman's noose. Yet here I am, the promise of gold dragging me back. Whispers follow me, sideways glances tight with suspicion. The butcher stands outside his shop, wiping bloody hands on an apron stained with more than just meat. He watches me with a grimace. A cluster of women fall silent at my approach, their stares sharp as thorns. One murmurs something, drawing venomous chuckles from the others.

MacAllister Hall sits along a small road west of the Square. Its silhouette an apology written in rotting timber and crumbling stone. It lost the will to live decades ago yet stands, indifferent to collapse. Weeds writhe across the path to the entrance, their roots infiltrating every crack. Paint, once dignified, now hangs in leprous strips. Windows form a patchwork anthology of decay—broken glass and makeshift repairs.

Only the front door maintains any dignity. Traces of artistry linger in the weathered stonework—serpents entwined with roses, now worn smooth, their details softened by time's patience. A wreath-shaped knocker clings to the door like the last vestige of respectability.

I stand before the door, contemplating my return. Do I go in, or turn back?

A voice cuts through my contemplation. "MacAllister—a detective, I hear?" The words drip with contempt. Drusilla Hobbert walks towards me from the forest, carrying herbs that look as lifeless as my prospects. She cuts an imposing figure, wrapped in a finely tailored cloak that catches mist like a spider's web catches morning dew. Those piercing eyes, framed by brows arched in judgement, dissect me with the clinical detachment of someone categorising specimens of decay. Her attire—beneath the open cloak, a charcoal-grey dress with understated embroidery.

"Thought you were dead?" she says.

The herbalist, and queen of the apocalypse, looks over me with the sort of suspicion you'd reserve for a blighted sprout.

"Not yet!" I say.

"Still can't keep out of things that don't concern you?" Her words drag up memories of me as a curious child, caught rifling through her alchemy journal.

"Don't fret Drusilla. I'm just passing through."

"Sure you are—Murder's been waiting for you, you know."

Her attention drifts skyward, reading omens in the gathering gloom. "The herbs knew you were coming. They've been restless."

I look up and sniff the air. "I reckon it's heaven sprinkles."

"No."

"Sky pillows, then? Maybe a gust of celestial tummy rubs?"

"...No!"

"Weather puffs, perchance?"

"Are you finished?"

"What about drift cushions?" I say.

She raises a hand to stop me from continuing. "I'm serious," she snaps as she walks off.

***

The front door of MacAllister Hall resists my kick, but then surrenders to a good shouldering—the universal language of unwanted homecomings. Inside, the Hall greets me with the chill of a mausoleum. News scrolls and advertisements block the entrance like literary detritus. Today's headline reads: *Pigeons Form Organised Circle—Villagers Fear Coup.*

A flock of the alleged connivers wing past the window.

I drift through rooms. Each floorboard's protest sends dust motes dancing like disturbed ghosts. The Hall exudes an air of faded grandeur; worn but not forgotten. Every piece of furniture, from the high-backed armchair to the mahogany writing desk, tells its own tale.

I make a mental note to expedite this inheritance—the past may be patient, but I'm not.

A knock at the door interrupts my thoughts.

The Mayor, a figure hewn from shadow and ambition, fills the doorframe like a living barricade. His thick dark hair and greying beard frame a face that smiles easily but doesn't warm the eyes—calculating pools that assess everything for its value. He's flanked by the miserable crone from the wagon.

"Him!" she shrieks, jabbing a finger my way like she's marking me for the reaper. "No, don't waste good money here—slice his throat and take the place, Ellington! One quick cut and the matter's settled!"

The Mayor exhales through his nose, not with weariness but with the controlled impatience of a predator. "Now, now, Aunt Agatha—it's rude to open negotiations with talk of murder."

She glares at him, jabs her stick into his ribs, and then turns her beady, bird-of-prey gaze back to me. "He's standing right there. Begging for it!"

"Oh, it's you again!" I say, my gaze flicking between them.

The crone, undeterred, hikes up her skirt and extracts the dagger she stole earlier. "Fine! I'll do it myself!"

I take a quick step back.

"This again..." the Mayor sighs.

She lunges forward with the grace of a spider, but the Mayor catches her by the throat before she reaches me. His hands move with speed, the kind developed through countless acts of violence cleverly disguised as necessity. His nails draw blood on her neck.

"Aunt Agatha," he says with infuriating patience, "we talked about this. Public spectacles are bad for business."

She thrashes, choking in his grip, blade slashing air. "Release me, you overgrown stump!"

He pries the weapon from her clawed fingers and pockets it. She rubs her neck, scowling at him like he's just kicked her favourite cat. "Perhaps we could focus on business," the Mayor suggests, wiping blood from his hands. "I trust the letter reached you safely?"

I cross my arms and lean against the door. "The one nervously slipped under my door? The one filled with legal prattle and images depicting thinly veiled threats?"

The Mayor's smile tightens, the momentary flash in his eyes confirming my suspicions. He's a man renowned for colourful threats. "Communication is an art form," he says. "I find drawings prevent... misunderstandings."

His fingers tap against his thigh. "I trust you've given my proposition some thought?"

"I have. It's in the garderobe for when I next unburden myself."

The crone snorts. "You always had an over-inflated sense of drama, boy. Just like your family. Thought you were better than the rest of us." She fixes me with the same vulture-like stare she'd had on the coach. "Didn't do them much good, did it?"

I flash her a smile that is all teeth and no warmth.

The Mayor lifts a hand, the gesture of a man who has silenced rooms with nothing but a glance. He steps forward, each movement deliberate, like an executioner measuring the distance to the block. "MacAllister Hall is a relic of an older time. A time that, dare I say, has long since passed."

"How poetic," I reply.

He offers a slow smile, eyes glittering with cold calculation. "The past has a habit of clouding judgment. But in time, even the most stubborn come to see the wisdom of letting go." His voice carries the weight of unspoken threats, heavy as a burial shroud.

"If we're trading wisdom, I'll need coffee and a chair," I say, glancing at the crone. "But why is she here?"

The Mayor gestures mildly. "Ensuring my dear aunt is taken care of in her twilight years is the least I can do."

"Twilight? Please. That spent old candle needs extinguishing."

Agatha snarls, revealing a set of teeth that look like they might once have belonged to someone else. "Still got a bite left in me, boy." She produces another blade from some dark hiding place beneath her garments.

I take another step back. "This feels excessive."

The Mayor intercepts her again with a heavy sigh. "Agatha, stop! We came for a chat, not decorate the floor with his entrails."

She strains against his iron grip. The Mayor wrestles the dagger away and mutters something under his breath. His patience is admirable. "Reunions," he says, his aunt still thrashing in his grasp, "such crucibles of joy."

"She's a delight," I say, looking at his aunt, now rummaging furiously in her pockets for another weapon.

"I'll feed you to my cat." She shouts.

The Mayor clears his throat. "My offer will come soon. I trust you'll give it your full consideration this time. It's prudent to agree."

"Then you'd better present a fair offer."

The Mayor's smile lingers, a slow, knowing thing, like a cat watching a bird with a broken wing. "Fair," he muses, "what a charming concept."

Agatha huffs, wrenching herself free from his grip and tries to bite me.

The Mayor steers her away from the door, a hand firmly back on her throat. With that, he strides out into the gloom, the crone hobbling in front of him, both leaving behind the chill of promised violence. I exhale as the door shuts with a heavy thud, leaving behind the scent of cabbage and camphor. I need some fresh air.

I venture out. Cobblestones glisten under my feet, each step echoing through the dark. Eyes track my progress from shadowed windows. The Square emerges from the gloom like a stage set for tragedy, existing in that liminal space between memory and nightmare.

The Market shutters its secrets for the night. Stalls close, their wooden frames groaning as vendors pack away their wares, leaving behind the ghost of commerce as scattered straw and the lingering scent of rotting produce. Across the square I see a figure emerging from The Corpse's Candle, staggering like a puppet with half its strings cut...

Chapter 5

Ulric Plenkovic, the village bard, moves with all the grace of a sack of turnips tossed down a staircase, each stumbling step a tragedy in coordination. His hair, a battlefield where silver wages war against brown, cascades around his face in untamed rebellion, partially obscuring eyes that swim in ale, but sparkle with undeniable charm. His cloak, once a verdant green and now faded to the colour of long-dead moss, tells its own story of faded glory. At his side, a worn lute dangles precariously, its strings as frayed as his sobriety. The familiar bouquet of stale tavern clings to him, announcing his approach.

"Noel... Noel MacAllister?" his eyes squinting at me as we approach each other. His voice rasps with the edge of a man who's spent more nights in the bottom of a tankard than under a roof.

"Plenkovic!" I step forward, offering a smile that feels both genuine and cautious.

He responds with a chuckle, but it quickly turns to a wheeze. "Drusilla's herbs told me you'd died! Good to see they were wrong... though, in Murder's Vale, who can say?"

"In Murder's Vale, we're all dead. It's just most of us haven't realised it yet," I say.

He raises his tankard. "Ain't that the truth! MacAllister Hall still standing, is it?"

"I don't think it knows how to collapse," I say.

Ulric smirks, but something in his expression shifts.

"Anything wrong?" I ask.

He fixes me with a look that suggests he's momentarily sober. "Noel, I'm worried. There's odd things going on."

"Odder than usual?" I ask.

"Dunno. I don't normally see 'em. But this was shadows creeping around the Mayor's place."

I laugh. "Scared by your own shadow?"

He sways like a laughing reed in a storm.

"Perhaps you should soak up some on that ale. Fancy a nibble?" I say, pulling a wedge of hard cheese from my coat.

"Aged to perfection!" I crack the cheese in half. The scent hits us—a sharp, tangy odour with a hint of barnyard. Ulric looks on, blurry-eyed, as I take a hearty bite straight from the wedge, fragments tumbling onto the ground.

"Bit dry," I mumble, spraying his shirt. "You know, this pairs well with ale. Like poetry for the stomach."

He hands me his tankard.

"No finer meal," I declare.

"Say, Plenkovic, how about filling me in on the usual suspects? Who's still hanging around here?"

We talk until his stories begin to circle back on themselves; the conversation drifting through the village's collection of scandals and oddities like a boat without a rudder. Finally, swaying like a candle flame in a draft, he wobbles back toward the Tavern, muttering about shadows and curses with the conviction of the truly pickled.

Here and there, gusts of wind swirl wayward drizzle until it slaps against my face; a reminder that there's no comfort to be found outside. Beneath torches and half-lit windows, water beads on every surface, each droplet flickering momentarily before rolling away as if it, too, wants to flee.

I turn to look over at the Square's dimly lit centrepiece—the Bitter Well, ancient guardian of secrets, its flint base slick with damp, with its usual crowd of miscreants. The Well's ancient pulley clings to a slimy water bucket. It's always been the Vale's favourite landmark. Around it winds a single road that circles the entire Square where carts, wagons and foot traffic will shuffle along its one-way loop like reluctant dancers, each forced to follow the same path. It's the one concession to discipline that everyone tolerates.

The noticeboard stands at the edge of the Square, just before the bustle of the market, leaning slightly toward the Tavern. A crude construction of two weathered wooden posts driven deep into the ground, with thick planks nailed between them like the ribs of some skeletal gate. I walk over to it. The wood is scarred and pitted, ink stains and the ghosts of past proclamations lingering where old notices have been torn away. Scraps of parchment and rough-spun vellum are nailed haphazardly to both sides—some curling at the edges, others sagging where the rain has bled the ink into illegible smudges. A few hang by a single rusted nail, flapping listlessly in the damp wind. Others are more securely fixed—some even reinforced with wax seals or twine.

At the top centre of one side sits the Blood Balance Dial—a crude but ever-present measure of Murder's Vale's debts and dues. A splintered wooden stick, darkened by age and handling, is firmly nailed at one end, pointing to an inked arc of tally marks scratched unevenly into the wood. The scale runs from one to four tallies—positive on the right, negative on the left. At either end, two pegs serve as final markers without a tally—off the scale. The boy was right. It's pointing to plus-one.

As I eye the dial, a villager mutters without looking up, "Don't get any ideas."

I smirk. "You think I'd meddle?"

She snorts. "Innkeeper's got a ledger. And a temper."

Beneath the dial, a note reads—"*To the individual who keeps replacing notices with their own poetry: The village appreciates your creativity, but no one understands your metaphors. Also, the Mayor is not a squid in a man's coat.*" And, in the neat, no-nonsense handwriting from the bailiff: "*A gentle reminder: The gibbet is for official hangings only.*"

Another, written in a distinct hand. *"To the person who 'borrowed' my shovel: Congratulations on your new property. May it serve you well in digging your own grave."*

I rub my chin. *I'd better monitor this board.*

From here, I can see the Well presiding over its congregation. They murmur their litanies of suspicion, their faces illuminated by the Tavern's light like specimens in a collection of the damned. Some glance in my direction, quick and sharp as a stiletto.

Among them stands Sir Roderick Highgrove, looking every bit the knight who's outlived his fairy tale. His armour bears the patina of neglect, and a thin scar races across his cheek, a signature of violence long past. Though time has softened his edges, authority still clings to him like a second skin, his shoulders squared against the burden of time and expectations. "Nibblenudge!" he calls out, his voice carrying the same corroded quality as his armour. "Didn't expect to see you back in Murder's Vale?"

I walk over. "Me neither. It's odd to be back," I say.

Sir Roderick looks me up and down like he's weighing a side of meat and not impressed with the cut. He squints, his brown eyes as sharp as nails hammered into rotted wood.

"I'll tell you what's odd," he says, "you arriving here today—the very day Mayor Crumley's body is found perchance dead."

"Perchance?" I ask.

"Some get up again. You can't always tell they're dead—unless it's obvious." He shrugs, like he's talking about the weather.

"Dead?"

He grunts; a sound filled with implication. "Maybe. Perchance. Who knows? Bit of an odd coincidence, though." Sir Roderick studies my face with the kind of suspicion that the Vale cultivates like a prized crop.

I shift, uncomfortable under his intense scrutiny. "Well... I just came back to resolve an inheritance matter."

"Oh, that. Just passing through, then, or maybe staying a while?"

"I haven't decided."

Sir Roderick's scrutiny holds me like a spider with a particularly interesting fly. "Well—what an interesting time to be... *undecided!*" His arms cross, slow and deliberate, like a closing trap.

I nod, noncommittally. The drizzle starts again—Murder's Vale's version of applause. Light, persistent, vaguely insulting.

"I need a drink," I mutter, more to myself than anyone else.

Sir Roderick sneers. "Then you know where to go."

"I do."

The Corpse's Candle squats at the eastern edge of the Square like a toad with secrets. Two floors of sagging timber and soot-stained stone lean slightly westward, burdened by the weight of its own stories. Its wooden sign dangles from a rusted bracket: a single candle burning atop a skull, forever flickering in the wind.

The thick oak door—heavy, iron-braced, and prone to groaning—offers resistance before relenting with a sullen sigh.

Inside, firelight spills across the crooked windows, distorting itself into shifting patterns. Regulars roost at their tables with the wary posture of men who expect betrayal. A single bar stretches along the far wall, battle-worn and stained with drink and misunderstandings. Behind it, the Innkeeper polishes a tankard with grim determination. His moustache does the emotional heavy lifting; his eyes, none at all.

The floor is thick with timber planks—uneven and stained by the kind of history no mop can erase. A massive hearth bellows at one end, while beams overhead crisscross like the ribs of a sleeping beast. Behind the counter, shelves cluttered with dust-coated bottles pose as choices. Above the bar hangs a painted scroll: *Warm Drinks, Cold Welcome.*

Corners lurk everywhere, some huddled close to the fire, others lost in deeper shadows. The centre of the room stands open—a makeshift stage for speeches, duels of wit or steel, and the occasional dramatic accusation.

Mismatched tables and chairs sprawl across the room like the remnants of a forgotten brawl. A staircase curves upwards along the back wall, disappearing into whatever remains of the inn's second floor.

The Corpse's Candle—too useful to burn down, too important to replace. Murder's Vale wouldn't function without it. I step inside, stomping damp from my boots, and wait for the welcome that never arrives.

Chapter 6

Morning, Eleventh Day of Gorst

In the distance, the village bells toll a discordant dirge, dragging themselves through the fog like a wounded animal. "Mayor Crumley," a voice splits the murk outside. "Perchance dead!"

I peel myself from what passes for a bed at MacAllister Hall—a defeated heap of straw beneath a sheepskin—and make my way toward the Square.

The news doesn't raise an eyebrow. To readers of *Murder's Prophecy Daily*, it's yesterday's news. Two days ago, they proclaimed, with characteristic temporal mischief, *Mayor Found Perchance Dead on the Morrow*. Such is the nature of foretelling—the Mayor perchance died last night, but the announcement of its perchanceness is today.

Crumley's dead. What a loss to society.

When we were children, Crumley was little more than a shadow to me—our families were never close. From my recent encounter, his death surprises me only in its timing and implications. I doubt he'll be mourned.

A crow's harsh call punctuates my thoughts—nature's own commentary. Soon enough, the vultures will descend, their appetite for conspiracy as ravenous as ever, spinning theories with the fervour of weavers at a cursed loom. Here, truth has always played second fiddle to a well-spun tale. And every good tale here demands an encore of *murderings*.

Standing at my window, I contemplate my next move as the bells continue tolling. This development threatens my plans. I need to meet with Darius Drummond, the bailiff, to see what becomes of the sale of MacAllister Hall now that the Mayor is dead. If he's gone, the deal might be too—unless someone else steps up to claim it.

His chambers lie north of the Library, along Manor Lane, but I doubt he'll be working on a day like this. More likely he's in the Square—the village's favourite stage for intrigue. I've never met the man. I need to find someone who knows what he looks like.

***

The Square serves as a grimy amphitheatre of human nature. The crowd swells like a festering wound, rumours coiling through the air as they await explanation. I hang around on the periphery, observing villagers huddling in mutual distrust. The bells offer one last note that hangs in the air like a *punctus interrogativus*. No one seems to know what it means. Instead, someone finds a message on the noticeboard. I wander over to get a view.

Mayor Perchance Dead!

Next to it, is scrawled in messy, looping letters, "*Again?!*"

And in neater script, "*Will he stay dead this time?*"

Such is the Vale's peculiar brand of humour.

I let my gaze drift down the board to the Blood Balance Dial. It sat at plus-one after my arrival but now points back to nought—reset by the Mayor's perchance demise.

Someone has scribbled beneath the dial in their usual brand of pragmatic pessimism: "*Balanced again. For now.*"

Amidst the layers of parchment, I almost admire the mordantly inspirational soul behind this observation: "*To those who navigate their way home from the Tavern purely by a process of elimination—congratulations on making it this far. Truly, an inspiration to us all.*" Before I can linger on what life choices lead to such wisdom, a woman's voice drifts from behind me. "Crumley's too stubborn to be dead. Remember his last funeral?"

Her companion releases a world-weary groan. "Crumley's got the better of Death a few times."

Curious, I edge closer to them. "How's that?"

Their response is silence wrapped in suspicion—like an uninvited guest at their murder party. They continue to stare at me until I turn away.

"Poison, they say," a woman's voice slithers through the crowd, each syllable dripping with delicious scandal.

"Or a curse," another whispers, the words crawling down my spine like frost.

The crowd thickens around me as I become the centrepiece in their theatre of accusations. Death here never lives up to its aspirations—it must be an event, a riddle, a labyrinth of possibilities with too many exits. Murder's Vale has elevated suspicion to an art form, with a generous portion of malice served on the side.

Theories multiply like maggots. "Could be the Midnight Crow. If it caws at your window, you're marked for the grave."

"More like the Sleepy Spectre," says another. "It sleeps on your back if you've had too many ales."

"Or perhaps the Mayor simply dies the same day I visit the village," I say.

Again, people stare at me in silence. With a weary sigh, I head over to the Well where I met Sir Roderick last night. If anyone knows the bailiff and his operating hours, it's that walking repository of village lore.

As I cross the Square, I see Drusilla where the Square becomes the market. She's arguing with some villagers. It's odd. Her sister, Ruthenia Hobbert or *Moondrop* as I used to know her—presents a stark contrast. She belongs to the whispers of the forest rather than the clamour of village life. Unlike her domineering sister, she appears indifferent to the Vale's daily dramas.

Two herbalists in a village this size—strikes me as excessive. I thought they'd go their own ways, rather than competing. A thought stirs. I turn to an elderly man lighting a pipe beside me. His smoke dances with the mist. It blurs edges, turning everything into a watercolour of suspicion. The elderly man's face is as weathered as cobblestones, though arguably less reliable to walk on in heavy rain. "Why do we still have *two* herbalists?" I ask him. He stiffens as he glances at me from the corner of his eye, his face creases up like old leather.

"Herbalists!" he mutters, his voice rough and smoky.

"Yes, why are there two in the village?" I ask, knowing full well the futility of the question.

"Herbalists!" he mutters again. Old Smokey isn't going to elaborate. He shuffles away into the crowd, mingling with other old smokers.

Nearby, pigeons arrange themselves into a perfect circle, all facing inwards as if passing judgment on an unseen crime. The mist gives the scene a shadow-play quality—a troupe of tiny phantoms rehearsing an unseen tragedy. I push the thought aside—there are bigger mysteries at hand. Like our recently perchance departed, Mayor.

At the north end of the Square, the Market hums, a chaotic hive of traders and noise. Stalls huddle like conspirators beneath weather-beaten awnings that snap like tattered banners. Trade is conducted in whispers, each sale a ritual of subtle implications.

The air is thick with competing scents: herbs that promise enlightenment, metallic tinctures that hint at oblivion. Questionable wares wink at me from every stall—roots twisted like petrified screams, small vials of ineffable liquids, and dusty tomes that might well read you back if you're foolish enough to open them. It's a place where rules, few that they are, grind to a halt.

One persists, however: the village's one-way system. A single road, known as the Ring, channels carts, wagons, and wanderers in a strict one-way flow around the Square. Traders enter from the north past the Highgrove estate filtering south past Milton's house before merging into the Market's west side. Departures follow the Ring around the Square, branching off north toward Drusilla's or south towards Moondrop's, before looping north again to Highgrove Hall. Without it, transport would snarl like hair in a furious wind.

I scan faces as I get closer towards the Bitter Well.

Drusilla steps into my path like an inconveniently timed prophecy, her dark eyes boring into mine with their usual intensity. I really can't tell if she's about to murder me or have a chat but—but the speed at which she found me suggests premeditation.

"Out for a stroll, are we?" she says.

Something about her commands attention—even when she's arranging herbs, she moves with the authority of fate itself.

"Just passing through," I say. "I'm looking for Sir Roderick."

"To hand yourself in?"

"Funny," I say.

"There's a shift. Something's coming," she says.

I glance skyward. "So you said yesterday. Perhaps it's snow?"

Drusilla stares at me, damp hair clinging to her face. "No."

"So it's not Heaven sprinkles?"

"No."

"The bailiff?"

"...Stop!" she says.

"Is this about the perchance death of the Mayor?" I ask. "I hear his condition has taken a dramatic downturn since our last chat."

Drusilla watches me, "You feel it too, don't you?"

I sigh. "If by it you mean the distinct chill of someone about to explain omens in vague and unhelpful ways?"

"This isn't just death. It's a change of order, a reckoning."

"A reckoning. Do the herbs think it be the existential kind?"

Drusilla's gaze sharpens. "You think this is a joke?"

I gesture at her basket. "I think it's hard to take impending doom seriously when it arrives in the form of damp herbs."

She exhales sharply.

"This village eats its own. It doesn't share with strangers," she says before drifting into the crowd, leaving me alone with that cheerful thought.

Sir Roderick looms by the Bitter Well as he studies the village's comings and goings. "Ah, Nibblenudge. Any theories?"

"No, but rumour has it I'm the villain."

He releases a grunt that sounds like disappointed gravel. "Can't blame them, can you? You show up after years away, and the Mayor turns up perchance dead the same day."

I cross my arms. "*Again with this*? It's a coincidence." The words feel flimsy as they leave my mouth. "And unless someone can produce a witness who saw me introducing the Mayor to an untimely end, I suggest broadening the suspect pool."

He grunts noncommittally, but the suspicion remains in his eyes like a stubborn stain.

A swell of movement pushes west off the Square and past the Library toward the Mayor's place, drawn by the arrival of his staff and the promise of answers.

Sir Roderick straightens like a puppet on tightened strings. "Better head over," he mutters, giving me a sidelong glance. "I need to secure the scene."

He turns to leave, but I hold up a hand. "Before you go..."

He pauses, clearly impatient. "Make it quick."

"I'm trying to track down the bailiff—Darius Drummond. Any idea where he might be?"

Sir Roderick's brow furrows. "Out of town. He left a few days ago on the Mayor's business. Didn't say where."

"Does he have a chamber?"

"Just north of the Library on Manor Lane, halfway to the Mayor's Manor. But the place'll be locked up."

I nod, filing that away. "What does he look like?"

"Stocky. Ginger hair like a bonfire."

And just like that, a thread pulls taut. *That's the man I saw striding out from my office in the city.*

He pauses with obvious reluctance and says, "You should come along to the Manor. Could be in your interest."

"I might," I say, certain it's a bad idea.

Chapter 7

Afternoon, Eleventh Day of Gorst

I linger in the emptying Square as the crowd drifts past the Library and down Manor Lane like a dark tide. With a resigned breath, I fall in with the stragglers, set on finding Darius. I try the bailiff's door as we pass—locked. I keep moving, carried along by the current.

The Manor looms ahead, a monument to intimidation. Its windows stare down unblinking. The grand façade presents an unsettling majesty, its architectural flourishes less an invitation than a warning. Nature, I reckon, shares my distrust—ivy writhes up the stone walls like desperate fingers, as if trying to drag this edifice of corruption back into the earth's embrace.

Its roofline bristles with gargoyles that disappear in shifting waves of fog, as though nature conspires with stone to obscure their sinister glee. These have watched over countless crimes, their weather-worn grins suggesting they've enjoyed every moment. Below them, the entrance is ringed with carvings that time has rendered cryptic.

My pace slows as I draw closer, the sound of voices blending with the soft patter of rain. I meld into the gathering throng, keeping an ear open to any news. Each voice competing to be the most shocking, the most plausible. Sir Roderick stands near the entrance, arms crossed. His sharp glance finds me. He dispatches a young messenger through the press of bodies.

"Sir Roderick says you should come over," the boy says, cool as you like, with a look that says he's got more important places to be. I acknowledge with a nod that sends him scurrying back.

As I approach, Sir Roderick's smile is as warm as a winter. "Nibblenudge!" he announces, voice pitched to carry. "Isn't timing a curious thing? You appear, and as if by coincidence, our Mayor's perchance dead. Some might call that... suspicious?"

The words float above the gathering like poisonous air, drawing hungry stares and muttered agreement from the assembled villagers. The realisation hits like a slap—he isn't an ally. He's staging a spectacle, casting me as the unwitting lead.

"No kidding," I say.

His armour groans a metallic sigh as he shrugs, the sound like old secrets being pried loose. "Well, guilty is as guilty doves," he says, each word another nail in my metaphorical coffin. "One might think if you've returned to settle old scores—such as arranging our dearly perchance departed Mayor's untimely exit?"

I fix him with a fierce stare, recognising the trap he's constructing. Every word feeds the village's suspicion painting me into an ever-tighter corner to do his bidding. My mind races for a counter. if I become the investigator, it puts me in control—it might help redirect suspicion.

"Guilty doves?" I say.

Sir Roderick's expression doesn't change. We pause, each weighing the next move.

I figure I have no good options. "I'm the detective, remember?" I say. "Best let me handle the thinking."

His eyebrow arches like a cat's back. "Really? In that case, with the bailiff away on business, you can deputise on this investigation for a while."

I let out a slow breath, tilting my head. "So, he's not expected back soon?"

"I wouldn't be wasting my time with you if he were.

I adjust my coat, squaring my shoulders. "Fine. But we do this my way."

"We'll see. You'll want to see the body *again*—I presume?" he says.

I don't react to his jibe. Sir Roderick gestures toward the doorway, offering an escape from the crowd's hungry stares. The foyer echoes with opulence, our steps ringing against marble worn by generations of the self-important. The walls whisper their history through intricate carvings, each groove a testament to when craftsmen laboured to impress master's long since dust. Above, a magnificent chandelier hangs like a crown, its crystals dripping onto the floor below. The corridor to the study swallows our sound, softening what waits beyond.

When I cross the threshold, the Mayor's inner sanctum reveals itself. It's a room that bleeds wealth from every corner, though not in the way I'd imagined. Oh, it's grand enough—but beneath the polish, chaos festers. Towering shelves of books, their spines cracked and peeling, gilt titles fading like dying breaths. Knowledge is a weapon here—cryptic tools for power and secrets. Overhead, ancient wooden beams twist like tortured confessors, their dark grain telling tales I'd rather not hear. An oak desk commanding the room's centre is a battlefield of bureaucracy. Ledgers sprawl like soldiers, scrolls curl like dying men, and abandoned quills stand as markers for the dead.

I can't help but wonder if the Mayor had been spinning a trap before someone sprang one on him. This isn't only a workspace—it's a shrine to ambition.

"Milton found him like this last night," Sir Roderick mutters, his gaze fixed on the Mayor's lifeless form. "He reckons the smell on the Mayor must be some sort of poison."

"Milton?"

"Milton Ledbury. Mayor's clerk and treasurer," he says, his expression edging toward amusement.

Mayor Ellington Crumley's corpse sprawls across his desk, his fur-lined robe flowing around him like spilled wine. Blood has made its own map on the floor, spreading under the desk in a dark constellation. His head hangs at an angle only the dead can manage, skin pale as winter frost, eyes fixed on whatever truth he found in his last moments. One hand dangles uselessly, the other rests on a quill, the ink's final stroke a testament to unfinished business.

The position of his body tells a tale of being caught unaware, a frozen snapshot of impertinent surprise, as if the last realisation to flicker through his mind had been stolen mid-thought. No signs of struggle mar the scene—just the abrupt full stop of a life caught between one breath and the void. The scent hits me as I approach the body—mint, sharp and clean.

Sir Roderick surveys the scene with all the concern of a man reviewing taxes. His sabatons rasp against the floorboards, a dry, grating intrusion in the thick silence.

"Mint..." he says, his voice flat. His nostrils flare as he leans closer. "Odd choice for a poisoner, wouldn't you say, Nibblenudge?"

"Not if it masks the taste of poison," I say.

"I've witnessed many ends," he says, drawing himself up like a tower. He looks over, "Never met a murderer with such... refinement." His gaze sharpens, locking onto me cold as a winter well. "With such... cunning."

"We're dealing with an artist, not an amateur," I say, gesturing toward the hearth where embers cling to life. "Time of death fits Milton's story—dead fire, spent candle on the desk. All adds up neat as a ledger."

"Though speaking of time..." I turn to face him. "You knew about this when I saw you at the Bitter Well last night. Care to explain where you were before our midnight chat? And how this news found its way to you?"

His armour protests as he stiffens. "Are you seriously suggesting I had anything to do with this?"

I raise a placating hand. "Everyone gets the same questions."

"I was with Milton in the treasury chamber before he made the discovery," he says, each word precise as a blade stroke. "Ask him yourself."

"Were you together the entire time?"

"I'm not one for aimless wandering."

"How convenient... You're each other's alibi."

Sir Roderick sniffs, fixing his attention on the body as if it has something very interesting to say. We both stare at it.

"That dagger," I say, gesturing toward the ornate blade in the Mayor's back, "rather spoils any pretence of subtlety, wouldn't you say?"

Sir Roderick's jaw works silently, teeth grinding with the gentle persistence of a miller's wheel.

"A poniard, if I'm not mistaken," I say.

Rain drums against the windows, its steady cadence underscored by a distant roll of thunder.

"You appear well-versed in instruments of death?" His words hanging in the stale air between accusation and inquiry.

"Just a hobby." My attention is caught by the intricate scrollwork adorning the hilt.

I crouch beside the body, studying the blade's trajectory. Its placement speaks of intimate knowledge—just below the left shoulder blade, driven deep: one clean thrust, no hesitation, no amateur fumbling.

"Murder by poison and dagger, then," I say.

"Or accident," Sir Roderick says, proud as a peacock. "Testing poison, stumbling backward onto your own dagger and collapsing onto the desk..."

"*Entia non sunt multiplicanda praeter necessitate.*" I let the words settle. "We learned that in Detective School—What was it now?—Something about being simple, I think."

"Indeed. Well? What is it then?" he says.

"Poison suggests a professional," I say, rising slowly. "But a dagger as well? That's *Amateur Hour Murder.* It lacks confidence."

"*Gilded Slaughter,*" Sir Roderick pronounces, crossing his arms as though he's solved the puzzle himself.

"Perhaps, but that's not an official murder category. It could be someone's idea of entertainment..." I say, prowling the perimeter of the scene to view the tableau from every angle.

"*Frustra fit per plura, quod potest fieri per pauciora,*" I say, unable to resist. "What can be done with less is done in vain with more. I think this has all the hallmarks of *Vanity Murder.*"

Sir Roderick straightens up, his outfit creaks into place, a mix of vague thought and irritation sweeping his face, like a man struggling to remember why he matters.

"*Vanity Murder?*"

"It's a process of elimination. Let me explain." I gesture toward the body with exaggerated patience.

"*Amateur Hour Murder* lacks finesse. *Vanity Murder*? has flair."

"Consider the use of mint poison—rare, expensive, unnecessary. It's not just murder—it's murder with a calling card."

I sniff the Mayor's head, inhaling it like a fine wine. "It could be *Jealous Partner Murder.*"

"Are you quite done?" Sir Roderick asks. "What if someone clever is trying to make it look that way? Like you, for instance. You met the Mayor, didn't you?"

"Just the one time." Another sniff of the head.

He grunts, unimpressed.

"Still, you arrive for some inheritance matter just as this happens. Suspicious timing. Perhaps you didn't like his offer?"

"It is." I shrug, casting an appraising eye over the Mayor's cluttered desk. "And it's certainly a narrative you've been nurturing. Having fun with that?"

Sir Roderick crosses his arms. "This is Murder's Vale, Nibblenudge. Fun isn't our business."

No argument there.

"We need to gather evidence," I say.

I approach the desk. Crumley's cluttered workspace is an orchestra of half-finished thoughts. A pile of cryptic parchments lies scattered, covered in strange notations—jagged, inconsistent, and unreadable, as though encoded. A quill rests beneath Crumley's lifeless hand. The parchment beneath it bears his final, cryptic scribblings.

Sir Roderick drifts away and scans the bookshelves and scattered scrolls with the intensity of a man seeking something specific. Less interested in the murder and more intent on satisfying his own unspoken curiosities.

From a shelf, he lifts the mayoral seal, turning it over. His fingers hesitate—looking like a moment's debate between pocket and propriety—before he sets it back. He moves to inspect the display case housing ancient coins and artefacts, their presence hinting that our killer's motives lie beyond mere profit.

The desk groans under the burden of books and scrolls. A dog-eared copy of *Murder's Prophecy Daily* lies splayed open to page twenty-four, dated the 9th Day of Gorst and crowned with the headline: *Mayor Found Dead (On The Morrow)*.

The words pulse with dark promise, a prophecy fulfilled in blood and mint.

Did Crumley see his own obituary in advance?

I nudge the journal with my knuckle. "Do you think he read this?" Sir Roderick grunts. "Crumley's never met a headline he didn't assume was about him."

I flip the page. "So where do these come from? The prophecy papers. Who writes them?"

Sir Roderick doesn't look up. "They arrive."

"Yes, but from where?"

He shrugs, inspecting a dusty coin as if hoping it'll whisper secrets. "Outside the Vale. Same wagon every morning drops them at the Library."

"Has anyone asked the courier?"

"No one cares. It's free, it's pretty accurate. Library just files them. Binds the monthlies, shelves them in order." He eyes the paper. "No one writes it. It just... arrives."

I raise a brow. "Comforting."

He grunts. "Only if it doesn't mention you."

A stick of dried mutton rests on a plate beside a half drank goblet of wine. I examine the leathery meat in the light. Sir Roderick flinches as I bend it with both hands, testing its toughness.

"This isn't evidence, is it?" I ask.

Sir Roderick looks at me with a hint of disbelief. I don't think he likes me.

"Waste not, want not," I say. The first bite resists, tough as old leather. I gnaw at it like a wolf worrying a carcass, my teeth clicking against the sinewy surface.

"Chewy," I say through a mouthful, spitting a string of meat onto the table.

Sir Roderick arches a disdainful brow. "A man's last meal? Were you raised by animals, man?"

I shrug and tear off another bite. I eat with chaotic pragmatism, blooming like a stain on society's tablecloth. I left Murder's Vale as a boy who refused to be tamed—a fork, slicing through the wreckage of etiquette.

"I'd offer you a knife, but it's busy," he says.

The relentless chewing begins to wear on my jaw, so I let the half-eaten strip of mutton dangle from my mouth, giving myself a reprieve.

My detective's instincts hum like plucked harp strings. Crumley's obsession with ciphers and secrets hadn't saved him, but it might decode the path to his killer. I extract a leather-bound tome from a desk drawer, its cover embossed with symbols worn from handling.

The spine's gilt lettering has surrendered to time, leaving no title or hint of its contents. Opening it reveals a more deliberate violation—all the pages have been cut out.

In the drawer, a cryptic runestone catches my eye. I lift it, feeling the rough-hewn edges. Its carvings are too precise to be mere decoration, too deliberate to be meaningless.

"Curious find," Sir Roderick mutters, materialising at my shoulder like an unwanted ghost. "What's that supposed to be?"

"Ritual artefact, perhaps."

His interest evaporates.

I move quickly, collecting anything that smells of intent. The runestone and the hollowed tome go into my satchel first, followed by the pile of cryptic parchments, scrawled with Crumley's spidery script—the symbols on them seem too deliberate to be idle doodling. They're connected, all of them. Something encoded, perhaps. If Crumley used a cipher key, it was probably in that hollowed tome. Which means it's gone.

Still... ciphers can be broken. Secrets leave echoes. Maybe there's enough left to dig out the truth.

I wrap the gathered evidence in a chair cover, bundling them with the care of a midwife handling a newborn. Each piece might hold the key to unravelling Crumley's demise—or lead us deeper into the Vale's secrets.

We check the cold hearth. A few charred parchment fragments cling to life along the edges, their markings still visible.

"Doubt you'll get much from scraps."

"Sometimes scraps are all you need," I say, securing them in my bundle.

With our harvest complete, we survey the scene one last time. Sir Roderick's face wears its customary mask of vague irritation.

"I think we've stripped this carcass bare," I say.

Sir Roderick pauses, eyeing the Mayor's slumped form. "Wait!" he says, "are we leaving him like this?"

"Depends. Want to allow our murder to collect their tools?"

He responds with a disgusted grunt and strides to the body. Gripping the ornate dagger's hilt, he yanks it free. Dark blood oozes from the wound like molasses, painting fresh streams across Crumley's robes.

"One poniard for evidence," he mutters, wiping the blade clean on the Mayor's garments with obvious distaste.

Turning back to Crumley, Sir Roderick steels himself like a man preparing to kiss a toad. He leans in, face averted, and pries open the Mayor's mouth. He grimaces at the milky substance inside. With an ivory spoon taken from the desk, he scrapes out the poisonous evidence, dividing it neatly between two small wooden boxes—one beech, the other birch. He snaps the lids shut as if expecting them to bite.

"Not exactly what I trained for," he mutters.

"Fine work," I say, letting a smirk play at the corner of my mouth.

He shoots me a look, passing me one box.

"Oh, and Sir Roderick," I say, nodding toward the body, "better alert the undertaker. No sense letting Crumley ripen any longer than necessary."

"Milton will handle that," he grunts. "Now, let's feed the wolves some scraps."

We leave the study. Portraits of former mayors line the walls, their painted eyes following us with the hollow disapproval of men who died believing their own importance.

At the entrance, he fixes me with a stare, his gaze lingering on my bundle of evidence. "Safeguarding the evidence is critical. Move fast once you're out there."

This will be interesting.

I adjust my precious cargo, offering a grim nod. "I'll find somewhere secure—away from MacAllister Hall. Every shadow holds a potential suspect. Including you."

Sir Roderick's mouth twists into a humourless smile. "Oh, do pace yourself, Nibblenudge. You'll run out of paranoia."

His attention fixes on my bundle. "Keep your head down and don't let them smell fear.

He opens the front door, using his bulk as a temporary shield, before stepping onto the threshold facing the crowd. His throat-clearing echoes like distant thunder, his voice carrying the kind of authority that can silence a mob—or at least make them think twice about becoming one.

"HEAR THIS! The Mayor is dead, beyond question, beyond perchance. This building is now sealed for investigation. None shall enter. More will be said at The Corpse's Candle this evening."

The crowd's buzzing dies to a muted hum, their curiosity temporarily smothered by Sir Roderick's iron-clad tone.

He raises a gauntleted hand, throwing me a pointed glance. "With the bailiff away, I stand in his stead. MacAllister is acting under my authority as deputy. This is official business—he's not to be harmed. Clear a path!"

Chapter 8

Head down, I slip through the crowd before their collective imagination crawls into action. I keep moving. The Library looms ahead, its door tall and unyielding. I press my palm against the damp wood, feeling the chill creep into my skin. It doesn't yield. Of course not. I lean in, shoulder braced, and push. The door resists, groaning like a thing reluctant to wake. Then, at last, it shifts.

Shelves tower into the heights, their content cloaked in the dim, reverent light that filters from above through the vaulted central arcade. Corridors branch like veins into darkness, their Gothic arches beckoning with promises of forbidden wisdom.

Row upon row of leather-bound malice stand ready to serve before me—treatises on curses nestled against manuals of coercion, botanical guides to deadly nightshade sharing space with well-thumbed texts on the poisoner's art. This is no mere repository of learning, but Murder's Vale's own reliquary of lethal knowledge. The scale of accumulated secrets imparts a reverent unease. I pause, noting the hush that has settled over the place. The patrons drawn away to the Mayor's courtyard, leaving only silence in their wake. A figure emerges from the rows with quiet, stern authority. Peregrine Sibberidge, the Librarian, adjusts a pile of journals with precise, economical movements. Her presence commands attention without demanding it; more knife than cudgel.

"Noel MacAllister," she says, recognition in her voice.

"Hello, Mrs Sibberidge. Good to see you after so many years."

"So, you've returned from the big city, then?"

"Just briefly. I received a message about MacAllister Hall."

We venture deeper, where shadows pool between the shelves. My gaze lingers on leather spines worn smooth by generations of seeking hands.

"I'm surprised you're not at the Mayor's place?" she says.

"Well, that's where I've just come from. Sir Roderick and I have been gathering evidence. It appears he was murdered. We're announcing it tonight at the Tavern."

Her eyes glint with a hint of intrigue. "How exciting!"

"I sense things are about to get a lot more dangerous," I say.

She nods thoughtfully as she returns a book to its shelf.

My stomach rumbles. It's mid-afternoon and I've had nothing to eat. I rummage through my coat and pull out a pear—lopsided, bruised and sticky. Mrs Sibberidge eyes it like a thing best left uneaten.

"Bit squishy," I say.

We walk to another shelf.

"When power shifts, everyone's agenda comes slithering into the light," she says.

I nod, taking a bite into the pear with a loud slurp, sending juice cascading down my chin. Mrs Sibberidge flinches as a piece of skin clings stubbornly to my lip, flapping like a flag as I chew. "Sweet enough," I say.

Mrs Sibberidge clears her throat. "Perhaps a *napkin*?"

A seed has lodged itself between my teeth, and I spend a good while digging it out with my fingernail.

We drift deeper.

"The Library seems to have grown since I left."

"Trade flourishes," she says, gesturing for me to follow.

"Flourishes?"

"I these troubled times, there's an insatiable appetite for the grim instruments of fate and associated knowledge," she says, each word weighted with subterranean implications.

She examines me quizzically, "though their appetite is somewhat... outmatched by your dietary impulses, Noel."

"Funny how trade's thriving, but the village isn't?" I say.

She exhales. "Taxes, protection, blackmail—you name it. People grumble. Some resist. Most learn to live with it."

"And the money?"

"Some goes to the Crown, or so the Mayor claims. The rest?" She shrugs. "I suspect stays with the Mayor."

We reach the stairwell. "Is that bundle you carry the evidence?" she asks.

"Yes. I need somewhere secure to store it."

"There's a strongroom below," she says.

A floorboard creaks near the entrance. Mrs Sibberidge's expression hardens.

"Here," she murmurs, pressing a stack of books into my hands. "Swap these with the evidence and head out. I'll secure your items below."

We exchange items.

She meets my gaze. "Tread carefully, Noel," she whispers.

I head toward the entrance, adjusting my pace to appear casual. To the left of the door, a wooden table sags under the weight of prophecy journals—free *Daily* editions stacked in uneven piles. Behind the table, a wall of shelves looms, filled with the heavier, leather-bound *Monthly* journals, arranged in strict chronological order, their embossed spines faded with time. Further up, the *Yearly* compilations rest in solemn ranks. The entire display hums with the quiet authority of history recorded and, inevitably, misread.

Nearby, a figure lingers with a *Daily* in his hands. He turns as I approach. It's the Innkeeper. I glance at the prophecy journals. "Checking what's happening tomorrow?"

He exhales. "You know how it is. Can't run a business blind." He flicks through a page, his expression giving nothing away.

His gaze shifts to the bundle slung over my shoulder.

"Looking to do a bit of reading?" he mutters.

"Figured I'd brush up on the Blood Balance."

He pauses, flipping a page he isn't reading. "So that's what you're after?" His thumb lingers on the edge of the journal, as if considering how much to say. "I keep track of the Blood Balance, as it happens."

His gaze flicks toward the door, then back to me. "Helps avoid... unpleasant surprises."

"Unpleasant surprises?"

His eyes lift from the page. "The village requires blood to balance. Well... living blood, anyway. That's the thing about the Vale—it demands balance. Likes its population fixed. If we don't act, it decides for us." His gaze flicks toward the door, then back to me.

"Wait... the Vale decides for you?"

He nods. "Too many, and some people die. It picks who and how. But we can act first to avoid all that. That's what the scoreboard's for."

"So it's a culling?"

A slow, humourless smile. "If you want to call it that. Blood's gotta balance."

"Why isn't the bailiff in charge of it?" I ask.

"Cos, I'm the best at numbers. He checks my ledger now and then."

"What about Milton Ledbury?" I ask.

"He's an accountant—his numbers are for comfort. This one's for consequence."

A brief silence, then—"What about traders and the ones just passing through?"

He shrugs. "Only seems to matter when people stay a while."

I exhale slowly. "And if people leave?"

"You'd better ask Sir Roderick about that."

A thought crawls up my spine. "So, me and the Mayor's aunt arriving... means two have to go?"

He tilts his head. "Well, the Mayor's dead. Darius is away on business. So, for now it's balanced."

I frown. "And if Darius comes back?"

A grin forms, like a man who enjoys the game more than its rules.

"That's when the fun starts. Watch out though. He's getting a new deputy soon."

He claps a hand on my shoulder, firm and familiar. "Nothing personal."

"Well, thanks for clearing that up. I'll see you later, then."

"Looking forward to it," he says. The Innkeeper leaves without ceremony. The door swings shut behind him, leaving only the unsettling notion that this village treats life and death with all the gravity of a ledger.

I exhale, long and slow, my fingers adjusting the bundle. My gaze drifts to the prophecy journals—the harbingers of doom vie for attention: *Murder's Prophecy Monthly* and its more impatient sibling, *Murder's Prophecy Daily*. The *Monthly* feigns respectability, offering its usual banquet of misfortune—market-trader proclamations sandwiched between grim prophecies. The *Daily*, a free chronicle in recycled parchment, provides yesterday's warnings to the literate.

Prepare Thyselves! the latest *Daily* screams. As my eyes trace the inked warnings, there's an unexpected lightness in my chest—no new prophecies of murder, yet. It's a shame they don't forecast further out.

Standing here drags forth an old memory of visiting the Library with my father. "Return when you're older," he said, "there is much you should know about this place and your heritage." I make a mental note—one that tastes of inevitability—to return.

I step outside without hurry, without deviation. But the prickle at my nape lingers. Eyes will be watching. I need to throw them off the scent of the Library. No choice but to return to MacAllister Hall until the Tavern announcement later.

Chapter 9

Evening, Eleventh Day of Gorst

I spent the time at the Hall pretending the walls weren't listening. Now the real performance begins—The village tavern, The Corpse's Candle, reeks of spilled ale and open wounds. If there's a grimmer place, I haven't found it. The rain follows me inside like a faithful dog, clinging to my coat, my hair and my mood. Perfect weather for facing down a room full of people who'd love to see me swing, but this is the best place to divert their growing suspicions against me.

My appearance stirs the room like cold gravy. The Tavern is packed, simmering with not-so-subtle glances my way.

"Can't believe the Mayor's dead," announces a woman at the bar, looking over at me. "And on the day *Nibblenudge* returns, no less."

Gossip is spreading faster than a buttered ferret.

"I hear the Mayor was poisoned," says a child, voice bright with macabre enthusiasm. "But who did it?" he asks.

That earns a few dark chuckles.

The Mayor cultivated enemies with the dedication of a gardener. Now he's perchance dead, the villagers breathe easier—except me.

A hush falls like an executioner's axe as Sir Roderick strides in, confidence gleaming in his eye. His sabatons strike a measured tempo against warped floorboards as he claims centre stage. He acknowledges me with a curt nod before addressing the crowd, his voice ringing with authority.

"WELL," he booms, his eyes sweeping over the eager crowd, "as promised, you'll get answers today—some of them, at least." He lets silence build like storm clouds before continuing, his gravitas settling over the crowd. "Naturally, there's been speculation about the Mayor's death and our... discretion until now. Let me assure you, this is no ordinary death."

His eyes narrow to stilettos, probing the gathered faces.

"I'll ask my assistant to enlighten us further." He beckons me forward as grumbles echo like distant thunder.

As I reach his side, he whispers with breath hot as forge-smoke, "Best keep your wits about you."

The room goes quiet, every eye fixed on me with predatory silence. No room for timidity now—they'll string me up for sport if I show weakness.

"Nothing says *welcome back* like a good murder accusation, eh, you bastards?"

A few laughs run through the crowd, but truculence still coils in the air like a serpent waiting to strike.

"Right, let's clear something up. The Mayor isn't dead..."

Before I can finish, the room erupts like a stirred hornet's nest, disappointment and irritation buzzing through the air. Sir Roderick glares at me. I raise a hand, promising more with silence, waiting for the crowd to settle like sediment in dirty water. Their eyes fix on me, hungry for what comes next.

"No!"

"What I mean to say is—he's not just dead—he's murdered!"

I let the words fall like lead weights. Relief floods the room, followed by a wave of grim exuberance and irritation.

"Proper murdered, or perchance murdered?" a teenage boy calls out, voice sharp with cynicism.

"Proper murdered," I say, baring my teeth in what might pass for a grin. "We can't give specifics yet, but the likelihood of it not being an accident in Murder's Vale is high."

"Higher than a hundred percent?" the boy presses, cocky as a rooster.

"A hundred and ten percent." I say.

"What—the likelihood of it not being an accident is a hundred and ten percent?" the boy asks, unconvinced.

Time to summon my battering ram of logic. "No... I agree a hundred and ten percent that the chances of it not being an accident are higher than a hundred percent."

Heads bob like buoys in a storm, some confused, others eager to move on. The moment breaks with a jubilant cry from the back—"Another murder!"

The Innkeeper gestures to the left of the fireplace, drawing my eye to the *Specials Menu* for today—*Lamprey Pie.*

The Innkeeper waves a hand downward. Below the menu I spot the *Murderboard*. "We've had a few recently." The Innkeeper says.

"Really?" I ask. "what, *actual* murders?"

Silence falls like a guillotine. The patrons look at me.

"Murder is serious business here, Nibblenudge."

He points to the Murder Board, a tracker on the day's activities:

Mr Thomas Tidwell
Bed Murder—Strangled himself with his own arm.

Miss Eliza Brookstone
Horse Murder—Kicked off a hill by Betty, the horse.

Old Harold Greeves
Old Person Murder—Drowned by a passer-by.

"I was too young to know about all this when I lived here. Won't the village run out of people at this rate?"

The Innkeeper looks at me and says, "We get by."

I stare at the board for a long moment. "Funny how everyone's desperate to find the Mayor's killer, but these three got filed under '*shrug.*'"

"Everyone dies. Not everyone causes paperwork. We'll need a new mayor," the Innkeeper says.

Murmurs of agreement drift through the Tavern like wind through a graveyard.

"Tell us more about his murder," the Innkeeper says.

Sir Roderick severs the anticipation. "Hold fire! There are procedures to follow before we can divulge further details. For now, the exact nature of the murder remains sealed to protect the investigation. All will be revealed when the time is right."

The Innkeeper slams his fist on the counter, voice sharp as broken glass. "Dammit, we need more than that, man! What kind of murder are we talking about? *Bed Murder*, *Desk Murder*—what?"

I step into the fray. "Let's put it this way. This has the hallmarks of either *Vanity Murder* or *Jealous Partner Murder*."

A villager surges forward from the crowd. "Why is Nibblenudge doing all the talking?"

Sir Roderick intervenes. "You raise a fair point. But I say we use him as my deputy. The bailiff is away on business. Nibblenudge is a detective and an outsider—more or less. Of course, it's likely he's the murderer. But better to keep him where we can all watch him—let him do the investigating and see this play reach its final act."

Sceptical murmurs dance like leaves in a whirlwind.

"The choice is yours." My palms raised in surrender. "But consider this—I have been to Detective School, so there is that."

The crowd's respond with uncertain grumbles.

"Look, I know I'm the outsider," I say, "but that's an advantage. No old grudges, no tangled loyalties. I'm as neutral as they come in this village."

An old man fixes me with eyes nested in a forest of eyebrows that long ago declared independence, the peak of his overly tall hat casting a narrow shadow down his face. "What can your meddling offer? The people of Murder's Vale know murder like farmers know soil!"

Agreement ripples through the Tavern, led by an enthusiastic nodding woman at the bar.

I raise an arm, palm facing the crowd. "Tell me this. With the bailiff not here, is there a single soul here you trust? Who among you won't twist this investigation to serve their own ends?"

Reluctant nods appear like mushrooms after rain, though doubt still clouds many faces.

A voice chimes in from the crowd, "Drumley, test what this outsider knows."

Old man Drumley's smile spreads, slow and condescending, the kind that suggests he's already decided I know nothing. He tilts his overly tall hat back a fraction, as if settling in for entertainment. "Why don't you enlighten us all on how to solve a murder? We're but simple folk, after all."

A few chuckles follow. Then silence, as every eye fixes on me like arrows nocked and ready to fly.

"Well," I say, treading carefully, "obviously, you start with the basics."

Drumley's eyebrow climbs like ivy up his forehead. "Of course! The basics. Old school," he purrs, sarcasm thick as honey. "You've got it all mapped out, then?"

"Er, yes—you know? How it was done—why—the usual things."

Drumley leans back, satisfaction creeping across his face like frost. "Means, Motive, and Opportunity, you mean? Oh! He's a sharp one, folks."

A few chuckles ripple through the crowd—some mocking, others thoughtful.

The stout woman at the bar slams down her tankard. "Everyone knows that much. What about alibis?"

"And evidence!" another voice shouts through the din. "Can't do much without evidence. Oh wait, that's not right."

"Witnesses!" the burly man by the fire joins in. "Someone must've seen something. Someone's always watching."

"Timeline!" shouts a scarecrow of a man from the back. "Who was where and when? Without that, you're pissin' in the dark."

"And what about a body?" growls a voice from the shadows. "No body, no murder."

I draw breath like a man surfacing from deep water. "Yes, there's a body. Alright. Means, Motive, Opportunity, Alibi, Evidence, Witnesses, Timeline, body and—"

"WEAPONS!" a man thunders, his fist meeting a table. "No weapon, no crime!"

A woman's voice surfaces above chaos. "Whose weapon was it?"

Silence falls as minds churn, before a leather-aproned young woman ventures, "Toxicology... fingerprints... and you know, forensics?"

Embarrassed coughs scatter through the room. A stern white-haired lady throws her tankard at the young woman and growls. "Quiet!"

"Well," Drumley chirps, bright as a raven spotting something shiny. "What about crime scene reconstruction? There's no reason we can't do that ourselves, right?"

Silence. Somewhere, a spoon clinks against the rim of a tankard, the sound unnaturally loud. A dog yawns in the corner. And then...

***

The Tavern erupts like a storm—boots stomp, chairs overturn, and the mob surges to the door, a contest of elbows and theories spilling into the night like a breaking wave. In their wake, the Tavern holds its breath. Only the Innkeeper remains, along with a few lost souls too weary or too wise to join the stampede. His eyes catch mine as he polishes a glass.

"The bell's rang for playtime," he mutters.

This place devours crime like soup—hot, messy, and full of chunks they don't fully understand. I turn back to the bar. Drumley nurses his drink, eyes sharp. "Alright, you run the investigation. We'll be watching."

"Maybe that'll stop me from getting murdered, too?" I joke.

"I doubt it," he scoffs.

My attention drifts to the Innkeeper's methodical movements, his rag traversing the bar's scarred surface in hypnotic circles. "So, why's this place called The Corpse's Candle?" I ask.

His hand stills mid-motion, eyes flicking up, sharp and assessing, before returning to his task. "It's what they do for the prematurely buried. And a reminder to not bury live ones," he growls, his tone walking the knife-edge between warning and fact.

"Since we're chatting, why is an Innkeeper running a tavern?" I ask.

"It used to be an inn. A man rents a bed. He expects a safe night. A man drinks at a tavern. He knows better."

He goes quiet after that, scrubbing at a stubborn patch on the bar like it owes him an apology. I take the hint, finish my drink, and leave.

In the distance, I can see Sir Roderick lingering near the Bitter Well, seemingly oblivious to the downpour. He sees me but looks away, radiating moody silence.

"Sir Roderick!" I call toward the Well. "Still guarding the village's most valuable asset?"

He snorts. "You think this village has assets worth guarding?"

"Good point."

I smile—a thin, humourless line, but he doesn't return it. His gaze lingers on the Well. Rain beads on his coat, but he makes no effort to move. I fold my arms. "So—the Innkeeper gave me the lowdown on the Blood Balance earlier."

He doesn't respond, just keeps staring into the murky black of the Well.

"He said I should ask you about it."

"The Innkeeper should learn to keep his mouth shut."

"Right, well, he didn't." I shift my weight, watching him closely. "And now I'm curious."

Sir Roderick exhales. "Curiosity's a dangerous thing around here."

I raise a brow. "And yet, here I am."

He shakes his head, water dripping from the ends of his hair. "Leave it, Nibblenudge."

I don't.

"So, me and the old crone arriving means two have to go?"

That gets him. Just the slightest shift in his stance. His fingers curl, knuckles whitening, but when he speaks, his voice is as steady as ever. "That's not how it works."

"No?" I press. "Then how does it work?"

A pause. Finally, he sighs, rubbing a hand down his face like he already regrets answering.

"You ever watch something rot?" His voice is quieter now. "Not just spoil, mind you. Proper decay. The kind that never quite finishes because something always comes along to gnaw at what's left."

I say nothing, waiting.

"The Well doesn't bury the past," he mutters. "It... restores it. And when the balance shifts too far, when we don't bring enough in to keep the ledger even." He gestures toward the oozing pit. "This. It coughs 'em back up."

I don't immediately respond. The Well wheezes, as if acknowledging him.

"What do you mean?" I say. "It brings back dead villagers for another go? They're born again?"

Sir Roderick studies me. "That's right. But not as infants. As they were before they died—when they were intact."

"I don't buy it. That's ridiculous."

Sir Roderick fixes me with a look reserved for the profoundly dim-witted.

"Everyone?" I ask.

"Seems so. And some better not seen again."

"What happens after they climb out?"

"I've said enough."

No point pressing further. I'll let him soften awhile. I leave him to his delusions and return to MacAllister Hall.

Back at the Hall, I light a single candle. Its weak glow licks at the edges of the dark, barely holding it at bay. There's a sound outside—soft, deliberate. A scrape. A pause. Then, closer. Footsteps.

I snuff the candle, plunging the room into darkness. Then the world tilts sideways.

Chapter 10

Morning, Twelfth Day of Gorst

My head pounds—a dull, insistent ache radiating from the back of my skull. A bump. A blow. A memory skimming just out of reach. What happened? Footsteps, a door creaking, the vague impression that I should have turned around sooner.

I'm bound, dangling upside-down from the chandelier in my study, swaying like a bat in the rafters of my own existence, left to ponder who had the audacity to flip the world.

The rope bites into my ankles—a lesson in my poor choices and someone's impeccable knot work.

Rain slips through the roof, dribbling onto timbers, gathering itself into trembling droplets before surrendering to gravity and splattering against my face. With each sway, I'm both comforted and alarmed by the creak of the chandelier—strong enough to hold me, fickle enough to reconsider. The whole arrangement feeling one misplaced creak away from calamity.

My first thought is not escape; it's how long the chandelier can hold my weight. The building sounds like it's wondering the same thing, groaning around me as if debating whether to hasten my demise or let me stew in the absurdity of my situation.

I guess I should have seen this coming. They could've slit my throat or burned the place down. If this was a message—it said everything and nothing.

Chapter 11

Evening, Twelfth Day of Gorst

By dusk, the ceiling surrenders. With a final, dramatic wrench, the chandelier breaks free, flinging me groundward in a symphony of splintering wood and crushed dignity. I lie there a moment, tangled in rope, wood and glass, choking on the settling dust.

Liberated, but alive, I stagger toward the village in search of something to numb the pain. Rain, relentless as ever, turns the cobblestones slick beneath my boots, conspiring to send me sprawling into the mud. Each step sends fresh waves of pain through my bruised and battered body, but the thought of relief—however fleeting—drives me forward.

At least the evidence is secure in the Library.

I reach Drusilla's shop. It's still open, perched partway along a winding lane of crooked houses, just visible from the Square. The lane flows off the northeast end of the Market, curling away like something trying to escape. Inside, Drusilla hunches over tender herbs. Behind her, shelves march in precise formation, bearing countless jars and bundles marked in her meticulous script. The air whispers of lavender and sage, a genteel mask over the earthier scents of her trade.

"Drusilla?"

She turns with the grace of someone who knows misery is part of her daily routine.

Her green eyes flick over me, assessing the damage, as if debating whether I'm worth repairing. "Still breathing, then. Pity."

My face cracks into a hollow smile. "The chandelier proved an unreliable captor."

I scan the shelves for something to ease my pain while she studies me like a specimen under glass. "Restocking your poisons?" I blurt out automatically.

"Do you have a particular fondness for poison, Noel?"

"No, but poisoners interest me."

She crosses her arms, frost in her stare. "Tread carefully. Many things in nature walk the line between tonic and poison, Noel. The difference lies in the hand that administers them."

"Would you say that's more Moondrop's area?"

Her expression thaws into dark amusement.

The air between us lightens. "It's good to see you in pain, Noel." She selects a vial and offers it to me with amusement. "Here, take this. Rub it on where it hurts. It's the non-lethal version."

"Thanks. You wouldn't have anything... *mintier*—by any chance?"

She pauses, fingers hovering near a jar. "Mintier?"

A knowing smile blooms. "I don't stock mint, Noel. There's no need, it grows everywhere."

"But you use it in things?" I ask.

"I don't. But would you like me to get you some, you seem very interested in it. I wonder why?"

I smirk. "Let's just call it a test."

I scratch the back of my neck. "So, the night of the murder. You weren't off murdering, were you? Like, say... the Mayor? I've gotta ask everyone this—it's procedure."

She arches a brow. "As fate has it, I was here brewing something unremarkable. Alone. No witnesses—unless you count the herbs." She returns to them.

A rattle of neglected armour announces Sir Roderick's entrance. The door clicks shut behind him, and he turns to face me. A small puddle forms at his feet, rainwater trickling from the gaps in his rust-speckled plate. He removes his helmet with a slow, deliberate motion, revealing damp, dishevelled hair clinging to his forehead. His face set in a frown.

Drusilla looks over briefly and returns to watering her tender herbs.

"Sir Roderick!" I say.

He snorts and sets the helmet on the counter with a heavy thud. "Rain," he mutters.

I stare at the puddle spreading beneath his sabatons.

"Nibblenudge," he growls, "Decided to grace us with your presence, have you?"

"I was tied up with things."

"You seem to be taking a very casual approach to this investigation, Nibblenudge. Some might say apathetic. Furthermore, after your theatrics at the Tavern, chaos has spread throughout the village. It might have bought you some time—but now anyone without a strong alibi stands suspect."

"Do *you* have an alibi?" I ask.

His frown cracks his knightly facade. "I was with Milton."

"Of course, a mutual alibi."

"I see. You don't trust my word. Well, that's useful to know."

He shakes his armour dry and scans the shop. His eyes dart to Drusilla's back. Leaning towards me, his voice lowers to a whisper, "You'd be well advised to pick your battles more carefully. It's clear where we need to focus our attention. She's cunning, hypnotic, and dangerous. A mesmerising serpent in human form. And her sister's worse."

I say nothing. My priority is redirecting suspicion. The more names on the list, the less likely I'll dance at the end of a rope. Instead, I exhale sharply and roll my shoulders. "As fascinating as this has been, I need food. And enough drink to make me forget I'm here."

Drusilla doesn't turn, but I catch the slightest shift of her head—acknowledgment, or dismissal—hard to tell.

Sir Roderick snorts. "Food? Thought you lived off sheer audacity."

I don't dignify that with a response. I step toward the door, push it open, and let the bell's jangle announce my exit.

Outside, the rain renews its vendetta. Puddles swell and merge, forming temporary alliances, each one a treacherous little saboteur lying in wait for an unsuspecting boot. Above, the clouds hang low and sullen, like an argument no one's willing to finish. Murder's Vale, for its part, appears entirely unbothered. My coat clings to me with the unyielding grip of someone who doesn't understand boundaries. Still, I press on, boots squelching in a rhythm that could generously be called jaunty, if it wasn't so miserable.

Hunger drives me towards The Corpse's Candle, where I hope the food will be warm and the ale strong.

"They're saying Drusilla did it," a leather-faced woman mutters.

"No, no," Ulric slurs his protest. "Word is it was Sir Roderick. Seen by the Mayor's that night. Shadows...shadows everywhere."

They'll tear each other apart soon enough.

Ulric staggers over as I sit. His eyes are glazed with a grin listing to port. "Noel... I've been thinking. About the murder." He leans in, his grin wobbling, but his eyes sharp.

I pull a boiled duck egg from my satchel and inspect it like a jeweller appraising a gem. Its shell cracked from travel but intact enough for my purposes.

Ulric raises an eyebrow. "Looks like its gone bad, Noel."

"Nonsense." I crack it open. The shell crumbles, revealing the sulphuric yolk inside. Ulric's nose wrinkles as the aroma wafts over. Bits of shell scatter as I peel the egg with grubby fingers. I pop half the egg into my mouth, chewing slowly as bits of yolk crumble onto the table. The rich, fatty taste lingers, but I swallow too quickly and cough, spraying bits of yolk across the table. Ulric flinches, his chair scraping backward.

"Dry food makes me cough," I say, scooping the remaining yolk with my fingers and shoving it into my mouth. When I finish, I hold up the empty shell. "Empty." I toss it onto the floor, where it shatters, leaving a faint sulphuric aroma in the air.

"It's not just dry food," he slurs, trying to wag a finger at me. "You was a mucky eater, even as a kid. Always eating too fast."

I smirk, taking a deliberate bite of bread, letting crumbs scatter down my tunic.

"Mucky or efficient? History will decide."

Ulric chuckles—"Efficient like a pig, Noel."

"Shut up and enlighten me on this theory." I laugh.

"It were someone who wanted him dead," Ulric slurs.

I stare at him long enough for his ale-addled brain to register my lack of enthusiasm.

"Brilliant, Ulric," I say, nodding. "You should take up detective work. You've got a gift."

He nods, self-satisfied. "I know."

"Speaking of brilliant insights… why were you lurking near the Mayor's place when you spotted those shadows?"

He blinks, grin faltering. Alcohol has eroded his self-preservation. "Me? Oh… just… passing by."

"Passing by?"

"Yeah… passing by… I pass by lots of things, Noel. You know me."

"I do. You still living at the stables?" I ask.

He shrugs. "Most nights. Ofttimes, I make do with the Mayor's barn. It's dry."

"Try not to freeze to death in a pile of hay. I don't want another murder to solve."

He raises his tankard. "Wouldn't be much of a mystery, would it?"

I snort, taking another slow sip. The Tavern hums around us, voices thick with drink and speculation. We drink, letting the hours slip by in a haze of ale and half-baked theories, the firelight carving deep shadows into tired faces.

It's late and I can barely hold the tankard. Ulric mumbles something about finding his way to the stables, or the barn, or whichever corner of the village will have him.

"You're coming with me," I say, draining the last of my ale.

He squints at me. "What for?"

"So, I don't have to investigate your corpse in a ditch tomorrow."

He considers the probability of this, then shrugs. "Fair enough."

We step out into the rain; the downpour muffles everything except our footsteps. The roads are empty, but as we make our way back to MacAllister Hall, one thing becomes obvious—some of the footsteps aren't ours.

Chapter 12

Morning, Thirteenth Day of Gorst

Morning slinks into MacAllister Hall like a thief with no sense of urgency. Pale light filters through rain-streaked windows, catching dust motes. The grand fireplace sits cold and neglected, its once-ornate mantle now cracked, speaking of better days. A thin layer of ash coats the hearth. Beside it, my coat—discarded carelessly the night before—hasn't dried, and when I reach for it, it greets me with the cold, cloying embrace of old leather and wet fabric.

We're both still alive, no signs of a break in. Ulric is sprawled across an armchair by the fire, one boot on the floor, one arm dangling to the side. He mutters something unintelligible in his sleep, then snorts and shifts, resuming the deathlike stillness of a man who's in no hurry to meet the day.

I, on the other hand, have work to do. A quick breakfast of bread and cheese, then I head out into the grey morning. The village is waking in fits and starts. As I reach the Square, a cart rumbles over the uneven road, its driver swaddled in layers against the cold air. A few traders set up their stalls, their movements brisk and purposeful. I buy a wrapped potted-pigeon thing for later and make for the Library.

I find Mrs Sibberidge. She doesn't greet me so much as acknowledge my presence. I reach into my coat and pull out the charred parchment fragments from the Mayor's fireplace. "I found these."

She takes the blackened pieces. "Burnt vellum, what a terrible waste," she says, voice as tight as a strangled throat. "Days of preparation, careful treatment of the animal skin— only for someone to burn it."

I grab a recent copy of *Murder's Prophecy Daily*, tapping the headline that screams *Mayor Found Dead (On The Morrow)*. My gaze finds hers. "He knew something was coming. No time to hide his secrets. I'm guessing he couldn't risk its discovery."

"I wonder what else do the prophecies have to say?"

She grabs the chronicle. "The Mayor was a fool. It's just attention-grabbing nonsense. A banquet of riddles, garnished with the bitter herbs of hindsight and washed down with the sour ale of fate. Whether they're uncannily accurate or self-fulfilling hardly matters—they exist to keep tongues wagging and minds chasing shadows."

"Quite the menu you're describing. Though it sounds like the sort of feast where everyone leaves hungry."

"And yet," she says with glacial precision, "they always come back for seconds."

Food metaphors make me pecky.

From my satchel I locate a waxed linen bundle, revealing the jellied potted-pigeon I bought at the market. Its consistency is best described as 'undecided.' Savoury odour wafts out. The gelatine trembles under my touch, producing a noise better suited to something escaping a swamp.

"Bit worse for wear," I say, inspecting the pigeon. My fingers sink slightly into the quivering surface, producing a wet schlorping sound.

Mrs Sibberidge eyes it with a mix of horror and disbelief, as though it might spontaneously flap away.

She waits for me to stop. "Just remember what I said before. When power shifts, hidden schemes uncoil like serpents in the sun."

"It'll be hard to find anyone without an agenda," I say.

I pry off a chunk of the gelatinous pigeon with my thumb. The jelly slides off in a sticky mass, landing on my boot with a soft *plop*. Mrs Sibberidge grimaces as I stoop to scoop it back up, bits of dirt now clinging to the wobbly morsel.

"They never use enough salt," I remark, stuffing the jelly-coated piece into my mouth. A loud slurp echoes in the quiet. Mrs Sibberidge covers her mouth with a handkerchief, her face drawn in a tight grimace.

She folds her arms and scowls. "For pity's sake! Please don't eat in the Library."

"Sorry, Mrs Sibberidge. I haven't eaten in a while. I'll finish up quickly."

I shovel in a large, final mouthful: a pocket of congealed juices erupts against my tongue.

Mrs Sibberidge exhales sharply, composing herself. She smooths her skirt pointedly, choosing to move on. We drift further into the Library depths and reach the stairs that go down to the basement.

"Your things are stored down there. One more thing," she says, her gaze lingering on me, "your father gathered quite the archive in his time. You should take time to look through it."

Before I descend, I clear my throat. "Mrs Sibberidge—I need to ask, formalities and all that. Where were you on the night of the murder? And can anyone vouch for you?"

She draws a slow breath. "I was here. Alone."

"Right." I nod, then turn toward the stairs, leaving her answer hanging in the still air as I descend into the basement's shadows.

***

I suspect the evidence is only the first thread I'll need to unravel. Inside the basement, scrolls crowd the shelves in drunken rows, their ribbons fraying like old bandages on ancient wounds. I see the evidence on a table. A chair accepts my weight with a protesting groan that echoes my own misgivings. The lantern's light performs its usual dance of deception, turning shadows into spectres and corners into covens. Something skitters in the darkness.

My fingers drum on scarred oak until the urge to dig deeper overwhelms my better judgement. Archives or evidence? Before logic can intervene, I've surrounded myself with books. Personal journals join the fray—family members, former mayors, village elders, all spilling their secrets. Most entries are dull: livestock tallies, weather records, petty grievances.

As I read, the village's true architecture emerges. Rivalries stretch back generations, feuds buried and exhumed, alliances forged and fractured. The mayoral records prove especially illuminating: scandals evaluated, favours tracked, debts erased. Influence is a game played in ink and blood.

The village wasn't merely governed; it was curated. Laws enforced or ignored with intent, families elevated or left to wither.

Then I find it—a note that stops my breath cold: *The balance must be kept. What is given must be returned, and what is taken must be replaced.*

The name at the bottom is faint. It's my father's hand. The blood balance isn't mentioned, but it's there if you know how to look—subtler than a ledger, more insidious than a grudge. Not a rule, but a rhythm. I wasn't told of this as a child. I haven't even started on the evidence yet, but I need to look through all the archives.

It's a shame I have no more food.

Chapter 13

Morning, Fourteenth Day of Gorst

I wake with my cheek pressed to the cold table, the damp air in the Library basement settling in my lungs like a whispered warning. My body protests as I shift. For a moment, disorientation grips me. The flickering lantern, now burned low, throws long, unsteady shadows across the walls.

I push myself up, shaking off the weight of the archives. They still hold more, and I've not even got to the evidence yet. But I've run out of food, patience, and optimism, in that order. I'll be back.

Outside the Library, I see people up near the Mayor's place. Drusilla holds court there, standing, arms crossed, wearing a self-satisfied smirk that could curdle milk. Her moment of glory has arrived.

"I told you," she announces to the crowd, her voice slicing through the murmurs like a knife, "it was poison. All the signs are there."

I suspect our mistress of alchemy knows her deadly brews well enough. But her eagerness to showcase that is unexpected. Her strategy is as bare as a winter tree: she'll position herself as the authority, the torch in darkness. If the villagers rally to her wisdom, they'll be less likely to see the venom beneath. I should know.

Sir Roderick's appearance before me drowns her words, his rusty armour screaming neglect with every movement.

"Nibblenudge," he grunts, packing a wagon's worth of suspicion into my name. "Finally decided to investigate? Or out for a stroll?"

"Just trying to keep pace with the village sleuths," I say.

He thrusts today's *Prophecy Daily* at me, parchment crumpled like his dignity.

A Goat Doth Gaze at Sir Roderick All Morning: Coincidence or Quiet Judgement? He snorts, crumpling the parchment further. "That damned goat again."

I smirk. "You know, goats have an impeccable sense of character."

His focus turns to Drusilla.

"What's her game?" he mutters.

"Self-preservation—a tactic we all dabble in, don't we?"

In these twisted alleys, where every shadow harbours danger and every glance carries betrayal's seed, suspicion isn't merely a visitor—it's the host. It pours the wine, lights the candles and plays the tune everyone dances to. Here, suspicion doesn't knock—it lets itself in, puts its feet up, and stays for supper.

"Any idea when Darius will return?" I ask.

"The bailiff returned last night. He acted surprised at the Mayor's murder."

"Will he be taking this investigation over now?"

"Says he's got the Mayor's affairs to deal with, plus his new assistant to train. Maybe—if you're murdered. Make sure you keep good notes."

"Great, so the Blood Balance will increase again."

"He asked me to tell you that the sale of MacAllister Hall is now void. Bad luck," he smirks.

"There's no reason for me to stay then."

"Not so fast, Nibblenudge. That would cement your guilt. We'd enjoy hunting you down."

I knew this fate would befall me.

"Back to business then. What do we do about that dagger?" Sir Roderick asks, his gaze pinned to Drusilla. "When do we let that particular piece of theatre take the stage?"

"We need to decide if it's the main act, or just set dressing?"

"I think it's derivative," he says, "... and ponderous."

We stare at the villagers, entranced by Drusilla's theories. The poison narrative has taken root like thorns in fertile soil. She basks in her role as keeper of toxic knowledge, while her audience drinks deeply of every word.

***

After a few minutes, I fade into the fog-wrapped lanes, another ghost among many. Somewhere in this maze of deceit lies a thread worth pulling, a truth that hides in daylight. Time is running out, and it won't be long before the fingers of suspicion knit a tangled tale that crochets me a metaphorical noose.

The village noticeboard looms ahead, a graveyard of long-held grudges. I'll just check the Blood Balance Dial. It's swung from nought to plus-one with the return of the bailiff.

Scrawled beneath the dial, in handwriting that looks both hurried and accusatory:

"That bastard, Darius, is back. Tremble accordingly." Of course, his return is an existential threat to everyone. But especially me.

Beside it there's a note saying, *"Lost: One goat. Answers to 'Greg.' If found, return him intact to the bailiff, or else."* On the other side, there's a note from Milton: *"Whoever placed a scarecrow in the Square with a sign reading 'I AM MAYOR NOW'—clever, but no."*

I head over to the Tavern. Inside, its usual symphony of gossip and scheming. My usual spot in the dark corner is free. I sit and let the conversations wash over me.

"Drusilla did it," rasps a leather-faced crone. "She knows her poisons."

"No," someone counters, "it's Sir Roderick. He's been after more power."

"What about Moondrop?" I ask.

The name lands like a stone in still water. Uneasy glances ruffle through the group.

"Ruthenia?" one murmurs. "She's no killer, not like her sister."

A knowing grin splits another's face. "Maybe the herbs aren't the only thing brewing."

Silence settles before a dark chuckle breaks it. "Sibling rivalry with a twist of venom—just our luck."

Murder's Vale's second joke of the day.

The conversations continue. The investigation is on the edge of chaos.

All it needs is a little nudge.

It needs a Nibblenudge.

Ulric staggers over, bleary-eyed but determined. "Noel," he slurs, collapsing into the chair opposite me. "I saw something… the night the Mayor died."

I pause, glass mid-tilt. "Oh? What's that?"

"A shadow," he mumbles, voice thick with conspiracy. "By the Mayor's house."

My mind is racing, but I keep my expression composed. "You've said that before. What did you see?"

Ulric sways like a reed in wind, words tumbling together drunkenly. "A strange shadow. Moving. By the Mayor's house—there was someone there. I swear."

Does truth lurk in his wine-soaked memories? Could he prove reliable when it matters?

"Interesting, but are you certain it wasn't imagination's trick?"

Ulric's eyes flash with drunken indignation. "No… no, I'm sure. It'll come to me. I know it will."

A faint smile touches my lips. "You might be our most valuable witness."

He blinks owlishly. "Me?"

"Did this shadow… have a villainous deportment?"

Ulric blinks again, uncertain. "I… I think so."

I pat his shoulder. "Every day you get closer."

Another slow sip of ale and my thoughts drift on a sea of half-formed theories looking for a lighthouse in an ocean of metaphors.

The Tavern's rhythm flows around me. I settle back, but something's shifted in the air.

Heads tilt in thought, voices lower further. Others have caught Ulric's tale.

**

It's evening. The last of the stragglers are herded from the Tavern, some through conventional exits, others making impromptu departures through windows. Fog creeps around like a predator's breath, swallowing even the sharpest cries.

In the distance, past the Market, Drusilla tends the damp herbs outside her shop as if they might reveal some deep secret. Her suspicion of me hasn't waned since I arrived, but with Ulric's shadowy sighting, I've got a fresh angle. I wander up to her shop. "Drusilla," I call out.

She peers up, her eyes narrowing. "Noel," she says, her voice flat as week-old ale. "What brings you slithering to my doorstep?"

"Know anything? Anyone creeping around the Mayor's place at night?" I ask.

"Is that an accusation?" The words drip from her lips like a poison toad.

"Ulric's latest tale. Claims he spotted shadows playing peekaboo near the Mayor's place the night he was murdered."

"And you're taking the word of the village drunk?"

"Ulric sees plenty, drunk as he is. He insists it wasn't just in his head." I shrug.

She folds her arms. "Don't be fooled by his tricks. You should dig into his debt problems instead of chasing his phantoms."

Sir Roderick appears behind me like a rusted weathervane, creaking with suspicion but pointing nowhere useful. His armour glistening with misty driblets.

"Nibblenudge," he grunts, "I'm heading to the Bitter Well. Word is you've been taken in by that bard."

"He claims he witnessed something interesting the night the Mayor died. A shadow with substance, you might say."

His eyebrow rises like an unconvinced drawbridge. "A suspicious shadow? Nonsense."

"A figure. Skulking near the Mayor's residence. Didn't get details, but presence implies purpose," I say.

Sir Roderick's hand twitches toward the hilt of his sword. "And you trust the ramblings of a drunkard? Shadows don't kill people, Nibblenudge. People kill people. Or did they not teach you that at Detective School?"

"But shadows make excellent accomplices, wouldn't you say? Ulric's sighting might be nothing but drunk's dreams—or it might be everything needed to crack this case," I say.

Sir Roderick doesn't look impressed. "Your methods lack backbone, Nibblenudge."

We part ways before the conversation turns the violence.

Back in MacAllister Hall, rain streaks down my grimy windowpanes. Drusilla's poison theories and Ulric's shadow story have taken root. For now, that helps my cause. Let them tangle themselves in theories like flies in a web. It keeps them occupied while I work.

I step back, rubbing a hand over my face. It's late—time for a drink and a rest in the study. The corridors of MacAllister Hall stretch before me. A candle guttering in its sconce casts flickering shapes along the walls. I push open the study door, its hinges groaning in protest. Faded tapestries hang like trapped memories, their colours muted by time, holding onto threads of past glory. The largest looms above a long oak table, where candle stubs stand in tarnished holders like forgotten soldiers.

There's a knock at the front door. It shatters my reverie like broken glass. Dagger in hand, I open it to find Drusilla. Mist twists around her figure, giving her the appearance of a spectre delivering bad omens—a spectre armed with a knife, its blade catching the lantern glow like a sliver of moonlight.

"Noel," she says, voice taut as a garrotte. "We need to talk. There's been a loud scream near the Mayor's place."

"I see. What sort of scream? Man or woman? How long ago?" The questions tumble from my lips with practiced indifference, though my pulse quickens—an old reflex I can't quite kill, like muscle memory for impending disaster.

"It was loud. Sharp. Not a scream exactly, more like... a cry. Pained. Cut off too fast." Drusilla's fingers dance at her throat. "I was still at the shop when I heard it. I locked up—and came here avoiding the area."

I lean against the doorframe. "Drusilla, screams and shouts are Murder's Vale's lullaby. It's normal."

Her eyes narrow to deadly slits. "This seemed relevant. It's your job, isn't it? The only point to your miserable existence and complete irrelevance."

Her fingers stroke the knife's handle with the casual intimacy of a longtime companion.

I match her stare. "I only worry when the screaming stops."

"Like now?" she says.

A pause. Just enough for her words to settle, to slip under my skin. Then, without a word, I shut the door, leaving darkness to its own devices. Mysteries are better left for morning—assuming one survives to see the dawn's indifferent arrival.

Chapter 14

Late Morning, Fifteenth Day of Gorst

Drusilla's words from the previous night still leech into my thoughts. Last night's commotion near the Manor, has left me curious. Perhaps I should return to the scene—it makes a useful subterfuge to drag along the man who found the body. I get my things ready and head on out.

I pass the village noticeboard to check on the Blood Balance. It's swung from plus-one to plus-two. From the announcements, it looks like the bailiff's new deputy arrived yesterday, tilting the scales. Knives will be out.

A fresh note has been tacked beneath the dial: "*A new deputy? Wonderful. Can't wait to be told what to do by someone with a badge and no sense.*" Further down, another entry appears to have been added in haste, as though the author was gritting their teeth while writing: "*To the person who left Gregory the goat outside my house with a note reading 'You Know What This Means'—I assure you, I do not.*"

I linger for a moment, resisting the urge to add a note of my own. It's getting close to lunchtime—I make a brief detour to the market, drawn less by appetite and more by the instinct to hoard something vaguely edible. I settle on a brined eel, curled in wax paper. The eel smells like low tide and probably counts as both a snack and a weapon. Still, I tuck it into my coat like contraband and look for Milton.

Milton Ledbury, keeper of coin and confidences, had long since claimed the Manor's treasury chamber as his domain. If anyone understood the Mayor's habits—his rhythms, indulgences, and concealed intentions—it was him. But the place is out of bounds at the moment. He could be anywhere. The Tavern, the Library, his home—but I think the most likely place just before lunchtime, is his chambers on the east side of the square. I head that way and spot him instead in the bakery next door, like a well-dressed church mouse methodically dismantling a breakfast roll.

At first glance, he is unremarkable—the kind of face that disappears in a crowd—but closer inspection reveals his cultivated appearance. His curly blond hair, already thinning at the crown, is combed with deliberate care, round spectacles balanced on his nose like a judge's scales. He's dressed with the air of quiet wealth—a waistcoat pressed sharp enough to draw blood, cuffs gleaming like fresh-minted coins. Every detail has been chosen with care to reflect the control he maintains over his world.

As I approach, he raises an eyebrow. He brushes an imaginary speck from his lapel. His gaze meets mine with the warmth of a winter sun—present but offering no real comfort. "Milton!"

He gives me a once-over, the way one might appraise a painting that's been left in a damp attic. "Noel! Welcome back to Murder. I've been waiting to catch up with you. Well—you've changed," he says, with a faint smile. "More... weathered than I remember. The Vale has a long memory, but I wonder if it would recognise you at all."

It's been years since we last spoke, but he doesn't dwell on the absence—only studies me as though trying to reconcile the boy he once knew with the man standing before him. I offer nothing. Let him guess.

Then he looks at me again, eyes sharpening. "I assume you're not here to reminisce. You've come about the Mayor's murder."

He doesn't wait for confirmation—just turns back to his desk, picking up a folded copy of the *Daily* with two fingers, like it might be contagious. "And this," he adds, "is what passes for commentary in the aftermath of a man's murder. Today's literary travesty." He shows me the headline from the Daily: Pig Escapes Butcher's Block and Declares Itself Mayor.

"Drivel," he mutters, but there's something else behind it. Not just contempt—resentment, unease. As if losing control over a village narrative disturbs him more than the murder itself.

A smirk threatens to crack my professional facade. "Well... Pigs *are* clever. And clean—not many people know that."

"People don't seem to understand that the Mayor devoted his life to this village, and this?—This mockery is how they honour him? A barnyard animal?"

"Pigs are resourceful."

He stares at me like a disappointed teacher.

"They're strong. Perceptive, too!" I say.

Milton's jaw clenches. "This village spits on both its dead and living."

"You're not wrong there. Someone needs to halt this mockery," I say.

His lips compress into a bloodless line. "Indeed. The masses should remember who keeps the wheels of this village turning."

I let him relish in his own importance for a moment and then turn to business. "Milton, there was a disturbance last night—a scream near the Manor." His eyes snap to mine, sharp as a coroner's blade. "I thought we should examine the Mayor's residence. You knew his habits. I could use your insights."

He considers this like an accountant weighing gold, then nods. "If anything's been disturbed, I'll notice."

"I appreciate it. Let's drop the formalities—Noel will do. Better to have someone who knows the place's secrets well enough to spot when they've been disturbed."

His scrutiny dissects my intentions like a butcher sizing up meat. "Of course."

We make our way toward the Manor. "Your assistance is valuable, Milton," I say, offering politeness like a loaded pistol.

"Fresh eyes—especially ones as sharp as yours might illuminate some shadowy corners."

"Always eager to serve truth's cause," he says, "the Mayor's affairs were complex; perhaps together we can make some sense of them."

***

The Manor looms ahead. Gothic carvings leer from the stonework, their frozen expressions more warning than welcome. Inside, our footsteps echo across marble floors, leading us toward the study where Ellington Crumley had penned his final chapter. The study crouches in darkness, its curtains drawn like a widow's veil, allowing only the most determined rays of light to penetrate its gloom.

Milton stays by the door. "We've not been allowed to return since that night."

"Let's look around for any disturbances," I say.

The study remains as I'd left it. The bloodstains on the floor have darkened to the colour of old wine, marking the Mayor's final contribution to the room's decor. We take our time checking the room.

Nothing looks missing or disturbed. The Mayor is gone, thankfully, though the odour lingers. Heavy drapes stay drawn in deference to death's privacy, wrapping the room in twilight.

"Mayor always preferred this room cloaked in shadow," Milton says, his familiarity with the space in every glance. "Said it helped him think."

"Fascinating," I say. "A man in his position must have had much to contemplate."

"The Mayor was a man of grand ambitions and even grander schemes. His mind was always several steps ahead, weaving plans within plans."

I gesture at the tower of documents. "I imagine he kept you busy?"

"The Mayor preferred to keep his hands clean of the minutiae—most of the time."

"A bit of creative accounting?"

A short, humourless laugh escapes him. "Nothing so crude. He'd slip things in—expenses, contingencies."

"For what?"

"Various projects," Milton replies. "Investments, land acquisitions, alliances. He was always seeking ways to expand our influence."

"That so? Did he meet any resistance?"

"Change is never welcomed in Murder's Vale."

I approach the desk, fingers hovering over a weathered ledger I'd left behind in my haste. The leather cover feels like old skin, its spine cracked and faded to the colour of dried blood. Inside, numbers march across yellowed pages in rigid formation, each entry a soldier in Milton's army of arithmetic. Scanning the entries, discordant notes emerge from the financial symphony—dates that skip like missing heartbeats, amounts that swell and shrink without reason, and in the margins, cryptic symbols dance like ancient runes. My finger traces an enigmatic symbol, watching him from the corner of my eye.

He leans forward. "That was a private venture the Mayor was exploring. He hadn't shared the details."

"Did the Mayor have any personal conflicts that you're aware of?"

He pauses in thought. "None that he mentioned explicitly. Though there were clashes with villages over tariffs. Minor disagreements, really."

"Nothing warranting bloodshed?"

"We prefer civilised solutions."

"We?"

He dismisses the slip with a shrug that's too casual to be genuine. "Well, after handling so many of his affairs, one develops a certain... investment in the outcomes."

"So you weren't just counting coins in the shadows?"

"If you're implying I aided in anything unsavoury, you're mistaken. The Mayor kept everyone at arm's length—even me."

"Let's talk about his final evening. Was burning midnight oil his custom?"

Milton rubs his spectacles with a cloth before responding, like a man testing thin ice. "He preferred starting mid-afternoon, working well into the evening."

"Walk me through that evening—start with your movements before finding him."

Milton measures me with a calculating glance before speaking. "I was in the Archive room hunting documents. Sir Roderick was in my treasury chamber." He pauses. "When I returned to the treasury, Sir Roderick mentioned hearing the Mayor's footsteps leaving the study, but he hadn't heard the Mayor return. I thought perhaps he'd stepped out for air."

I raise an eyebrow.

"We searched everywhere—corridors, dining room, kitchen. Nothing. I returned to the study, thinking he might have circled back."

He gestures toward the massive desk, a wooden altar to bureaucracy. "At first, I thought he'd passed out, but that dagger..."

A shudder ripples through him, his voice dropping to a whisper. "I shouted to Sir Roderick. He confirmed my fears. Then I caught the scent of poison—didn't dare breathe too deeply. We... left him until morning."

His eyes dart to mine like trapped birds. "That's everything." His fidgeting hands betraying the calm he's trying to wear.

"While you were playing archivist, did he stay put in the treasury?"

"He did, while we shared the space. His movements during my absence... I couldn't say."

"And his footwear preferences? does he wear socks, do you know?"

"Socks?" Confusion clouds his features.

"Nevermind. So, you can't account for his movements for the entire period?"

"No," he says, thoughtful shadows crossing his face. "I cannot."

"Must've been a tough call—letting the Mayor marinate in poison all night. Didn't occur to you he might still be breathing?"

"Look," Milton stammers, his composure cracking. "There was a big dagger in his back. He wasn't moving. A killer was loose in the Manor House. We smelt that poison..."

He swallows hard. "You don't take chances with such things around here. Sir Roderick insisted we withdraw. Let matters... settle until dawn brought clarity."

His eyes dart away from my unwavering stare. "We were... certain he was finished."

"That dagger... did you recognise it?"

Milton blinks. "Recognise? No, why would I?"

"Thank you, Milton. That's been enlightening. That's all I need for now."

It's getting late in the day. Milton returns to his treasury chambers and archive rooms to check on them before he heads off, and I survey the quiet study, letting each clue simmer in my mind. With a last glance around, I step out into the early evening and let the study's oppressive atmosphere slide from my thoughts.

"Time to hear what the tavern dwellers have to say about our friend Milton." A few ales are sure to loosen tongues. Milton is a man of intellect and precision, capable of manoeuvring through complex situations with poise. If he was involved in the Mayor's demise, it won't be easy to prove.

***

The Tavern wraps me in its cloak of spiced ale and simmering stew. Local faces huddle around worn tables like mourners at a wake, trading whispered secrets over amber-filled tankards.

I scan the crowd; each face a potential key to unlock the maze Crumley left behind.

The Innkeeper acknowledges me with a nod as weighty as judgement. "Nibblenudge. What do you want?"

"Your finest," I say, settling onto a stool scarred by countless nights of similar conversations. As he draws my drink, I extract a brined eel in waxed paper from within the folds of my coat, its leathery surface shimmering in the dim tavern light. The Innkeeper recoils as the sharp, briny aroma wafts between us. His face twists like a man confronted with a corpse.

"Found this beauty at the Market," I say, holding it aloft as though it's a prized relic, it flops limply in my grasp.

"No outside food. You want to eat that here? It'll cost you."

"A levy? For the privilege of eating my own eel? What's next, a breathing tax? A surcharge for existing?"

"You won't be needing a breathing tax."

"Fine," I say. "Add it to my tab."

The Innkeeper makes a show of wiping his hands on a rag, eyes narrowing. "You don't have a tab."

I shrug. "Start one."

The Innkeeper pulls a knife from beneath the counter and places it on my little finger. "If you want a tab, I'll need collateral. Otherwise, it's two silver for the food."

I slide over the coins, staring at the Innkeeper as I slip the eel's tail into my mouth. I bite into it, tearing at the meat with enthusiasm that borders on violent. Brine dribbles down my wrist, pooling on the bar counter. The Innkeeper looks at me, the corners of his mouth twitch as though suppressing the urge to hurt me.

"Is it always this busy?" I ask.

"Aye."

I continue to chew the eel with my mouth open, letting the juices seep out onto my chin. "Bit tough," I say, spitting a sliver of skin onto the counter. It lands with a wet *plop*, but I pay it no mind, tearing off another bite. This time, a sliver of flesh dangles from my lip, *flapping* as I speak. "Want some?" I waggle the remaining eel vaguely toward him.

He shakes his head.

Perhaps he's already eaten.

"You could at least peel it," the Innkeeper mutters as I chew, the sound of squishing meat mingling with cracking bones.

"Peeling's for the weak," I say, tearing off another chunk. A stray bone catches in my throat, and I cough violently, spitting out the offending shard onto the counter. The Innkeeper cringes as it skids toward him. He responds by throwing a cloth at my face and points to the *spillage*.

"Was the Mayor overdue a reckoning, do you think?" I let the question float like bait while mopping up brine and bone from the counter.

"Of course, but he paid people to protect him," he says, leaning in, sharing confidence like contraband. "People that aint getting paid now."

"Any particular people?" I ask.

The Innkeeper shrugs. "Enough. They'll want recompense. In blood or coin."

"Didn't he also tax heavily?"

The Innkeeper leans against the counter, voice now a whisper. "He did. Give with one hand, take with the other. If you didn't help, then life got tough. Plenty helped."

"Interesting. Fear and favour. Was Ledbury involved?" I ask.

"What do you think?" Without waiting for an answer, he wipes his hands on a rag and steps away, turning his attention to another patron leaving me to my thoughts.

As expected, Milton's fingers reached deeper into the pie than he'd admitted. Conversations swirl around me as I nurse my drink. Milton was not just a treasurer in his book-lined cage, but a spider dancing on threads of his own spinning. The Mayor had played his ruthless game, squeezing blood from stones until the stones grow legs and decide to strike back. His aggressive plans created a garden of motives, each one blooming with deadly potential. Even the most loyal servant might snap under such pressure. Who better to exploit the Mayor's vulnerabilities than the man who kept his secrets? He had access to everything—the books, the contacts, and most importantly, the Mayor himself.

Another drink, the ale bitter as truth on my tongue. The warmth of the Tavern wraps around me like a false comfort as I contemplate my next move.

Two men settle on stools either side of me at the bar, their coats dripping, their faces carved from old leather. They don't speak. Just sit, looking ahead. My thoughts coil, ready to strike, but my face remains still. I study my empty glass like it holds the answer to a question I'd rather not ask.

When I rise to leave, they rise.

Outside, I pull my coat tighter; drizzle conspires with the night. Rain doesn't care about hunters or prey—it only knows how to fall. I quicken my pace—no use. A hand clamps onto my shoulder and spins me around.

The first punch comes from nowhere, followed by another, then another—no drunken sloppiness, just cold efficiency. I don't see faces, only the blur of movement and then the sharp snap of pain. When it's over, they leave me in the mud, my ribs aching, blood trickling from my lip. There's no calling card. Is this a warning, a punishment, or their idea of fun? Who sent them?

I stay down for a breath, then another, listening to their retreating footsteps. No taunts, no whispered warnings—just the rain swallowing the evidence. When I finally move, pain flares sharp and insistent, mapping out each place they left their mark. I drag myself back to MacAllister Hall, each step a reminder of the night's unanswered questions.

Inside, I bolt the door, pressing my forehead against the wood for a moment. The hall is silent except for my own ragged breathing. My fingers twitch—habit wants to check for broken ribs, but I already know what I'll find. Pain, bruises, and no real answers.

Murder's Vale doesn't offer answers, only resistance. It's a puzzle, but not a clever one—more like a rusted lock, corroded shut, unwilling to be pried open. But even the most stubborn locks break, eventually.

And I'm not done picking.

Chapter 15

Morning, Sixteenth Day of Gorst

This morning is as persistent as the painful bruises across my body—its tiny daggers pierce my skin with icy indifference. I trudge through the Square, each step sending up a small rebellion of mud and filth. The fragments of gossip and half-truths I've collected tumble through my mind, like bones in a fortune-teller's cup, rattling against each other but refusing to settle into anything resembling clarity.

Sir Roderick is standing by the Bitter Well in his rusted armour, looking like a suit of armour someone forgot to empty. His face wears its usual expression: the look of someone who's discovered his favourite chair has developed opinions, most of them unpleasant.

"Nibblenudge," he grunts, my name scraping past his teeth. His eyes perform their customary inventory of my supposed sins, his jaw tightening—a tell I recognise as his internal monologue with suspicion.

"I've been meaning to speak with you."

"Ah, Sir Roderick, what's on your mind? Found a cursed chicken?"

"There's something you need to see." He growls. "But tell anyone about this and you'll hang in the gibbet."

"Before we go, I need to know more about the Well."

He grunts. "I wish you'd ask someone else."

"Is the Well the centre of it all? Like a volcano spewing out the dead?"

He sighs. "Something like that." His gaze lingers on the abyss. "Rebirthing them." He pauses, then adds, almost casually, "You'll climb out of it again one day. You won't remember the first time—too young."

I frown, searching my mind for some buried trace of that grim horror, but there's nothing. Just the Well, staring back.

I watch him carefully. "What happens after they climb out?"

He exhales, rolling his shoulders like he's trying to shake something off.

"Depends."

"On what?"

He looks at me like I should already know the answer. "On who they are. Now can we return to the other matter?"

I file away the Bitter Well's grim revelations for later.

His voice is brisk now, businesslike. "Come with me." He turns without another word. I follow, curiosity prickling at the back of my neck like a premonition with icy fingers. Whatever's got Sir Roderick bothered enough to seek my company must be worth investigating—or at least worth remembering for future leverage. We leave the Bitter Well behind, threading through the Square and past the Market's restless stirrings.

The road winds ahead, skirting Milton's house and the farmland stretching beyond. From there, it arcs east, curving past the main village road before snaking toward Sir Roderick's estate. Inside Highgrove Hall, it feels like a museum of Murder's Vale's discarded memories. He leads me through the corridors to the study at the rear of the building. On a hulking slab of dark-stained oak, polished to a sullen gleam, sits a broken crest. Its surface is marred with dried mud, clinging to the jagged edges.

My finger brushes against the rough limestone as I look close. "What's this?"

Sir Roderick crosses his arms, his face settling into its default expression of profound disappointment.

"It's my family crest. Or what's left of it. It was found at Crumley Manor yesterday afternoon buried in mud, as if someone had dropped it in a hurry."

Once pristine white limestone has aged to a tired grey and split through its centre like a broken promise. A lion's head snarls from its heart, its mane transforming into wild vines and branches—nature and nobility locked in eternal struggle. Above, the family motto, the words: *Semper Fidelis Fortis*—broken as the stone that bears it. Shattered like a porcelain vase in a pig's pen, leaving fragments of reputation for everyone to tiptoe around.

"Who found it?"

"The new deputy bailiff," he growls.

"I take it he's taking over this investigation?" I ask.

"Why would you want that? You're more likely to be named the killer," Sir Roderick mutters.

"Another fresh face. That'll tip the Blood Balance. When do the villagers start sharpening their knives?" I ask.

Sir Roderick reaches for a nearby decanter, pouring himself a measure of something dark and accusatory. "Anytime. People usually give it a few days to avoid being hasty."

He gestures vaguely toward the crest. "Perhaps this is saying I'm next."

Its break isn't natural; these edges speak of deliberate destruction rather than time's slow erosion. One half lies flat in surrender, while its partner tilts upward, revealing spiderweb cracks that threaten to reduce the whole thing to rubble.

My fingers trace the break's jagged path. "You're right. Broken like this... *it's not only theft. It's a message.* Someone wants to make their point in stone."

I catch the momentary twitch of Sir Roderick's eyebrow before his face resumes its usual fortress of disdain. Something catches my eye—a faded rust-coloured stain in the crack. Old blood, maybe. "Did you notice this?" I tilt the crest toward what passes for light in this gloom.

He doesn't answer, and I don't press him.

His scowl deepens. "The point is that it was attached to the wall in my study. Someone took it—and finding it near the..." He lets the implication dangle like a noose.

The logistics alone are interesting. Moving something this substantial, breaking it, and depositing it outside the Mayor's residence suggests premeditation. Whether it's meant as a threat, insult, or something more arcane remains to be seen.

"I see your frustration, but it doesn't seem connected to the investigation. It wasn't there when we visited the Mayor's place after the murder, although we didn't check around the outside."

His eyes meet mine, hard as winter frost. "I don't trust anyone in this village, Nibblenudge. Least of all you. But I wanted to see what you make of it. If it was your doing after our little spat outside the Mayor's, then face me like a man."

"Nice to know where I stand," I mutter, studying the crest. Even broken, it radiates the kind of authority that comes from centuries of looking down on common folk. A family lineage whose influence has faded but whose pride hasn't noticed its irrelevance. I adjust the larger piece, feeling its weight. "Whoever did this wanted the act seen. But who?"

He shakes his head like a man trying to dislodge an unwelcome thought. "Could be anyone in this cursed place."

"Someone's trying to draw a line between you and the Mayor's death," I say.

His eyes narrow. He leans forward, his bulk turning the simple movement into a threat. "You're saying it *wasn't* you?"

"I'm an outsider. I had no stake in either you or the Mayor."

He doesn't look convinced. He gestures toward the crest. "It might be connected to the murder. Let me know if you find anything. But keep it quiet."

***

The road narrows as I make my way back into the village. The clouds sulk above, heavy with unspent spite, and the wind smells of wet stone. I take the lane past the Corpse's Candle, boots squelching in familiar mud, when a flicker of movement near the hedgerow catches my eye.

Moondrop is there—half-hidden in the undergrowth, bent low as she plucks something delicate from the earth. Her basket rests beside her, already brimming with stems and roots, their scents faint but familiar: nettle, valerian, maybe the bitter edge of widow's root. She hasn't seen me. Or if she has, she chooses not to show it.

I pause. Not to startle her—just to watch. She works without hurry, without hesitation. Every movement is quiet and assured, like she belongs more to the earth than the village behind me. The rest of us are tangled in theories and panic, but she's still gathering what the ground offers, as if murder hasn't shifted the soil at all.

I step closer.

She glances up then, only briefly. "Noel."

"Moondrop."

She returns to her work without another word. The silence that follows isn't cold, just… habitual. Neither of us rushes to fill it.

I watch her fingertips brush dirt from a pale green stalk.

"Mind if I ask some questions while you work?" I say.

She doesn't answer at first. Just breaks off a stem and places it carefully in her basket. Then a quiet, "Of course."

I nod, though she isn't looking. "I've been wondering what the Mayor's death might mean for the village."

She moves to the next patch, kneels again, begins parting the leaves. Still no reaction. So I ask again—carefully.

"Do you think the Mayor's murder will change anything?"

"What a shame for my sister," she says, as if continuing a conversation we hadn't started. "All that care she gave the Mayor and now he's dead," she adds, turning back to the plants.

I watch her for a moment, waiting to see if she'll say anything else. She doesn't.

"I should be going," I say, and pull my cloak tighter. "But before I do—just a formality. I need to know your movements on the night of the murder."

She doesn't stop. "You mean, do I have an alibi?"

"I'm checking everyone's whereabouts."

She leans back on her heels and wipes her hands on the hem of her cloak. "I was at home. A quiet night. No witnesses, I'm afraid."

That familiar ghost of a smile crosses her lips—barely there, but real. I search her face, but as always, it gives me nothing.

"Fair enough," I say.

"Have you satisfied your curiosity, Noel? Or will you be back—with more questions and even fewer answers?"

I nod. "Probably."

Moondrop turns back to her gathering, already vanished into the foliage like the conversation never happened.

The rain follows me as I leave, insinuating itself into every seam of my coat. I walk on, boots squelching through the soft mud. Another empty alibi—calm, polite, and entirely useless. It's the same with all of them—answers that reveal nothing, smiles that conceal too much.

I need somewhere to think.

Chapter 16

Later, Sixteenth Day of Gorst

The Tavern beckons—perhaps a drink and a dark corner will help me untangle this web of deceit and decide where to rake next. But this afternoon, the mist has ambitions. It's not content to skulk like a stray cat; It's plotting. It settles over the Tavern like a brooding spectre, roosting with patient malevolence, as if waiting for the patrons to stagger out the door. Meanwhile, rain pecks at the roof in arrhythmic fury, like an irate woodpecker, restless and unsatisfied.

Inside, a drink offers clarity—or at least a temporary illusion of it.

Milton Ledbury. That's my next move.

If the Mayor's murder was about money, his ledger will be its confessor—or its alibi.

The Mayor's Manor includes offices for the treasury and archives where Milton spends most of his working days, but his business chambers are wedged between the butcher's shop and the bakery, where the stench of raw meat mingles with scorched bread. A fitting place for a man accustomed to figures—both financial and dismembered.

I push back from my table, abandoning a half-drained tankard. Milton's chambers lie just east of the Market—a short walk, yet long enough to reconsider whether I'm truly prepared for the man's particular blend of self-importance.

Outside, the sky sags beneath the yoke of rain clouds, their collective grumbling settling into the sodden lanes. Water slithers through the cracks in the cobbles.

I cross the road off the Square toward the narrow row of shops tucked beneath the library. Milton's door sits small and smug between them.

I knock. Wait. Nothing. Typical. I push the door open and step inside.

He's hunched over his desk like a monk at prayer, his quill scratching numbers with the desperate energy of a man trying to calculate his way out of damnation. Leaning against the doorframe, I take in his scroll-strewn sanctuary and look for somewhere to sit.

Abandoned quills litter his desk, and the butcher's signature perfume hangs thick in the air. "It smells like the aroma of a man slowly drowning in his own calculations in here." I say.

He sniffs like an offended undertaker. "Numbers don't manage themselves."

He points to a chair across from him. I sit. The desk before me is a war zone: ledgers sprawl open like bodies on a battlefield, quills stick out of an inkwell crusted with the remains of battles past, and a lone candle stands, crying wax tears onto a saucer that's seen too many vigils to count.

The walls tell their own story of neglect, bare except for the ghost of what might have been a map, its features worn away. A window near the ceiling admits just enough light to mock the darkness below, though the shadows creeping across the floorboards suggest they're winning the daily battle.

Milton himself appears to be practising the art of disappearing into his own shadow. Sweat beads on his forehead despite the chill, and he mops at it with a handkerchief so worn it's more memory than cloth.

"Relax. I'm not here to accuse you of murder." I grin with a wink, "—yet." That gets his attention. He peeks up, paler than usual—which for Milton is like saying the dead look tired.

"Good," he says, sounding irritated. "I didn't kill him. And now I've got twice the work trying to hold everything together."

"Together?" I ask.

He deflates like a punctured wineskin, slumping forward as though his spine's finally given up the fight. He retrieves a massive ledger from a drawer and slides it across the desk like a peace offering. "Look at this," he says, his hand lingering on the cover as if reluctant to let go of his last defence.

"Another ledger?"

"This is the one from his desk, I asked Sir Roderick to retrieve it so I can maintain the village affairs while the Manor is out of bounds. This what I call the formal ledger. It's for the tax collector's eyes. Look at all the alterations. Money playing hide-and-seek without rules."

"You said he often made changes."

"He wasn't to alter formal accounts, only to the detailed ledger. This will raise questions. Criminal investigation. From the Crown." His hands hover over the ledger like a father over a fever-stricken child, trembling before clenching into fists. Emotions chase each other across his face—rage, fear, desperation.

"I can't fix it." His voice climbs like a cat up a tree. "The ledger is bound with the royal seal. Once written, any edits are visible." He exhales, hands dancing across the ledger's surface like nervous spiders. "So here I am, keeper of chaos, waiting for judgement. I'm the only one accountable now."

A lone candle on Milton's desk flickers defiantly against the siege of the weather outside. Milton slides over another ledger.

"Here's the detailed version—what I call the informal ledger."

The ledger groans as I ease it open, its pages worn with use. I read the first page. Columns stand at attention, each figure placed with care. If bookkeeping is an art, Milton is its tortured maestro. Every transaction recorded with religious devotion; each coin accounted for like a precious relic.

"Lantern oil," I say aloud, savouring the mundane words. "Stable repairs. Sepultra fees. Market taxes." My finger pauses on strange marks beside each entry. Each with its own little symbol. A crescent moon guards the lantern oil entry, a slashed circle brands the stable repairs. Sepultra bears a cross. At first glance, harmless shorthand.

"And Sepultra is what, exactly?"

He glances up. "Cemetery supplies."

I murmur acknowledgment, moving down the page. "These taxes look vague. How do you track who owes what?"

Milton sighs. "There's a process. Every merchant, vendor and taproom have their mark. The Mayor insisted on symbols instead of names."

"Symbols. Efficient."

"If by efficient you mean needlessly baroque," he snaps. "His preference, not mine."

Baroque, something about the word makes me hungry.

"I think it's time for a little pick-me-up, Milton," I say.

I pull a wrapped sausage from my coat pocket, its greasy surface gleaming in the firelight. Milton stares at it as if I've pulled out a snake.

"How long have you had that?" he asks.

"Long enough to know it's still good," I say, taking a hearty bite. The casing bursts with a faint *pop*, and grease dribbles onto my chin. I wipe it away with my sleeve, leaving a shiny smear.

"Watch the pages! That grease will stain!" he shouts.

Humming, I leaf through pages. The ledger is a study in contradiction—Milton's obsessive order disrupted by the Mayor's cryptic additions.

I read more entries, letting boredom coat my voice. "Parchment, bulk order. Candle wax from market vendors. Three crates, personal delivery."

Milton flinches as I take another bite, this time biting into the middle of the sausage rather than the end.

He glances over. "You eat like a barbarian."

I chew noisily, savouring the spices. "Baroque, barbarian—call it what you like. Either way, it's efficient," I say, holding up the remaining sausage like a trophy before shoving the rest into my mouth.

The last ledger entry snags my attention. The writing is jagged, ink smeared as if written in haste. Its numbers dance to a tune that makes no sense—too much coin for such a vague description. I tap the entry. "Your handiwork?"

He stiffens. "No. As I said."

I grunt, returning to the pages. My eyes track the mysterious symbols scattered in the margins. "Never occurred to you to question their meaning?"

He massages his temples with ink-stained fingers. "Why would I? The Mayor was very secretive."

"Was the Mayor skimming off money?" I ask.

Milton swallows hard, his eyes dart to the rain- spattered window as if the answer might escape into the rain. "No! Of course not," he stammers, then hesitates. "He might have... guided it. Not theft, of course—just ensuring the right pockets stayed heavy, the right hands remained open. Politics, Noel. Just politics."

My chair protests as I lean back—it punctuates the silence. The ledger squats between us like a toad hoarding snails. I slam it shut with a sound like a coffin lid dropping. "And you played along, kept the numbers neat while the Mayor turned the village inside out?"

Milton leans forward, "Listen... who could I tell? In this place, trust is rarer than sunshine. The Mayor said it was for the village's good."

I drag a hand across my face, tasting the frustration. "I need names. Who owed the Mayor?"

He straightens; his eyes drawn to the ledger. "It's all there. Debts, payments—everything he made me record. But don't expect clarity."

What will kill me first—talking to Milton or being lynched for the Mayor's murder? I stand, tucking the informal ledger under my arm. "I've seen and heard enough for now."

"You're taking it?" His voice cracks like thin ice.

"Evidence." I move toward the door.

He protests, but the look I give him says I'm not in the mood. Milton collapses into his chair, glaring at the ledger like a betrayed lover.

"Relax," I say. "I'll bring it back. But you should keep a low profile." I adjust my grip on the book. Stepping outside, I pull my coat tighter against the drizzle. The evening air hits me like a slap. The ledger weighs heavy under my arm. Somewhere between the salted fish and candle wax, truth lies waiting to be uncovered. But not tonight. The day has bled out, and soon the village will turn its attention to the Mayor's funeral.

Chapter 17

Morning, Seventeenth Day of Gorst

Dawn arrives grudgingly, dragging a sullen light. The Cemetery stirs with figures, drawn not by grief, but by the promise of spectacle. The Mayor's burial is less a farewell and more a morbid punctuation mark in a long, festering story.

The Cemetery sprawls at the edge of Murder's Vale, its rows of graves—some marked, some bare—like a matrix of missing teeth. Headstones lean and list like drunken revellers: some crumbled to mere suggestions of markers, others swallowed by the hungry earth, and many with no stones at all. Scattered among them lie ledger stones—some grand and engraved, others small and blank as unspoken sins—flat slabs sunken into the soil, as if the dead beneath had tried to keep their heads down. Around it all, the perimeter fence sags in rust-flecked vigil, warped as if the iron had once tried to flee but gave up halfway through.

One by one, the villagers filter in. The procession winds up from the fork in the road by Milton's house, where the road splits eastward around the farmland beside Highgrove Hall, and west, leading to the Cemetery gate.

From the gate, a path snakes through the burial ground, bordered by wild ivy and overgrown grass that whispers in the breeze. At the heart of it all stands an ancient yew, its dark branches clawing at the sky as if trying to escape into the heavens. At the far end of the Cemetery, newer graves stand in militant rows, betraying the pragmatic efficiency of the villagers.

This is no ordinary funeral—it's the Mayor's bow, and the legacy of corruption hanging over the proceedings as if grievances themselves have come to witness his descent into the dirt. Centre stage sits the coffin—a monument to tastelessness. Dark wood gleams with an unnatural sheen, its edges festooned with carved ivy and roses better suited to a boudoir than a hole in the ground. A gilded crest adorns the foot, its lacquer cracking like the Mayor's promises, while atop the lid, red roses and thistles arrange themselves in garish display.

The whole affair gives the impression of a poorly staged tragedy, its theatricality bordering on parody. The villagers make little effort to hide their scorn.

Stepping away from the crowd, I drift toward the undertaker—a wiry spectre in a mud-stained coat studying the *Daily's* news with professional detachment.

"Seen tomorrow's headlines?" the undertaker drawls. "Market Day Tumult: Turnip Tossing Sparks Fistfight," he quotes, tossing it aside.

"Busy week?" I ask.

His sunken eyes flicker my way like disturbed moths. "Fairly quiet at the moment. Work comes in clusters."

"The Blood Balance must help?"

"Sometimes. Not everyone can afford professional services. There's a lot of do-it-yourself business around here. Works fine, mostly. Long as we don't get... surprises."

"Surprises?"

"People not following the Grid System." The undertaker gestures at the arrangement of graves like a proud architect. "Keeps things orderly. No one wants to dig up... *leftovers*."

"Did the Mayor pay for your services in recent times?"

"I don't think so."

"So not him, his bookkeeper, or the bailiff?"

"Don't think so."

"His ledger mentions cemetery supplies. Seems odd, though, given he was a man who could afford your services."

The undertaker shrugs, attention already sliding back to the news. "Less odd than you'd think. Some prefer discretion. Quiet burials, no names. Happens more than you might expect. Folks have their reasons."

My thoughts churn like maggots in a corpse: Supplies, secret burials and discretion—the Mayor had buried something more than his conscience. *But who?*

"Any chance you'd know if he carried out a burial? The location, perhaps?"

"No chance at all." The undertaker's response cuts like a sexton's spade. "That's the point. So long as people keep to the grid, everyone's happy. 'Nullae mirae' is our vision statement now." He pauses.

"Course, it used to be 'Primum non nocere'," he says and goes quiet again.

"Before that, it was 'Noli esse malus'."

"Why all the changes?" I ask.

"There was trouble sticking to the earlier ones?"

"Have they embraced the sentiment?"

"Who cares? It's all a load of horseshit, but it keeps them in check for a while."

My mind moves onto the implications of nameless burials without ceremony or record as I head back to the edge of the gathering.

With no house of worship in Murder's Vale, a vicar from another region presides. No one cares—faith, belief, and obedience are all absent. He stands by the coffin, draped in black, eyes shadowed beneath the brim of his hat. His voice, thin and hollow, cuts through my musings like a dull knife—slow, blunt, and unwelcome.

"Friends and... well, all those who knew our beloved Mayor Crumley," he says, raising hands skyward, "we gather to honour the life of an irreplaceable leader of grand vision."

The crowd's response is a symphony of stifled laughs and coughs, punctuated by knowing glances.

Above us, the clouds conduct their own funeral—first a gentle patter, then a crescendo of spite that drowns out the vicar's platitudes.

Among the mourners stands Drusilla Hobbert, her attire a perfect match for the funeral's theatrical nature. Her glare is as sharp as a blacksmith's chisel, carving lines of regret into anyone foolish enough to meet her gaze. Beside her, Sir Roderick Highgrove shifts in his armour, which catches what little light penetrates the gloom. His keen eyes patrol the crowd like a guard seeking escapees. Further back, Moondrop murmurs incantations, scattering herbs toward the grave as if feeding invisible pets. In the front row, Milton Ledbury radiates unease, his constant fidgeting marking him like a beacon.

"Let us remember the integrity, the... ambitions of this remarkable man," the vicar soldiers on, struggling to hold his listeners' attention as he forces praise from each line. "Let us cherish his contributions and preserve his memory... for what he was."

Reactions rustle through the crowd—unable to suppress its collective scoff. If Crumley's memory is preserved, it will be as the man who made enemies faster than friends. Some roll their eyes skyward, while others, Drusilla chief among them, savours the absurdity like fine wine. She lets wolfsbane slip through her fingers like an afterthought, but her eyes hold intent. Her arched eyebrow and knowing smirk suggesting she's enjoying her own private joke. Then, with slow deliberation, she tosses a sprig of mint—directly into the grave. A warning? A mockery? Or a message meant just for me?

The vicar's monologue finally grinds to a close. The pallbearers step forward for their grim duty. They thread thick ropes through the coffin's ornate handles, nervous hands gripping frayed ends. They exchange glances, then begin their careful choreography. Slowly, they lift the coffin from the trestles and inch it toward the grave. The polished monstrosity hovers briefly above its destination, then begins its descent.

But then—

A crack of splintering wood ricochets through the Cemetery. The pallbearers stagger as the coffin's bottom surrenders, dumping its contents into the waiting earth. Gasps scallop through the crowd as the Mayor's body makes its ungraceful final appearance—followed by an unexpected encore. The mist swirls backward as a wild-eyed stowaway bursts from the within the open grave like an undead jack-in-the-box. Rain, ever the opportunist, makes escape slippery as it gleefully turns the edges treacherous.

"WE'VE GOT A RUNNER!" the undertaker announces with professional dismay.

The crowd erupts in uproarious applause, embracing the impromptu gladiatorial spectacle as the runner claws through the slop, shoving past mourners in a frantic bid for freedom. The runner vanishes into the mist, and a cheer rises in their wake, the mourners' macabre delight suggesting this is less a funeral and more the opening act of a cabaret.

"Fast as a snake," an elderly woman cackles.

"What mockery is this?" the vicar cries out.

"Did anyone recognise the runner?" the undertaker calls.

I do, but I'm saying nothing. My eyes stop on something amid the wreckage—a small burnt candle stuck on Crumley's forehead.

The crowd presses forward, faces painted with a mix of amusement and morbid fascination. The vicar raises his hands in a futile attempt to restore order. "Let us remember, friends, that today we honour Mayor Crumley." He glances nervously at the chaos below. "Regardless of... unforeseen circumstances."

"Finish this farce," a villager growls. "Drop what's left and be done."

The pallbearers are chasing the runner. Several villagers take matters into their own hands, sending the broken casket tumbling unceremoniously into the ground.

The vicar steps forward, hands trembling. "May he find eternal rest," he says, voice hollow as an empty grave. "And may this... unusual day remind us all of life's ephemeral nature."

The gravediggers, Rufus Hedgerow and Galen Twilthorne, attack their task with unseemly enthusiasm. Shovels bite earth, and dirt rains down on the broken casket and its remaining occupant.

The vicar offers a final blessing, his words drowned out by the crowd's muttered conversations. With the ceremony complete, the villagers begin to file out of the Cemetery.

Sir Roderick appears beside me.

I lean close, pitching my voice low. "Notice any *absences*?"

His frown deepens like a well-worn groove. "Ulric. Haven't seen him all morning."

"Unless he was our impromptu runner," I say.

"No, too sprightly and thin for Ulric," Sir Roderick says.

As the last mourners dissolve into the mist, I move towards the Cemetery gate. The three of us exchange glances before parting ways, each mind already dissecting the possibilities sprouting from Crumley's wake.

By the gate, my thoughts circle back to the undertaker's casual mention of discretion and that curious ledger entry marked Sepultra. A weathered signpost near the gate draws my eye. Below it hangs a guide, its lines drawn in fading ink—the undertaker's precious grid system. Each plot arranged in neat columns and rows, marked with cryptic symbols.

A note in faded script adds: *Burials must needs be paid aforehand at the undertaker's quarters.* Discretion, the undertaker had said. Quiet burials, no names. My fingers tap the edge of the signpost as the memory sharpens. What if the symbols aren't just random markers? What if they tie to something? *The Mayor's cryptic runestone?* I withdraw it from my coat pocket, studying its precise etchings. Holding it against the guide's faded grid, my pulse quickens as patterns align.

The symbol matches one among many on the guide. A subdued whistle escapes my lips as understanding blooms like nightshade. I transcribe the grid and its vital markers. My hand moves with efficiency, translating faded mysteries into something portable. Stepping back, I roll up the parchment and slip it back into my coat. My gaze lingers on the signpost, as though expecting it to yield further secrets. For now, it remains silent, but the puzzle it hints at is anything but.

I'll have a few drinks at the Tavern this afternoon for courage and return at dusk to continue this investigation.

Chapter 18

Dawn, Two Days Earlier (Fifteenth Day of Gorst)

Rufus and Galen stood in the pre-dawn slop. Sprawled before them was Ulric's body near the Mayor's doorstep. Rufus was stocky and weathered, his face a permanent scowl of discontent. His patched coat, once black, hanging off him. A scraggy beard clung to his jaw, defying the wet chill of the morning. Beside him, Galen, built like a question mark, was wiry and nervous, his thin frame shivering beneath his threadbare cloak.

"Well, here he is, like the note said…," Rufus muttered.

Reluctantly, Galen edged closer, each step accompanied by the wet squelch of boots protesting their mistreatment. His gaze darted across the ground until it snagged on something beyond Ulric's outstretched arm. Something unnatural interrupted the churned mud—a hard edge where there should only be sludge. Galen frowned, nudging it with his boot. Rain had washed enough of the dirt away to reveal a faint carved edge, the telltale lines of something man-made.

"Uh… Rufus?" Galen called, his voice tight.

Rufus prodded the object with the tip of his boot. The stone shifted, revealing its fractured edge. Galen leaned down, squinting until the shape became clearer: a lion's head, snarling through a tangle of vines, split in two.

"That's… Sir Roderick's crest, isn't it?"

Rufus looked up sharply, his mood darkening. He rose to his feet with a grunt and stomped over, his boots sending splashes of filthy water in every direction. "What are you talking about?" He followed Galen's pointing finger, his eyes narrowing at the broken crest. "Yeah... looks like it," Rufus muttered, crouching for a better look. His thick fingers brushed away more of the dirt. Rufus frowned, his voice laboured with suspicion. "What's it doing here?"

"Maybe an accident," Galen says.

Rufus cast him the kind of look reserved for village idiots and optimists. "What, you think he slipped on a big, heavy crest lying about on the ground?"

Rufus returned to Ulric, squinting at the scene. He shook his head and muttered under his breath, "Typical."

Galen's face drained of what little colour it had left. He shifted uneasily, his boots sinking further. "So... what do we do?"

Rufus stood, his boots squelching with all the enthusiasm of a man who's seen this play before and knows the ending's never good. "What we always do, Galen. Hide it and let someone else find it. If we get spotted, we'll say we thought he was drunk and were being sorta kindly; getting him out of the rain. Now let's get him inside the barn over there."

Their plan was as sturdy as a butter knife in a brawl—sure to make a mess, but not in the way you'd hoped.

Galen hesitated, his hands clenching and unclenching at his sides. "But why move the body? Why not just... leave it here? It's filthy, I'll get covered in shit."

Rufus sighed, rubbing a hand over his beard like he's trying to comb sense into the situation. "Because that's what we've been told to do, Galen. He needs to be out of sight. If he's found dead in a barn, it looks like he just died drunk and alone."

Rufus crouched beside Ulric, grabbing the body under the arms with resignation. "Come on. Quick. Orders are orders. Now help me lift."

Chapter 19

Evening, Seventeenth Day of Gorst

The Cemetery at night is a different place altogether from the funeral this morning—tense, furtive, and thick. The moon's pale light cut jagged shadows through the gnarled branches of the central yew tree.

The rusted gate bites cold as I lean against it. I light my lantern, let the glow push back the dark. Then the creak of iron as I step into the graveyard. My eyes trace neat rows of gravestones, ledger stones and fresh mounds. The crunch of gravel marks my progress along the path, the map I sketched earlier tucked into my satchel. Its lines have burned themselves into my mind.

The grid system demands I work methodically, but I pause to pay my respects to the more verbose residents:

Hic iacet Eldrick Fortis—fortior in nomine quam in facto.

Verity Granger: May her pies ne'er be forgotten.

My attention snags on a grave marked with an odd symbol. It looks like one from the cryptic runestone. The dirt is freshly packed, and the ledger stone carries no name, just a blank, polished face. My gloved fingers trace the edges of the soil, but there's no sign this grave is any different from the others.

I move to the next plot. Nothing. I press on, my mind turning the Mayor's Sepultra entry over like a coin. Was it just a burial expense or something encoded? Am I seeing too much into the symbols—they are used for many purposes after all? But knowing the Mayor there has to be more. It's getting late, and the cold has rooted in my marrow. Six graves with rune marks, six dead ends. *Could the Mayor have layered another clue over the symbols? Or perhaps none of these graves are the right one.*

A distant sound—a muffled groan—breaks my thoughts. My hand finds the dagger under my coat. The noise repeats itself, a drawn-out sigh that could be the earth settling or something less natural remembering how to breathe. The sound tracks to a headstone that reads *Here rests Edith P.—Finally.*

Another sound rises from below a nearby ledger stone—a gasping thing that shouldn't be. My spade taps the stone, a gentle interrogation. The noise cuts off like a candle in a draft. Could be the damp earth shifting, coffin wood giving up the fight against gravity. I scan the Cemetery, but nothing moves. *Could it be ghosts or the prematurely buried?*

I force my mind back to the task, moving through the graves, watching out for unexpected company. Cold burrows deeper, and night bleeds across the sky like spilled ink. I stop by the yew tree and pull out the runestone, turning it over in my palm. It's hard to see the markings properly. Frustration bubbles up.

The rain has grown teeth, turning the graveyard into a sodden maze.

Then—

A crack—wood surrendering or something more deliberate. I snap my head toward the sound, but darkness keeps its counsel. In Murder's Vale, the unwary tend to join the Cemetery's permanent residents sooner rather than later. The sound comes again—closer this time. My hand grips the spade like a weapon.

Whatever's buried here isn't ready to slumber. It's time to leave. I'll be back—armed and preferably sober.

Chapter 20

Morning, Eighteenth Day of Gorst

Sleep eluded me after the Cemetery's whisperings, but morning arrived all the same. Wrapping myself in a heavy robe against the chill, I navigate the Hall's arthritic corridors. My destination: the upper garderobe, that peculiar temple of contemplation so revered by generations of MacAllisters.

The door at the corridor's end protests as I shoulder it open, admitting me to the wooden chamber that clings to the Manor's flank like a desperate lover. Perfume from its primary function lingers. A shaft of light from the narrow window blesses the seat like a reluctant benediction. More thoughts have been loosened here than bowels.

Over the years, it's earned its reputation as a sanctuary of sudden insight—epiphanies born in life's most humble moments. Above the seat, a shelf sags beneath dog-eared books and charcoal stubs, tools for capturing those fleeting revelations. The walls tell their own story, etched with the midnight musings of past occupants. My rear settles onto the wooden throne, grimacing as the draft from below makes its presence known. The things we endure for clarity.

The air feels different here, charged with possibility. Maybe it's the confined space, but my mind begins to sharpen as cold wood works its magic, the whistle of wind below adding a certain... urgency to my contemplation. Thoughts circle back to the artefact pieces: the ledger's mysterious entry, the runestone's arcane symbols, the map—all tantalising fragments of a larger mystery. The clues orbit my mind—then a jolt.

'That's it!' I bark, nearly unseating myself. I scramble downstairs, pulse quickening with the thrill of discovery. *There's work to do.*

***

The Hall's ancient door whines a protest as I step into Murder's Vale's latest meteorological tantrum. Rain isn't just falling—it's launching a full assault, as if it has finally grown tired of its own predictable downward trajectory.

Passing through the market, I can see Drusilla outside her herb shop, locked in verbal combat with a farmer. Their argument spirals upward like smoke from green wood, choking everyone nearby with its acrid futility. The farmer's face a shade of sunset red, his arms whirling like a baby bird.

"Poisoned my pigs, you did!" he bellows, spittle flying.

She maintains the weary expression of someone who's survived far too many similar accusations. "Your pigs couldn't distinguish between a mushroom and a boot. They likely ate something unfortunate all on their own."

The farmer's scowl deepens. "Two are missing 'n all. That you're doing?"

Drusilla shrugs. "They don't seem very bright. Probably just lost."

"Don't be stupid. Pigs are intelligent."

She crosses her arms. "Only compared to you."

The farmer's complexion deepens to beetroot. "I know what you're about, Hobbert! Those... potions you brew. Perhaps it's time we have a proper look inside that shop of yours!"

A gust of wind hurls a sheet of rain sideways. Drops *plink* against Drusilla's shop windows with the intensity of a thousand tiny fists demanding justice.

"Pigs, Drusilla? Really? What's next—are the chickens planning a coup?" I say.

She fixes me with a withering look. "Don't you start! Half this village is one bad turnip away from a witch hunt."

The farmer storms off, muttering dark promises about curses and cabbages.

Drusilla straightens, brushing manure from her arms, then reaches into her apron, pulls out a chunk of cured bacon, and shoves it into my palm. The gesture is quick, almost dismissive, but her eyes hold a flicker of amusement.

"They're getting restless," she says, nodding toward the Square. "The Mayor's death leaves a void, and folk don't like voids—they start filling in their own answers."

"They're working out who to blame," I say, giving her a knowing look.

Her eyes narrow. "And you think it's going to be me, rather than you?"

"If not one of us two, then who?"

She exhales heavily. "Crumley collected enemies like villagers collect stones."

The late Mayor had elevated antagonism to an art form, often delighting in it.

"Word is, Milton Ledbury's been acting peculiar," she says. "More skittish than usual."

It seems that Ledbury has always been twitchy as a rabbit in a wolf's den, but when your boss gets murdered, paranoia's a reasonable response. Unless, of course, you're the one who did the murdering.

I glance at the meat. Dark-rind, well-salted—good quality. Suspiciously good.

She notices my hesitation and snorts. "From the farmer's finest, or what's left of them."

She's either trying to kill me or flirt. Possibly both.

I lift a brow. "Is it one of the poisoned ones?"

She shrugs, already turning back toward her shop. "Let me know. And keep an eye on Ledbury." The door shuts behind her.

The village Square enters its midday routine. The aroma of fresh bread and bubbling stew mingles with wet stone and woodsmoke. Without warning, the sky erupts with turnips, pelting Drusilla's shop roof and display racks. Herbs flail in vegetative indignation, while puddles reflect the turnip-laden sky like portals to some vegepocalyptic realm—where tubers reign with soggy, starch-fuelled tyranny and the air reeks of damp rebellion.

Should I check on Drusilla?

My stomach decides I should head toward The Corpse's Candle instead.

The Tavern greets me with its familiar embrace of muttered voices, suspicious eyes, and a cracking hearth fire. Inside, the air is thick with stale ale, roasted meat, and the musty undertone of rain-soaked wood. My eyes scan the room and find Milton sitting at a table near the fire. His drink sits untouched, his fingers drumming on the table's edge.

I collect a pie and a tankard of mead from the Innkeeper and head over to Milton. The rickety surface wobbles as I set down my lunch. Breaking through the pie's flaky armour reveals a fragrant treasure of pork and herbs.

"Mind if I join you?"

He startles. "Noel!"

"What's the news?"

"The *Prophecy's* outdoing itself. Look at this: *Farmer Misjudges Puddle: Drowns in Two Inches of Water*.

I glance at it, shaking my head. "Oh, Drusilla…" We share a knowing look.

"Milton, I've been hearing things." I lean back in my chair, chewing fervently on the pie. "People are talking."

His fingers freeze mid-tap. "About… me?"

"They say you're acting strange. Nervous. Drawing attention. I warned you about keeping your head down."

He grips his glass. "But I'm not the murderer."

I take an enormous bite of pie, stuffing my cheeks like a squirrel preparing for famine. Milton squirms as I chew with deliberate slowness, scattering detritus like breadcrumbs in a fairy tale. I gesture for him to continue; mouth too full for words.

"Look, I didn't know half of what was going on! The Mayor kept things… separated. I suspected he occasionally did questionable things, but I just kept the books."

I finally swallow, washing down the pie with the mead. "Kept the books? Interesting choice of words. Something in those books might be what got him killed."

His face achieves a new shade of pale, but his voice remains steady. "Why would someone kill over bookkeeping?"

"Don't worry about it. No one's pointing a finger."

Milton deflates. He mutters something about his coat and hurries away. His ledger lies forgotten, a nervous breadcrumb in his wake.

Perhaps I'll add an incriminating entry.

Milton returns moments later—too soon—searching for the ledger. "Nothing adds up, Noel. It's too messy. Too deliberate."

"Messy how?"

"I saw the murder scene. The dagger. Why is everyone focused on poison? It makes little sense."

"A dagger is an unremarkable murder weapon. The poison tells us more about the killer," I say, maintaining neutrality. "We're keeping the dagger quiet for now to avoid confusing things."

"Fascinating... I shouldn't be speculating..." he says, backing away. He thanks me for listening and leaves, disappearing into the downpour.

With Milton gone, I step back into the deluge, I need an afternoon nap after no sleep, a full stomach and mead. I'll try the Cemetery again later when it's dusk.

Sleep came in fits, like a drunk trying to dance. The mead helped, but only enough to let the aches settle in. I rise groggily, grab my things, and light a reluctant lantern.

The rain has achieved a spiteful sentience, finding every gap in my clothing with unerring accuracy. Each step sends up a spray of water that hangs suspended, as if considering which direction would cause most discomfort before striking.

As I trudge, I ponder that the village is fraying at the edges—turnips taking flight, accusations gathering weight. Someone's bound to crack under the pressure. The only question is—who, when, what, and why—because when the bell breaks, it's not the silence you hear, but the toll it takes.

Chapter 21

Evening, Eighteenth Day of Gorst

After a short nap, I think another go at the Cemetery is needed. The chill of dusk settles in as I navigate the winding roads. Rain beats against the cobblestones, each drop a tiny assassin sent to slowly drown the world. Perfect weather for washing away grave robbing sins. The Cemetery waits like a patient predator, its wrought-iron gate baring rusted teeth against the dying light. I can't start digging until it's darker, but I can scout my quarry—assuming none of the Cemetery residents object.

The gate shrieks as I push through. I pull the map from my satchel and examine its grid, scarred with yesterday's failures. I pause at each headstone, cross-referencing the runestone's cryptic markings against notes I've taken from the informal ledger.

I keep wandering around, but the graves offer nothing useful, and doubt gnaws at my certainty like a hungry rat. I think the Mayor was sly—too sly. Perhaps he added a layer of misdirection. Or maybe I'm still missing a key that makes sense of it all.

I step over an unassuming grave, no headstone to speak of, just a small ledger stone shrouded in dirt and vegetation, like dozens of others. Something about its plainness and size draws me. My fingers brush away dirt and debris from the stone base, each swipe revealing more of the stone as rainwater streams between my knuckles.

At first, nothing. Then, under the grime, my fingers catch a whisper of something more: seemingly meaningless cuts etched into the stone. But I've spent too many nights studying the runestone to mistake their significance. My hands tremble as I pull the runestone from my coat. It's hard to be sure by feel alone but I feel there's an undeniable similarity.

The stone refuses to yield to direct force, but my probing fingers find a groove marking the means of opening. A hard pull, and the top stone slides back. I ease my breath out and pull again. A gap emerges, just enough to mock my curiosity.

My shovel, my trusty companion in these grim excavations, becomes a lever to reveal an open space. No corpse waits in this cradle of secrets—but it's not empty. My fingers close around something heavy. I pull it free—a book wrapped in oilcloth. The cover is embossed with symbols, it's dark but they seem like those on the hollowed tome from the Mayor's drawer.

The pages are brittle but intact, it's hard to make details out, but it appears to be filled with diagrams and dense text written in a spidery hand. This is no ordinary thing, this is something the Mayor thought worth preserving, yet too dangerous to keep close.

I wedge the tome inside my coat. Something about its weight feels prophetic. With this tome pressed against my ribs like an extra heart, I might finally decode the late Mayor's grand scheme. Tonight, the Cemetery holds its breath around me, though the rain shows no such restraint. I peer at the shadows, half-expecting some guardian of the dead to emerge and demand restitution for my theft.

But the graves keep their own counsel, at least for now.

Time to get out of here.

My mind churns as I head back to the Hall. The burnt fragments from the Mayor's study might be enough to confirm whether this is its twin. The Mayor's fingers must have trembled with the magnitude of his choice—this damned tome burning like cursed gold in his hands, too lethal to cradle close yet too precious to feed to cleansing flames.

Thoughts churn like dark waters as I reach the Cemetery's edge, every step bringing me closer to a truth that refuses to crystallise. The puzzle hovers beyond comprehension, taunting me with near-clarity, and this cursed tome might be the key.

My pace back is brisk, but not so as to arouse interest. The Hall looms before me.

The oak door protests my entry with an arthritic groan. Inside the Hall, the familiar perfume of ageing wood and creeping damp wraps around me like an old friend's embrace. A single sputtering lantern burns near the grand staircase, its light pooling in the shadows like spilled honey.

I shed my waterlogged coat and make my way to the study, where a dusty bottle of port sits beside a tarnished glass—tonight's companions in contemplation.

Though the draughty Hall will steal any warmth before it settles, the growing chill convinces me to light a fire. I arrange the logs and touch the sulphur splint to the kindling, watching as hungry flames begin their dance.

On the central oak table, tarnished silver candlesticks catch the firelight like distant stars, surrounded by the ghostly trails of melted wax. I place the port and the recovered tome on the table, alongside the fragments of parchment and scattered notes. A high-backed chair accepts my weight with familiar resignation, its cushions long since beaten into submission.

MacAllister Hall's silence settles around me. Here, separated from the whispers and watching eyes of Murder's Vale, my thoughts might begin to take shape. My fingers trace the embossed symbols of the tome's cover, seeking answers through touch alone. Their patterns spark recognition, too precise to be coincidence.

I inhale, steadying myself, then open the book.

The pages resist at first, reluctant in their bindings, the parchment thick and aged. Most of it is the mess of diagrams and symbols. But then, just past the first few pages, something different. The ink is old, dark as dried blood. Its script sharp and deliberate—the work of a steady hand with no room for hesitation. The passage reads:

The Vomitus of the Earth: A Sacred Record

And lo, the earth did tremble, and the void did stir. And the silence that had lingered for centuries, waiting, biding, craving, did open its maw. A tremor. A convulsion. And the land did purge itself of what should never have been.
In one breath, Murder's Vale was spat forth. Roads writhed into place. Stones fell like dislodged teeth. The Bitter Well, emptied of its bile, was then left barren, a mouth sealed mid-scream. And then, as the universe stilled, time lurched—And they crawled forth. Unbidden. Unclean. You now walk among them.

I read it again, hoping it might soften on the second pass. It doesn't. But brooding over this won't give me answers.

The ink glistens in places, though whether from age or something less explainable, I can't say. Some words—Bitter Well, spat forth, unbidden—are rubricated in a deep, faded red, as if meant to draw the reader's eye to a singular, inescapable truth.

I run my fingers over the lettering. The texture is wrong—thicker in places, as if the scribe had pressed harder over certain words. Not hesitation. Emphasis. Whoever wrote this believed every word.

I read the passage once. Then again.

My fingers tighten around the tome's edges, the parchment rough beneath my skin. The words pulse in my mind with a terrible certainty, a history that should not be history.

I exhale slowly, resisting the urge to snap the book shut. It's absurd. It's ridiculous. And yet... the Vale itself—the Blood Balance, the way people seem to crawl from the Bitter Well as if placed rather than born—feels like the aftershock of this grotesque birthright.

How does this tome relate to the charred fragments? I push past the unease and retrieve the brittle remains, each one no larger than my palm, edges blackened and curling inward like dying leaves. Firelight catches on their markings—some jagged, others flowing in elaborate curves.

I begin the delicate work of comparison. Pages of dense text and intricate symbols await examination, each one potentially holding the key.

The first fragment trembles in my hands, its burnt edges shedding like dead skin. The markings curve inward with deliberate purpose, though their meaning remains opaque. I hold it to the firelight, memorising each line before beginning the painstaking process of searching the tome's pages. Hours blur together as I work. The spidery script begins to swim before my eyes, offering tantalising matches that dissolve under closer scrutiny. The sheer volume of text threatens to overwhelm my senses, but I force myself to remain methodical. Finally—a match. The curve stares back at me from the brittle parchment, a whisper of something undeniable. Not perfect, but close enough to steal my breath.

"One down," I murmur to the empty room, setting the fragment aside like a played chess piece.

The next proves more challenging, its markings almost imperceptible. Frustration gnaws at my patience, but I resist the urge to rush. The room closes in as the hours tick by, the creak of the chair and the occasional crackle of the fire my only companions.

The second fragment proves more elusive. Its markings are faint, imperceptible against the charred edges, and the tome offers no immediate match. Frustration gnaws at my patience, but I force myself to remain methodical.

I tilt the fragment at different angles, trying to catch the light just right, and work through the tome again. Another hour passes before I find what I'm looking for—a partial match hidden in the book's back pages, the alignment imperfect but undeniable. This discovery feels monumental. Then my stomach reminds me that hunger trumps all other pursuits. From my satchel, I extract the cured bacon Drusilla gave me earlier, its greasy surface sticking to the lining. I imagine Ulric chastising me, saying, "That's probably poisoned."

I sniff the bacon. It smells like salt, smoke, and bacon. I give it a suspicious squint, then a shrug. If it's poisoned, it's subtle—and frankly, I've had worse. Either I'll die, or I'll be full. "I'm sure it's fine," I say to myself, taking a hefty bite. Grease smears onto my chin, and I wipe it away with the back of my hand—and onto the chair. The bacon dangles from my mouth before I tear it clean in half, the taste momentarily drowning out any intellectual pursuits. Bits of fat fall onto the table, but I pay them no mind as I lick my fingers one by one to avoid grease getting on the unread parchments.

Replete, I focus on the third and fourth fragments, these demand even more time. My shoulders ache from hunching over the table and my vision blurs from squinting at faded ink, and my stomach doesn't feel impressed with the bacon. Yet each successful match builds a growing certainty: this tome isn't only similar to what the Mayor tried to destroy—it's its twin, perhaps even the original itself.

As I finish with the final fragment, the fire has burned low, casting more shadows than light. My hands bear the marks of my labour—soot and ink creating a map of their own across my skin. But the evidence is irrefutable. Every fragment aligns with passages in the tome, fitting together like pieces of a shattered mirror. My mind drifts to those long hours spent in the Library's basement, poring over forgotten archives. One book, mentioned only once, as if by accident. "The codex..." I whisper.

Firelight dances more urgently across the embossed symbols on the cover, as if acknowledging their true significance. What I hold isn't a mere book; it's a key to understanding not only the Mayor's usual schemes but the very foundations of what's playing out in Murder's Vale. I sit motionless for a while, letting the implications wash over me. "The Mayor had the codex," I say, tasting the words' bitter significance.

The fire sputters its last breath, leaving the room lit by candles alone. I stand to snuff out the last when a flicker of motion outside the window catches my eye. Through the rain-blurred glass, figures gather in the lane, torches carving streaks of firelight into the night. They do not move. They do not call out. They simply stand, watching,

waiting. The night holds its breath. I sit, careful not to disturb the silence, and wait.

Chapter 22

Morning, Nineteenth Day of Gorst

The miasma hanging over the village this morning carries a fresh note beneath its usual bouquet of doom—a cloying sweetness that clings like morning dew on deadly nightshade.

The crowd is gone. No knock, no confrontation. If they came with purpose, it seems the night talked them out of it. Maybe they just wanted to scare me or check what I'm up to. Or maybe they were just making sure I'm safe and well—wouldn't want anything happening to me before I've wrapped up the investigation. Very thoughtful, really.

I peer out the door, half-expecting the night to rearrange itself into something less ominous. The lane is empty now, wet and glistening like a freshly scrubbed conscience. But something shifts in the front hedge. I step into the drizzle.

It's a goat.

Tied to the gatepost like some woolly harbinger of doom, chewing with the blank intensity of a philosopher who's forgotten the question. Rain drips from his horns. His eyes, as ever, radiate pure indifference.

The goat stares at me, then lets out a long, nasal bleat. He tugs at the rope.

I squat down beside him, inspecting the knot. No note, no explanation. Just left here like a sacrificial offering or an unwanted gift from fate. "You're not even waterproof." What am I supposed to make of this?

I sigh, step back inside, and collect my things—satchel, coat, hat, whatever scraps of dignity remain. When I return, the goat is still chewing.

"Come on, then," I mutter, untying the rope. He falls into step beside me like we've rehearsed this—hoofbeats soft against the cobbles, breath steaming like a disapproving kettle.

We make our way toward the Square. I don't know why. Instinct, maybe. Or maybe because if you've just been mysteriously delivered a goat in the dead of night, the Square's as good a place as any to return it to public consciousness.

By the time we reach The Corpse's Candle, the rain has mellowed to a steady drizzle. I loop the goat's rope around the post outside the tavern, where he resumes chewing with the air of someone who fully intends to outlive us all.

I linger, half-tempted to step into the tavern—warmth, noise, and the reliable stink of yesterday's beer. A pair of villagers shuffle past me, heads bent close.

"Whatever she's stirring, it ain't soup," one says, voice low and damp with disapproval.

"Poison," hisses the other, the word curling out like smoke on a cold stove. "They say she's been testing it on livestock, maybe villagers."

They disappear into the tavern without noticing me.

Drusilla's recent attempt to seize control of the poison narrative has curdled. What makes poison more interesting is that it's more calculated, more patient than your garden-variety murder. For the killer, it lacks the brutal satisfaction of a blade—but to the villagers, it offers something better: intrigue.

Now the village has locked its serpentine eyes on her. She might be more inclined to talk. I give the goat a final glance. He blinks at me. "Stay put," I tell him. Time to pay Drusilla a visit while she still has a voice left to use.

As I reach her road at the top of the market, I can see her standing in her shop's doorway, arms folded like a fortress against an incoming siege. Her glare slices through the cluster of villagers like a scythe through dry wheat—sharp, practiced, and just as merciless. As I approach, a look of exasperation flits across her face.

A bead of rain slides off the awning above, hesitates for a fraction of a second—perhaps reconsidering its choices—then *plops* onto her shoulder with an insolent splash. She exhales sharply, brushing it off.

"Noel, come to join the witch hunt?"

It seems her plan public relations plan has backfired.

"I'm not here to accuse."

She clutches her arms tighter, as if warding off a chill. "I try to educate them, but now they think I'm a rampant poisoner."

"Well, you can understand their reasoning to fear you. I mean… I see from the news that a farmer's going to drown in a two-inch puddle later. You know—for example."

A sharp smirk crosses her face. "Tragic, but necessary," she says.

"Thanks for the bacon, by the way. Still alive," I say.

She lifts a brow, wickedly dry. "Pity. I must have given you the wrong one."

She eyes me. "So what brings you to my door today?"

"A goat," I say. "Tied to my gatepost. I don't need a goat. Thought I'd bring him into the village. He's outside the tavern now. Chewing with conviction."

Drusilla exhales. "Gregory."

"He's got a name?" I ask.

"He's an omen," she says.

I frown. "How does that work?"

"He wanders around. Sometimes he lingers," she says.

"What's the omen mean?" I ask.

"No one knows. He has a following who are trying to interpret the omen. They tie him up so they can find him again later."

"Right," I say. "Wouldn't want the prophetic goat going missing."

"Is that all, Noel?"

"Look, while I'm here. Could you help me understand your dealings with the Mayor?"

"I didn't kill him, if that's what you're angling at," she snaps. "The man was greedy, vicious, and insufferable—but *Overt Murder*? Please. If I'd wanted him dead, it would look like natural causes."

She drums her fingers against her arm—a tell, perhaps, or the habit of someone who spent their days measuring precise amounts of herbs and powders. Drusilla is many things—sharp-tongued, persistently irritated, and perhaps too enamoured with her mysterious brews—but something about her denial rings true, though it's too soon to rule anyone out.

"I believe you, but you've made yourself an obvious target."

She lets out a dry laugh, like a shattered bell, scattering echoes like startled doves. We head into the shop. I was too battered and bruised on my last visit to take it in. Shelves groan under a regiment of jars and bottles, each bearing labels in script that look more like ancient runes than proper writing. My gaze sweeps across the rows of containers, noting how some labels have faded to ghostly whispers while others bear the sharp clarity of fresh ink.

She re-pots some plants at the counter. Plants, at least, put a smile on her face.

"What manner of darkness is this?" I say, gesturing toward a jar filled with what appears to be twisted twigs.

Drusilla glances at it. "*Mugwort*. Harmless as a newborn lamb. Good for dreams, if you want that sort of thing. You'd need to consume an entire barrel before it'd do you any harm."

She bangs an empty clay pot onto the counter. "Listen," she says, her voice dropping. "I know they don't trust me. They never have. But I didn't poison the Mayor. If death came to him in a bottle, it wasn't one of mine."

An army of jars stand on their shelves before me shouting poison. In Murder's Vale, truth is as slippery as an eel in moonlight, and it's shaped more by tavern whispers than facts. It doesn't matter what I believe—only what the villagers decide is true.

"Fine, but was there nothing between you and his mayorship that might raise eyebrows? Better to air it now than have it surface when the mob's mood turns ugly."

"Nothing beyond remedies," she says. "Ointments and digestive aids."

My gaze lingers on the mysterious collection of bottles. "Can you show me what you gave him?"

She frowns, her sharp features tightening. She crosses to a shelf laden with mysterious vessels, snatching two containers and placing them on the counter with enough force to make the nearby bottles shudder. "There. Joint pain ointment. And this," she says, lifting a ceramic vessel like it's evidence at her own trial, "the digestive remedy."

I lift each container, weighing more than their contents as I examine them. The labels bare her distinctive scrawl, the edges of the jars show the patina of regular use, and each carries that peculiar herbal fragrance that marks her work. "How were they sealed? Wax? Cloth?"

"Wax seals on both," she replies, irritation crackling in her voice like static before a storm. "I run a proper establishment, whatever the gossips might say."

"Then you won't mind sampling them, just to prove they're safe to everyone."

"Safe!" she screeches, opening the jars with practiced ease. She dips a finger into the powder, swirls it against her tongue, then pauses—just long enough for my mind to leap to conclusions. Her lips press together, as if tasting something unexpected, before she smirks. "Tastes like grave dirt."

"And the other?"

With an eye roll, she dabs the ointment on her wrist. "There!"

"I'll need samples to compare against whatever the Mayor was using. If they match, you're in the clear."

Her jaw clenches, but she begins measuring out samples. "Here," she says, thrusting them at me. "Don't say I wasn't cooperative when they're lighting the pyre. But know this, organics degrade over time."

"I'll send the knight over to the Mayor's to test against the originals."

"Let's hope the fool doesn't test rat poison on himself," she snaps.

"Just remember, we've never said poison was used. You planted that seed yourself."

Her voice cracks like a whip in the enclosed space. "Your techniques are too transparent for Murder's Vale, Noel. Please—asking for something *mintier*?"

"Fair enough," I say, maintaining steady eye contact. "But remember—you fed the flames, and fires have a way of spreading beyond control."

She crosses her arms, eyes narrowing to deadly slits.

"You think I don't know about fires spreading? For years they've been stockpiling kindling for my witchcraft trial. Silence would have damned me faster than words. But you knew that, didn't you, Noel? Convenient how the shadow of suspicion now barely seems to darken your doorstep."

And there it is—truth sharp as a blade between my ribs.

"We'll be in touch on the results," I say as I leave her shop.

Time for another drink at the Tavern.

***

The Tavern hums with the energy of scarcely contained hysteria. The poison theory has taken root in fertile soil, and the room crackles with possibilities. Every eye in the place tracks my entrance the moment I cross the threshold.

"She's been skulking about," a voice whispers from the shadows, thick with conspiracy. "Saw her near the Mayor's house the night before he stopped breathing."

Another voice trembles with excitement. "She's been poisoning us all along."

"My pigs!" The farmer's voice cracks with urgency. "They've been acting strange—wallowing more than usual. They know something's amiss—pigs are very intelligent animals, you know!"

Murmurs of agreement rumple through the crowd, as if swine are well-respected oracles in Murder's Vale. Our village's talent for spinning paranoid fantasies would be impressive if it weren't so damned dangerous. I make my way to the bar, where at least the drinks are honest about their intentions.

The Innkeeper leans across the wooden counter. "What's your reading of it, Nibblenudge?"

"I think the village is too fond of its own paranoia," I say, taking a sip of ale against the bar.

He hunches closer. "Can't be too careful, though. I hear she keeps all manner of strange things in those jars of hers."

Setting my tankard down with deliberate care, "Strange things, you say?"

"You and Sir Roderick should do a proper search of her shop—and her sister's one too. There's something off about those two. And folks are thinking you appear a little too familiar with them."

"That's a good idea. I'll suggest it to him. With the villager's help, we'll have this case cracked in no time," I say, hoping that'll pacify him.

The Innkeeper lowers his head to mine as I lean over the bar to whisper. "While I've got your ear, I need to verify everyone's whereabouts. Routine business."

He surveys me, confused, "And?"

"Well, perhaps I could start with you. Where were you that night?"

He straightens, offence clouding his features. "Me? Right where I always am, serving drinks and collecting secrets. What are you implying?"

"Nothing," I say, swirling the ale in my tankard. "It's all part of the investigative process. One last thing—can anyone vouch for that?"

He turns to the crowd. "Oi! You lot! Where was I the night our beloved Mayor met his maker?"

"Watering down our drinks behind that bar, you bloody fool!" a woman's drunken voice carries over the din, followed by scattered laughter.

"What day is watered-down drinks night?" another shouts, laughing.

"Every day!" they all cheer.

"You're all barred!" the Innkeeper shouts back, turning to me with a grin. "Satisfied?"

"I expected no less," I say, leaning on the counter, "but you must feel vulnerable in your position, you know, drunken secrets heard across the bar, inebriated confidences shared with a man they think they know."

His grin faltered like a candle in a draft. "What are you playing at?"

"Truth has a funny way of getting tangled in places like this," I muse. "And if this murder goes unsolved, some might say you know more than you let on. Others might wonder who you're protecting—yourself included."

"You're playing a very dangerous game."

"I've got evidence and a creative imagination," I say, my voice cold as a midnight grave.

He stares at me, knuckles white against the bar's edge, "Everyone! Nibblenudge here wants to know where you all were on the night of the murder and your alibis," he shouts.

The Tavern erupts with laughter.

"I'll return for that list in due course, then," I say, settling back onto my stool.

Mocking dissipates and chatter resumes. The Innkeeper busies himself in glass-wiping, though his fiery stare finds me more often than necessary.

I finish my drink in contemplative silence. Every move here is a gamble, and sometimes you have to play with poisoned dice.

Yeah, I used to think I was smart, but here I am threatening the man who handles my daily food and drink.

Chapter 23

Afternoon, Nineteenth Day of Gorst

As I step outside, the sky glowers—unsteady, brooding, and unreasonably persistent. Villagers scurry about Murder's Vale with their heads bowed. None spare me a glance as I tug my coat tighter, a futile defence against the inevitable deluge.

Sir Roderick arrives cradling something wrapped in cloth—a gleam in his eyes hints at excitement. He halts before me, splashing the puddle at our feet. He unwraps his precious cargo. A metallic glint beneath the cloth confirms my worst suspicions—it's the dagger.

"Nibblenudge," he announces, "I've been reconsidering this dagger. Perhaps we were too quick to dismiss it. Its craftsmanship is... extraordinary."

"I thought we agreed it was derivative."

"Initially, yes..." he says, his eyes drawn to his deadly treasure. "But upon closer inspection—the patterns, the workmanship—there could be vital clues here. If we examine it thoroughly—"

My raised hand cuts through his fervour.

I put my hand on the wrap to stop him. "We're brandishing a murder weapon in the open air like a prize at a fair? Need I remind you we decided to withhold how he was killed? You know... to maintain some control over the investigation."

Sir Roderick hesitates, "Well...I thought it prudent to discuss this immediately."

He blinks, reality penetrating his enthusiasm. "Ah... perhaps this discussion is better suited elsewhere..."

"The Library," I say, scanning the Square for unwanted observers.

Drizzle escorts us to the Library's entrance, leaving the prying village eyes behind. We navigate to a back room that serves as the village's unofficial museum. Glass cases line the walls, housing everything from yellowed scrolls to ancient weapons. In this shrine to the past, Sir Roderick unveils the ornate dagger once more.

"Listen, before we look at the dagger, I found this." I show him the eldritch entry from the codex.

Sir Roderick reads in silence. "Utter nonsense," he says, voice clipped. He pushes the codex back to me as though it offends him. "The work of a lunatic—or worse, a scholar who fancies himself a poet."

He leans over to me. "You'd do well to forget you ever saw this," he adds. "People who ask too many questions about the Vale's past don't fare well."

I catch the flicker of something in his eyes. Not fear, exactly.

"Fine. But I want to know more about the Well. Is there a pattern—who returns, when they show up?" I ask.

He shakes his head. "This again?"

"If the murdered return mid investigation, how can we ever wrap it up?" I say.

"There's no pattern on who returns." His voice is tired but not resigned—like he's explaining something he's said too many times before but still hopes won't be true the next time. "They come back when a Blood Balance is required." He rubs at his chin. "It's not a bloody resurrection service. It's more like... a ledger that a body slips from, given time."

"It must cause problems?"

"Sometimes it lets out those who should have been gone for good."

I raise an eyebrow. "What do you do?"

His eyes narrow slightly, as if assessing whether I really want the answer. Then—"There's always someone at the Well." A pause. "We re-bury the bad ones quickly."

"And what about the others?" I ask.

"I grow tired of this. We should return to the dagger."

We look at the dagger before us. The poniard catches what little light filters through the grimy windows, its surface polished to mirror-perfect clarity. Precious stones wink from the hilt like knowing conspirators, set in gold filigree that writhes in hypnotic patterns.

We lean in, studying the artistry etched into the hilt. A serpent winds its way around a rose, its body twisting elegantly with a sense of quiet menace. The craftsmanship speaks of wealth, power and something more sinister lurking below the surface.

"This symbol here," I murmur, tilting the ornate dagger to catch the details, "it's more than just decoration. It's a crest—a family seal, or perhaps a mark of an organisation. Something old, something powerful. You don't see work like this on common blades."

Sir Roderick's frown deepens. "A noble house, then? Or one of those shadowy cabals that fuel tavern gossip?"

"Precisely," I say, studying the way light dances along the blade. "This isn't just a weapon—it's a message. Whoever wielded this wanted their handiwork recognised. A blade like this carries weight beyond its steel. History. Loyalty. Secrets."

"A bloody proclamation in the Mayor's back," he mutters.

The blade grows heavier in my hands as I turn it, examining every detail. "This, my friend, is a clue wrapped in riddles and dipped in gold. A serpent entwined with a rose... it's the kind of symbolism that points to old money."

My attention catches on the etchings along the blade's length. They form patterns within patterns, like a language meant only for initiates. This weapon belongs in someone's private collection, not left carelessly behind at a crime scene.

Taking a rest from the poniard, I look into the distance to think. A glint from one of the display cases draws my eye—a long, gilded box lined with a few jewels, sitting beside similar containers. Its proportions beckon, a silent invitation.

The long box aligns well to the size of the dagger.

Sir Roderick looks at it suspiciously. "Rather convenient to find its case so close at hand—as if someone wanted us to find it."

I inspect the box, my mind working. "Or cleverly hidden in plain sight."

I set the box aside and return to the dagger, turning it in my hands. This isn't just a weapon; it's a part of an unfinished story. Its jewelled hilt and intricate engravings tell of a purpose beyond mere violence.

Returning to the box, we examine it more closely. "The markings don't match the dagger. Interesting."

An eagle spreads its wings across the lid. The corners bear four distinct symbols: flame, anvil, bear and tree—elements disconnected from the dagger's serpentine motif, suggesting that the box might have a separate origin or purpose.

Sir Roderick peers over my shoulder, his scholarly instincts fully engaged.

Using my notebook, I sketch each symbol. "We need to trace this back to its source—find out who had access to both box and blade." I pocket my notebook, mind already racing down dark corridors of possibility.

"Let's get this somewhere more secure," he says.

"We will," I say. "But first, there's something else I need to ask you."

He exhales, already wary. "Go on."

"The Well. You keep holding back on the detail."

His expression shifts, just slightly—a flicker of something less readable, something guarded.

"Again? What about it?"

I lean back against the nearest case, crossing my arms. "You've told me what it does. You've told me it spits people back up when the Blood Balance demands it. But what happens next? When they climb out?"

Sir Roderick exhales through his nose. He glances toward the room's small, fogged-up window, like the answer might be out there instead of here, pressing in on him.

"It's managed," he mutters.

"Managed how?"

"There's a house nearby," he says finally. "Where they're—" he waves a hand vaguely "—cleaned up. Given clothes. Given time to understand what's happened to 'em."

"And?"

His mouth tightens. "Not all of 'em take it well."

I watch Sir Roderick closely. His posture is still, but there's something else beneath it. A weight. A memory.

"It's a messy business," he says at last.

I wait to see if he'll add anything more. He doesn't.

I nod, letting it go—for now.

"Alright, I'll secure this in the basement," I say. "Wait for me by the entrance."

After locking the dagger and box away, I meet Sir Roderick, and we leave.

***

Threading through the Market, the discovery lingers in my thoughts. The ornate dagger, its mysterious box, the cryptic symbols—all point to a conspiracy deeper than a simple killing. The pieces are there, but assembling them will require more than perceptive deductions.

At the Market's edge, we pause as a gust of wind shoulders its way through, rattling shutters. A merchant curses as his awning flaps like a dying bird.

"What now?" Sir Roderick asks.

"We'll need more than clues to crack this case. I'll start with those markings—see where they lead us."

He nods and peels off toward the Bitter Well, his footsteps leaving ripples in his wake.

I linger, watching the villagers hurry past. But as I turn to leave, something catches my attention—a familiar voice. Moondrop. She's holding an impromptu performance close by on the edge of the Market. This isn't like her, this public spectacle. Her voice carves the damp air like a rusty blade, and the locals gather to feast on her words. The village loves nothing more than a good tale.

"Everyone knows Drusilla never liked Crumley," she proclaims. "But it goes deeper than that. She's been planting seeds of chaos for years. Mark my words—this is no coincidence."

"What's she been doing now?" a market trader asks.

Moondrop raises her arms like a carnival mystic unveiling dark mysteries. "Poisons! Curses! She's been brewing things far darker than mere remedies, and Crumley knew it. A Mayor doesn't threaten to shut down an honest healer."

Villagers can't agree whether Drusilla and Crumley's relationship was forged in mutual hatred or a friendship gone septic. And Moondrop has now entered the fray, weaving her gossamer threads of innuendo.

Fascinating. Drusilla sits at the centre of the storm. Let's see how she's weathering it. As I thread through the market, thoughts circle over Moondrop's motives. Why is she stoking the flames against her sister? Maybe she's positioning herself not just as a truth-teller, but stealing control of the narrative for herself, I imagine she's just as capable a poisoner. Whatever game she's playing, Drusilla's under threat. And if she's rattled, she might provide more information.

Drusilla is scowling before I'm fully through the door. I step in, lean lightly on the counter, and pretend this is a friendly visit.

"Your sister's been uncommonly chatty in the Square."

"With Crumley dead, she has the perfect opportunity to attack me."

"She's convinced you and Crumley had... unfinished business." I say.

A snort escapes her, sharp as breaking glass. "It's been like this since we were young. My only crime was healing his ailments."

"If truth doesn't satisfy, they'll manufacture something that does. Anything else you want to share?" I ask.

She doesn't respond, her fingers drumming on the counter as she stares at me.

I take that as my cue to leave.

***

The Tavern's warm glow pierces the gloom ahead, a siren song for lost souls and loose tongues. It's where secrets slip free after one too many drinks, where truth floats to the surface like bodies in a well. With a sharp exhale, I adjust my hat and make for the welcoming light.

Inside, the Tavern pulses with bleak cheer, a haven from the murk outside. I shed my coat like a snake's skin and scan the room as I walk to the bar for a drink. "Seen Ulric lately?" I ask, watching the Innkeeper's hands still—just for a moment. He resumes polishing, slower now.

"Not for a while. Figured he's sleeping it off somewhere."

I claim a chair near the fire, where shadows dance like guilty men. Conversations wrap around me, theories and accusations swirling. I let it wash over me, sipping my drink and watching the door with disinterest. Three drinks in, the fire's warmth begins to dull the edges of the day. The villagers' theories rise and fall with the flames, their voices lowering as night deepens. When the hearth dims to embers, I drain the last of my drink and step into the rain.

The road to MacAllister Hall stretches ahead, slick with water and doubt. The rain's steady rhythm is my only companion—until the sound of footsteps appear behind me.

My pace slows. The sound slows too. A glance over my shoulder discloses nothing, the flicker of lanterns barely illuminating the road. I quicken my step. By the time I reach the Hall, my pulse matches the tempo of my boots. Inside, I bolt the door and exhale, the silence wrapping around me like a borrowed alibi.

Then—thud.

A soft knock. Followed by a low, nasal bleat.

I press my ear to the door.

Gregory.

Chapter 24

Morning, First Day of Widders

It's mid-morning, and the Square has transformed into a speculative cesspool, with locals huddling under rain-sodden cloaks and dripping hats, their concerned faces likely masking excitement. Some say it's obvious—Sir Roderick struck in a fit of righteous indignation.

"Two murders!" A woman's voice carries across the Square, treacle-sweet with performative horror.

Another shakes their head, "I always said he'd talk himself into a grave. Guess someone finally listened."

"It was the butcher's boy who found him," mutters an old woman from beneath a shawl. "Went into the barn chasing that damned goat again."

At the Square's edge, I adopt the stance I've perfected over years of investigation—the outsider who holds the most pieces of the puzzle, even if half of them might belong to different games entirely. The rain, unimpressed, takes it upon itself to drip down my collar. It's less precipitation, more petty sabotage.

A sharp gust of wind unfurls the corner of a rain-warped notice on the noticeboard. It flaps like the feeble protest of a condemned man. My gaze drifts over the usual offerings—someone's lost a goat, someone's accused of finding a goat but refuses to admit it. Then I see that the Blood Balance Dial has moved again. It had gone to plus-two with Darius back and the new deputy, but is now back to plus-one.

Villagers are saying Ulric's been killed.

I tuck my collar higher and turn away. The board has told me everything it can for now.

Drusilla, ever the opportunist, sidles up to me with all the grace of a one-legged spider who knows exactly where her web is leading.

"Noel," she purrs, "remember the scream I told you about the other night?"

"The one where you banged on my door?"

"It came from near the Manor. I was tending the herbs outside my shop. The lavender was restless."

"Milton and I checked the Manor the next day. We found nothing out of place."

"Well, that may be so, but a scream came from that area. Sir Roderick heard it too."

I study her words like a suspicious coin, testing their weight. Her flimsy alibi ready to disintegrate at the first real question.

"Is that so?" I say, reaching into my satchel for a snack. My hand locates a waxed cloth package.

"How fortuitous that you were both far from the scene," I say unravelling a greasy coil of blood sausage from the waxed cloth. The dark, congealed links glisten.

Drusilla stands open-mouthed as I bite into one of the links. The casing bursts, releasing a gush of oily, metallic-tasting blood and fat.

"Yes, it was fortuitous! What about you? I don't suppose you have an alibi?" she sneers, her face twists with visible revulsion at my sausage sideshow. "Perhaps you had time to return to MacAllister Hall before I visited you?"

She's lashing out. That means she's nervous.

The blood sausage texture is soft and gritty. I chew, savouring the taste.

"Rich," I declare, holding the sausage up like a trophy. "Want some?"

She waves her hand as if to shoo me away.

I shrug and take another bite. Bits of sausage filling stick in my teeth, and I pick them out with my fingernail, flicking the remnants onto the ground.

"If I follow what you're inferring, the three of us are witnesses to each other's innocence—like these linked sausages. A tidy little chain of alibis, all neatly cased up in convenient timing." I wave the empty casings now dangling from my fingers.

"It may seem convenient, but it's the truth." She walks off, irritated at either my lack of enthusiasm, or how right I am. Or maybe something else.

**

It's afternoon and the village sleuths have moved to the Mayor's barn, their collective breath fogging the damp air as they dissect the latest bloodletting with all the care of amateur butchers.

They have now reached a consensus: Ulric, the village drunk and professional irritant, is perchance dead, having met his fate at Sir Roderick's hands—bolstered by the discovery of a broken crest bearing his family's insignia at the scene by the deputy a few days ago.

But the real conundrum on everyone's mind is the twisted skein of possibilities that Ulric's death has created. Are we hunting one killer with varied tastes, or did someone lower the Blood Balance before the village decides for us? Ulric's death teeters on the edge of Mundane Murder. The only reason to investigate is his standing in the village—few disliked him. Which makes his murder even stranger. There were many more deserving.

Outside the barn, the Mayor's courtyard hums with tangled theories—even the rain joins in, slapping against my face with the enthusiasm of a wet-handed debtor. Murder matrices sprout like poisonous mushrooms, each more byzantine than the last.

Adding to the chaos, Sir Roderick, the favoured culprit, has become more aggressive. The proximity to two corpses has painted a target on his aristocratic back.

Some claim they'd spotted him skulking near the Mayor's residence on the night of the first murder, while others whisper about peculiar interactions with Ulric. His noble bearing, once an asset, now appears more damning than a bloodstained dagger.

Ulric might have been several rungs below the Mayor on the Vale's social ladder, but his death promises an avalanche of fury to break loose. The murder reconstruction group is loitering at the barn just off the Mayor's courtyard. The supposed murder weapon, Sir Roderick's Family Crest, is notably absent—presumably back at Highgrove Hall. I wonder why the bailiffs aren't holding onto it as evidence.

Drusilla and I make our way to survey their handiwork. Rain drums against the barn's weathered boards as accusations fly thick as arrows.

Galen pipes up—"Maybe Ulric was trying to steal it!"

"Sir Roderick knew it was Ulric." Rufus says. "He's been watching Ulric's movements."

The Innkeeper has closed the Tavern to join the others. "It all points to Sir Roderick catching Ulric with the crest and bashing him with it?" he says.

I watch events and turn the facts over. The crest—four feet of solid plaster, neither sharp nor subtle—as murder weapons go, it lacks finesse, but passion rarely concerns itself with practicality.

Sir Roderick storms in, drenched and defiant. "Listen to me. I wasn't anywhere near Ulric that night," he snaps, voice rising above the murmurs. "I was in the Square—the herbalist saw me. If anyone's guilty, it's whoever stole my family crest!"

"Sure, Sir Roderick," Perrin drawls. "And maybe that scream was your partner-in-crime setting up your alibi—staged to offset the true time of death and bought you an alibi with Drusilla, who, incidentally, is the Mayor's murderer. How tidy."

Sir Roderick's scowl deepens. "Look at whoever has the most to gain from Ulric's silence. Because I had nothing to gain from it!"

"Except getting your crest back," Perrin says.

I decide to retrace Ulric's last journey from the Tavern. The last night I saw him, he'd been talking about remembering something. Before leaving, I corner the Innkeeper. "What exactly was Ulric say the last time you saw him at the Tavern?"

"We heard him goin' on about shadows," he says, wiping muck from his hands with all the enthusiasm of a man who had given up on hygiene years ago. "Said he saw something."

Ulric seems like an unlikely candidate for The Blood Balance settlement. Maybe he was silenced for what he knew—for what he was about to remember. Whoever killed him was listening, waiting, ready to act before his memory caught up. Perhaps retracing the path from the Mayor's place to the Tavern will reveal something. The route offers a dozen perfect spots for an ambush, yet the broken crest turned up outside the Mayor's residence—right where Drusilla claims she heard that scream.

Everything points to Ulric met his end via Sir Roderick's crest.

The wind responds with a deep groan, rattling doors left ajar. It's a cruel joke—murder by ornament, they'll add it to the Wall of Death. Sir Roderick makes the perfect suspect, yet why would he show me the murder weapon instead of hiding it? And who'd choose something so conspicuous and unwieldy unless they wanted to point fingers at its owner?

Rain intensifies as I near the Tavern. Good, it's closed. I need silence, space to think. My feet carry me back to MacAllister Hall. I light a candle and coax the hearth to life, watching shadows retreat to their corners. A worn chair by the fire welcomes me like an old friend.

My mind drifts to when we were all younger—unburdened by secrets and suspicion, still pretending the world could be explained with lessons and lunch breaks. Drusilla and Moondrop arrived in Murder's Vale during my last year of school—orphans, newly returned from their years at convent education. They came under the Mayor's protection and were sent to work for the herbalist soon after.

I didn't see much of them—I left the Vale not long after finishing school—but during the time I was there, Moondrop haunted my dreams. Her laughter, like wind chimes, was rarely directed my way. When it was, her knowing smile both acknowledged and dismissed me in a single breath.

Drusilla was tough to like—she was a storm in human form. Her tongue could flay the skin from your bones. Quick to scorn, she had no patience for our games.

Our school days shaped us in different ways. Ulric, Milton, Roderick—and I—spent our formative years at a makeshift school beyond the village walls. Austere, unyielding, stripped of warmth and comfort. The lessons carved order into us, leaving little room for imagination.

Ulric was the exception, always scheming, always smiling. He turned the school's rigid rules into opportunities, running dice games and trading contraband, his smile never dimming. That same smile stayed bright even as they expelled him, his voice echoing down the hall:

"You'll beg me to come back!" They never did, so he made the Tavern his kingdom, his music its heartbeat.

Milton was a steady presence. He'd watch Ulric's escapades with silent amusement. Milton's friendship with Ellington Crumley had been strong, though I never understood it. Crumley, privately tutored and proudly distant, inhabited a different world. Friction between the Crumleys and the MacAllisters ran deep for reasons never spoken of.

Sir Roderick's life had been harder. His path was paved with his father's expectations, each cobblestone a bruise. I saw the shadows in his eyes. His conscription came young, his father's military legacy a chain around his neck.

The Library archives tell of MacAllister and Crumley families fighting for leadership. But the Crumleys entrenched themselves under baronial favour. Now the Self-Determination Charter threatens to uproot that well-tended garden.

Rising from the chair, I let out a long breath. The fire is dying, its embers glowing dim in the hearth. Tomorrow will come soon enough, bringing with it the demands of the present, but tonight I indulge in remembrance's bitter wine. I climb toward my bedchamber. The candlelight flickers like a guilty conscience.

Chapter 25

Morning, Second Day of Widders

Storm clouds churn above like a pot of over-boiled gruel, ready to spill without warning. The Library looms ahead. The door protests, as always. Inside, a handful of villagers skulk between the stacks. Behind her desk sits Mrs Sibberidge, her razor-sharp focus dissects the gloom to pin me like a butterfly to cork. Our little dance begins, as it always does. Her head tilts a fraction—that precise angle of ambiguity that can mean anything.

"Mrs Sibberidge," I murmur.

"Mr MacAllister." Her eyes flick to my coat and back to her work.

Taking the cue, I head for the back staircase.

The basement greets me like an old friend. Ancient beams creak overhead. The central table still bears the scattered remains of my previous visit. I lay the codex on the table, shrug off my coat, and roll up my sleeves like a man preparing for surgery.

"Right," I mutter to the waiting darkness. "Let's see what secrets you've been hoarding."

The codex lies open before me, its cover embossed with arcane symbols, its binding brittle, its ink faded to the colour of dried blood. Each page is an enigma: dense diagrams, impossible geometries, and spidery script that veers between mysticism and madness. It smells faintly of mildew and earth, like the grave I dug it from.

Beside it, the Mayor's parchments sprawl in chaotic contrast—more recent, but no less confounding. Jagged notations scrawled in haste, margins crammed with obsessive annotations, symbols and glyphs repeated like compulsions.

As I scan the parchment, I begin to notice familiar shapes—fragments that echo the codex. Certain symbols appear in both, though the connections are tenuous at best. I flip through pages at random, searching for anything resembling sanity. One spread displays circles within circles. Another shows what might be a cipher key—if ciphers were designed by madmen. I turn to the margins, where faint scratches catch the light, revealing a sequence of numbers that emerge like ghost writing on a tombstone.

The numbers appear to correspond to specific pages, though the logic behind their sequence remains elusive. I flip back and forth, my fingers tracing the spidery marginalia that creeps across each yellowed page. Another dead end—or is it? A pattern emerges, faint as a bruise. Certain symbols recur, each marked with a subtle dot.

My hands move with fevered purpose, copying these dotted harbingers onto fresh parchment. Column by column, they form a grid that whispers of purpose. When I lay one of the Mayor's documents beside it, the match hits me like a fist to the gut—one perfect row of symbols, aligned as neat as graves in a churchyard.

These aren't mere letters or words scattered across the page—they're coordinates, each pointing to a symbol in the codex. Third row, second column. Fifth row, first column. Piece by piece, a message takes shape.

My hand cramps from hours of scribbling, but pain is a small price for progress. Still, what I uncover is maddeningly opaque—each answer breeding two more questions. The codex isn't just a book with secrets. It's a warden, locking truth behind bars of ink. Every word a riddle, every page a snare. And yet, no prison is perfect.

As I trace the links between codex and parchments, one word keeps surfacing like a body refusing to stay buried: *Accord*. It appears in both texts, always beside an intricate symbol—a circle imprisoning a triangle, with lines radiating outward like the spokes of fortune's wheel. Its meaning remains just out of reach.

For hours, my quill scratches across parchment. Cross-referencing symbols. Mapping connections. Until, like a whisper from the grave, three words emerge—clear, undeniable, and heavy as a death knell: *The Final Accord*.

This is it. The codex has given me the key.

I grab a boiled beetroot from my satchel. Its deep purple skin glistens in the candlelight. I bite into it. "Full of flavour," I say. The beet slips from my grip, leaving a sticky trail in its wake. By the end, my hands, mouth, and tunic look like they've been dipped in wine.

"Beetroot's always worth the mess," I say, grinning.

The Final Accord isn't just some dusty municipal document—it's a blood pact, a constitution written in ink and intent. It codifies what this place has always been: a stage where murder is both art and political currency. Leadership would no longer pass through bloodlines but be seized through cunning, carnage, and survival.

The parchments spell it out with chilling precision. In exchange for self-determination, the Crown demanded regular elections. But Crumley had twisted that edict into a deathmatch—a game of deception where no one is exempt and no one can refuse. Power here belongs not to the just or the wise, but to those cunning enough to survive the rules. The rules he wrote to suit himself. And the rules that would reveal any threat to his control.

In Crumley's own words—"To lead, one must command the tools of power: manipulation, intimidation, ruthlessness, and deception. In Murder's Vale, governance belongs to the serpent, not the lion."

"He had the whole thing sewn up," I mutter. "Designed the contest. Controlled the votes. Our dear departed Mayor was playing chess by himself with everyone else as spectators."

His plans read like a manual for aspiring tyrants. My quill hovers over one line that catches the lamplight—"To win the game, one must be the shadow, not the blade. Let others wield suspicion while you wield the illusion of truth." Poetic.

A detail catches my eye—symbols on a particular parchment that strike a chord in memory. Rifling through the Mayor's notes with renewed purpose, I find it. A codex entry bearing the same star symbol—one that translates to *Sanctum*.

The word means nothing at first... until memory strikes. I've seen that symbol before. Carved in stone above Sir Roderick's study. Whatever secrets Crumley hoarded, Sir Roderick's *Sanctum* may hold the next piece.

My mind races through the implications like a rat through a maze. I close the codex with the finality of sealing a tomb. What began as a murder investigation has twisted into something that makes plain murder feel quaint. First the Mayor. Then Ulric. The body count is rising like floodwater—and here such things rarely stop at two.

Every face in the village wears a potential mask. I catalogue the players. Mrs Sibberidge, with her suspicious interest in the Library's holdings—is she what she seems, or simply another piece on the board?

And Sir Roderick's *Sanctum* is looking less like a study and more like a spider's web.

The village itself performs the role of co-conspirator, its every citizen an actor in a grand, terrible play. Every conversation I've had needs reviewing. The village is a powder keg in a lightning storm. The Mayor's death leaves a vacuum. Ulric's murder has only added fuel. Without Crumley's grip, this place teeters on the edge of its own cunning. Unless the Final Accord is already in play.

Murder doesn't feel like a village preparing for an orderly transition of power—it feels like a beast about to turn on itself. Crumley was the architect of the process, but who, if anyone, is directing its macabre performance now? I pack up and climb the basement stairs.

Time to visit the Sanctum.

Chapter 26

Evening, Second Day of Widders

Clouds overhead seethe like a crowd on the verge of riot, each billow turning darker. Now and then, a swirl of wind rakes through the village, as if testing how easily the sky's fury could tear roofs from their beams.

I reach Highgrove Hall, its silhouette looming on the outskirts of the village. The front door stands half ajar—an invitation or a trap? I cross the threshold into the foyer. "Sir Roderick?" My voice dissipates into the hungry silence. Inside, I shed my rain-soaked coat, each droplet marking my presence on marble. The air carries an acrid whisper—smoke—the perfume of desperate men covering their tracks. Wind and leaves spiral into the foyer, a rude reminder of the storm beyond. I close the door with a deliberate thud, hoping the sound will summon someone—anyone—to spare me the indignity of standing here like an intruder.

My footsteps betray me as I head towards the study where Sir Roderick had revealed the broken crest. Nearing the door, I regard the star etched into the frame above—the *Sanctum*. The burning scent intensifies. I pause at the threshold, taking in the scene of chaos before me. Desk drawers gape like open wounds, spilling their viscera across polished wood. Books lie scattered in positions of surrender, some splayed open as if caught mid-flight, others face down in final repose.

The fireplace crackles with satisfaction, digesting what I suspect are far from mere outdated records. Milton stands before the hearth like an amateur arsonist at his first burning. Another set of scrolls feeds the flames under his methodical hand.

"Busy?" I inject the word with casual menace, stepping into the room's warmth.

Milton turns, surprise flickering across his features before his bureaucratic mask slides back into place. His gaze performs a nervous dance between me and the fire.

"Noel," he says with artificial coolness, "what brings you here at this hour?"

"I could pose the same question," I say.

"Sir Roderick is occupied," Milton says his words like a man rationing truth. "You shouldn't be here."

"Burning secrets, Milton?"

His eyes flicker with irritation. "These are out of date. It's perfectly normal administration."

"Perhaps," I say, watching another page curl into ash, "but timing's a curious mistress, isn't she?"

His jaw tightens like a hangman's knot. "The Mayor's passing necessitates... housekeeping."

A small pouch of hazelnuts sits restless in my pocket. I pour a handful onto the table, their hard shells rattling like dice. Milton looks at me in silence as I grab the first nut.

"So, just following orders?" I say, rolling the nut between my fingers.

Milton exhales sharply. "It's easy to sneer from the sidelines, Noel. Some of us have obligations."

I crack the nut with a lazy bite, letting the shell splinter like the fragile excuse he just offered. "Obligations, or debts?"

"Use a nutcracker," he says stiffly.

I spit the shell onto the floor and crunch on the nutmeat with audible gusto. "I've got all the tools I need," gesturing vaguely at my teeth.

"It seems that Sir Roderick's picked up the puppet strings?" I say.

"Some people have a talent for remaining atop the heap. I do what is required of my role."

Another nut meets the same brutal fate, its shell joining the growing pile under the table.

"You're making a mess!" Milton shouts.

I grin, fragments of shell clinging to my teeth. "That's how you know it's a good snack."

A cool voice slides into the room—"Nibblenudge, I trust you're not making mischief?"

We turn in unison. Sir Roderick stands in the doorway, composed as a cat at a crime scene. He closes the door with deliberate grace, his eyes performing a dance between Milton and me.

"Sir Roderick, I'd like a word," I say.

"That, I gathered," he says, gliding toward the brandy decanter like a man who knows precisely where every weapon in the room is hidden. "Though it appears you've found ways to entertain yourself."

His demeanour exudes confidence, sharp and deliberate, a stark contrast to the usual grim, determined air I've noticed on him elsewhere in the village.

Milton shuffles sideways, gathering scrolls with exaggerated care. "Just disposing of outdated materials, as discussed."

Sir Roderick sips his brandy, his gaze lingering on Milton like a noose. "Efficient as always."

The undercurrents between them are thick enough to choke on—resentment and fear tangled like lovers in a death grip. "Quite the reorganisation effort. Everything ship-shape?" I ask.

"Preparing for the changes our dear departed Mayor set in motion," Sir Roderick responds, smooth as poisoned honey.

"Fascinating timing, given we're still picking through the Mayor's murder like ravens at a feast," I say.

"Do you have a point buried in that observation, Nibblenudge?"

"Perhaps it might appear less suspicious if we suspended the impromptu bonfire until after we solve this murder.

However, my reason for dropping in is to enquire about the Mayor's remedies you were to test."

Sir Roderick's expression darkens. "Ah, our beloved herbalists."

"Have you compared Drusilla's samples to the Mayor's?"

He nods with the slow deliberation of a judge considering the gallows. "I conducted the tests myself. The remedies in the Mayor's possession were different in every measurable way—colour, texture, the very stench of them," he says, his words precise as autopsy cuts. "His ointment carried a sharp, malevolent odour—deadly. Either they're lying through their teeth, or these treatments have a nasty habit of turning into something lethal."

"They've been meddling in dangerous substances for years," Milton says, his stare distant.

I look at Sir Roderick. "Yet you survived? How fortunate."

"I destroyed the poisons so no one else could be harmed. A thoroughly dangerous business it is," he says.

"THAT WAS EVIDENCE!" My words explode like trapped steam.

"It was too dangerous," he says with the patronising calm of a schoolmaster. "Focus, Nibblenudge. What matters is catching them red-handed."

My anger cools into calculation. "We'll need to search both shops, leave no vial unturned, no drawer unopened."

"We must exercise caution," Sir Roderick says. "They're craftier than garden snakes, venomous, and twice as slippery."

"No more impromptu bonfires please, Milton, 'til we've laid this case to rest," I say.

His eyes seek Sir Roderick's face like a compass seeking north.

Sir Roderick's attention flickers between us like a guttering candle. "As you wish, Nibblenudge. Now, unless there's something else pressing…"

"Actually, I'd like to discuss the Final Accord."

Sir Roderick's posture calcifies in bureaucratic discomfort. His spine straightens as though someone has threaded steel through his vertebrae.

"I see." His voice carries the particular strain of a man trying to stuff an inconvenient truth back into its box. "Well, that's... official business. Not the sort of thing we broadcast from the bell tower, you understand."

He pauses, choosing his next words like a man selecting stepping stones across treacherous waters.

"But since you've stumbled into this, let me be clear—it's not a conspiracy, if that's the trail you're sniffing down."

"Then what would you call it?"

"Order," Sir Roderick snaps, wielding the word like a shield against chaos. His voice holds the certainty of a man who's repeated this explanation so often it's become a prayer. "And order is essential. Without it, this village will unravel."

He releases a sigh like a confession. Then his eyes find mine. "But you already know that, don't you?"

"Order, or control?" I ask.

"They're two sides of the same coin," he replies, cold as a winter moon. "Control maintains order."

Milton's voice flares, then fades—conviction and cowardice playing tug-of-war behind his spectacles. "The danger is that order can be manipulated," he says.

Sir Roderick shoots him a warning look. "Careful, Milton."

"Schemes are simple enough to devise," Milton says, his voice trembling. "But some of us must sweep up the wreckage."

"You chose your path. Don't seek sympathy now," Sir Roderick says.

I watch their exchange like a chess match where both players hold poison-tipped pieces. "Trouble in paradise?"

Sir Roderick eyes Milton. "A difference in perspective—requiring resolution, it seems."

Milton adjusts his glasses; his fingers just shy of steady. Bravery evaporating like morning dew under a dragon's glare, leaving only the faint outline of misplaced valour.

Sir Roderick exhales, voice lowering. "The Accord isn't some tyrant's whim—it's structured. A panel of villagers oversee the transitions. It lends legitimacy, appearances... It keeps the masses calm."

"Interesting perspective," I say, leaning against a bookshelf. "It's poetic in its pretence of democracy."

"Why shroud it in secrecy?" I ask.

"Secrecy maintains integrity," Milton replies. "Though an outsider might struggle to grasp our methods."

"Try me," I say.

Milton hesitates, his fingers conducting a nervous symphony on the desk's edge. "The Final Accord is designed precisely to not be fair," he says, sounding pleased with the concept. "It's designed to be a structured process. Fairness constrains ingenuity. Murder's Vale thrives on ingenuity and cunning."

"Structured, or choreographed?"

"A method appropriate for our unique circumstances," Milton says, pride eclipsing his fear. "Under committee oversight, naturally."

"A process that eschews fairness is ripe for manipulation, especially by those intimately familiar with its mechanics," I say.

"That's—" Milton catches himself like a man stepping back from a precipice. "Your interest in this matter seems... excessive."

"Professional curiosity, that's all, Milton. Murder investigations have a way of illuminating hidden corners."

Sir Roderick steps in. "I think you should be focused on the poisonings, Nibblenudge. We need this case solved quickly. After Ulric—who knows how long before another of us is inexplicably murdered? The herbalists should be your focus."

"Of course, I say, watching the subtle interplay of power between them.

He raises his arms to usher everyone out of the room, a conductor ending a dark symphony.

As Milton walks past me to leave, he mutters, "Dig too deep and you'll find more than you bargained for."

"Don't mind him, Nibblenudge, he's adjusting to new direction," Sir Roderick dismisses, his words polished smooth as river stones.

"I understand the Mayor had quite a grip on your own direction, didn't he?"

Sir Roderick takes a sip of his brandy. "He tried. Baseless accusations."

"And Milton caught in the crossfire?"

"He makes his own choices," Sir Roderick says coolly. "As do we all."

"Talking about choices," I say, "I have a couple more questions on the Well."

Sir Roderick raises his hand. "I grow tired of this conversation, Nibblenudge."

"It's just a couple more questions."

"Be quick about it, then. I have things to attend to."

"You said the bad ones are reburied quickly. What happens to the others? Do they cause problems?"

Sir Roderick snorts. "Oh, they cause problems."

His fingers drum against his belt. "Grievances. From past murderees. From those who were buried alive. From the present villagers. Some weren't finished with their business, others had business unfinished for them." His jaw tightens. "People who were wronged. Or the ones who did the wronging."

"Sounds complex. There must be property arguments, relationship complications, all sorts," I say.

His mouth twists in something that's not quite a smile. "Meaning more murders. More thievery. Over and over. Unless they make up."

"Does that happen?" I ask.

He gives me a look.

"Do they age?"

Sir Roderick's expression darkens. "Not after they've been in the ground." He exhales through his nose. "One benefit, I suppose. This conversation is over, Nibblenudge."

I hold his gaze a moment longer, waiting for something. But he offers nothing. Just silence.

I turn and leave him alone in the study. I need to finish this investigation before victims and murderers reappear. Not that murder seems to count for much here. In Murder's Vale, death isn't so much a conclusion as it is an inconvenience—one that comes with baggage, unfinished business, and grudges that refuse to stay buried.

Outside, my thoughts whirl like autumn leaves in a storm. Milton looks like a man drowning in secrets, each one a weight drawing him deeper into whatever game Sir Roderick is playing. The knight himself moves like a grandmaster, sacrificing pawns, unconcerned by the bodies left in his wake.

By the time I reach MacAllister Hall, the weather has settled. Clouds still boil overhead, a swirling congress of gloom and ill intent, but the downpour holds its breath as though waiting for the next movement. My hand reaches for the door, hovering over the handle. Something's off—a footprint.

Seems like MacAllister Hall entertains visitors when I'm not here—it's the ones who visit when I am here that concern me more. There's no sign they came in. Maybe that's worse.

Chapter 27

Morning, Third Day of Widders

Now I sleep in shifts and change rooms like a fugitive with commitment issues. Whether they're hunting me or just rummaging for information, I'd rather not be the curiosity that bleeds.

Breakfast sits in my stomach like a dare. Everything tastes faintly of threat these days—brine, bitterness, and the lingering suggestion of poison. Either the eggs were off, or someone's getting creative. Great, now I'm wondering if I've been poisoned. I suppose I'll find out soon enough. Which reminds me—Sir Roderick's poison findings don't match Drusilla's samples. It's time to search the herbalist shops properly... and dig deeper into this Final Accord shenanigans while I'm at it.

As I cross the Square, mist veils everything, leaving the townsfolk squinting at each other like uncertain betrayers. One moment, you see a familiar face; the next, it dissolves into nothing. Drusilla's shop crouches before me. The warped windowpanes catch what little light filters through the mist, transforming it into writhing patterns. Even from outside, I can sense the cloying sweetness within.

The village's furore over poisoning has peaked, and we need to respond, particularly as Drusilla's remedies, according to Sir Roderick, don't match what was found at the Mayor's place. If

Drusilla's remedies were perchance, tampered with, someone wants her framed. If they weren't...

Wrong texture, wrong colour, wrong smell. Fatally wrong, or so he claims—hard to verify once it's all gone up in smoke. But if he's right, there are two possibilities: either she gave me the wrong treatments, or they degraded—just as she warned—though she never suggested they could become toxic.

Sir Roderick arrives beside me like an armoured shadow. "We need to handle this with care," I say, keeping my voice muted. "Push too hard and she'll either clam up or feed us pretty lies."

He responds with a grunt, his hand drifting to his sword hilt.

"Restraint is not for me, Nibblenudge."

Nothing like a friendly interrogation to start the day.

***

Time to find out whether Drusilla and her sister's poisons are calculated or careless—though in this village, carelessness is its own kind of crime. A bell tinkles as we enter—a sound too innocent for this place. The air inside is thick with herbs and something sharper, something that makes my nose twitch in warning. Drusilla stands behind her counter like a queen at court, dark hair severely pulled back, eyes gleaming with the kind of mischief that ends in a funeral.

"To what do I owe the pleasure, gentlemen?"

"I think we all know why we're here," I say.

Her eyes narrow. "Do we?"

Her counter becomes a handy place to lean against while my fingers find a jar labelled 'Sweet Dreams'—no doubt, the least honest label in the shop.

Sir Roderick steps forward. "Those treatments you gave the Mayor—they don't match."

So much for our delicate approach.

"Please, forgive his enthusiasm, murder accusations are rather weighty fare for breakfast, aren't they? That aside, we'll need to search your shop. With poison on every tongue and a concerning discrepancy in your treatments, we need to determine whether your treatments played a role in the Mayor's death."

"Search the shop?" Her eyebrows arch. Her fingers dance across the bottles behind her like a pianist selecting their next note. "How thrilling. What kind of search?"

"The kind where we need to check your shop for anything… minty," Sir Roderick booms, proving yet again that diplomacy isn't in his repertoire.

She blinks, mastering her expression with the skill of a professional liar.

"Minty? Are you suggesting the Mayor's treatments contained mint?—show me." She crosses her arms.

I shoot Sir Roderick a frustrated glare.

"We're not here to discuss the evidential chain of custody, Drusilla. We need to examine your inventory—the poisons, the dangerous herbs, all those little bottles you keep for special occasions."

Her eyes narrow.

"You know, mint grows wild in the fields. Anyone can harvest it."

"May we look around?" I ask.

"Be my guest." She gestures with theatrical grace. "Though I should warn you—sniffing concentrated concoctions can drop you to the floor, it doesn't make them poison."

Drusilla's shelves hold an encyclopaedia of bottled fate, from the mundane *Pain Balm* to the ominous *Drowsy Nightshade* and *Whispersleep*. Nothing screams murder—or minty.

Sir Roderick yanks open a drawer, revealing bundles of dried vegetation that look like they've been harvested from a witch's garden. He holds up a twisted root that resembles a hanged man's hand. "What's this supposed to be?" he barks.

Drusilla's sigh could wither plants. "*Mandrake*. Perfectly harmless unless you're fool enough to chew it raw."

A high shelf draws my eye, where liquids in every hue imaginable wait in apothecary jars—pale lavender like dawn mist, deep crimson like fresh wounds, murky green like stagnant pools. I tilt one gingerly, watching the liquid inside slosh. The label reads *Euphoria Draught*.

"*Euphoria Draught?*"

"Exactly what it claims to be," she says. "One drop makes you think you've got friends. Two drops helps you forget Murder's Vale exists. Three drops and you wake up in a buried coffin several days later."

Sir Roderick slams another cabinet shut. "And people trust you with their health?"

"It's me or my sister. Which would you choose?"

Sir Roderick grimaces.

Crouching by a lower cabinet, I uncover rows of glass vials sealed with wax. "Anything in here we should worry about?"

"Worry?"

"Enough games," I snap, rising to fix her with my best investigator's stare.

Her smile flickers like a candle in a draft. She nods toward a locked box on the highest shelf. "There are some interesting items are up there out of reach."

Sir Roderick reaches for it, but Drusilla clicks her tongue. "Careful now. Those vials are fragile."

I climb a stool and retrieve the box myself, setting it on the counter with exaggerated care. "The key?" I ask.

She produces an ornate key from her apron, passing it with mock reverence.

Inside, nested in midnight velvet, lay vials labelled with precise handwriting: *Doomflower Extract, Shadowbark Distillate*.

I lift one to the light. "And what does *Shadowbark Distillate* do, other than shimmer?"

"That depends on your ambitions. A few drops calm the nerves. A few more, and your skin parts way with your body. Quite definitively."

Sir Roderick sneers, "A dangerous thing in the hands of someone with your... reputation."

Drusilla winks at him.

I replace the vial, unease growing.

"What's this?" I lift the vial labelled *Doomflower Extract*, turning it in the dim light.

"A mild sedative for troubled nights."

I uncork it and take a careful sniff. Lavender, yes, but underneath—something sharper, familiar. The same scent Sir Roderick had described from the evidence. "Smells stronger than a mere sleep aid."

"Only if you take too much."

We've found nothing directly incriminating, but as we prepare to leave, Sir Roderick's attention is drawn to a plant tucked behind more common herbs like a secret between lies. He reaches for it, bringing it into the light.

"And what's this supposed to be?" he asks.

Drusilla moves with sudden speed.

"Step away from her," she says, voice sharp as broken glass. "That's *Little Mimsi*."

It's a plant with black leaves that drinks in what little light touches them. He leans closer, his hand hovers above it, caught between curiosity and instinct.

"STOP!" she says.

Sir Roderick stiffens—his grip jerks toward his throat. My breath stutters as I catch the edge of a bitter-metal tang from *Little Mimsi* and the taste of blood.

Sir Roderick retreats, his hand jerking away like he's touched a serpent.

Too late.

Sir Roderick collapses to the floor.

From my satchel, I dig out a small, pickled turnip, its vinegary scent an uninvited guest.

Drusilla wrinkles her nose. "Are you quite sure this an appropriate time to snack, Noel?"

"Your plant has left a nasty taste in my mouth," I say, biting into the pickled turnip with a loud crunch. Pickling juice squirts from the turnip, splattering onto Sir Roderick, who lays motionless on the floor. A droplet lands on Drusilla's sleeve, and she hurriedly dabs at it with a handkerchief.

Sir Roderick begins to groan.

"Welcome back," she says, her tone as sharp as the tang of the air. She stands over him, arms crossed, with *Little Mimsi* safely tucked back into her corner.

Sir Roderick coughs on the floor. He cradles his head and clutches his chest as though he's surfaced too quickly from deep water.

I chew slowly, the vinegar tang making my eyes water.

"Do you have to eat so loudly?" he says.

I finish the turnip with another sharp crunch, then lick the remaining vinegar from my fingers with theatrical zeal.

We consider helping him but decide against it.

She looks at him, arms crossed. "You're lucky. You made her anxious. She's a breath stealer."

"Murder without poison," he mutters, adjusting his armour as he puts more distance between himself and the jar. "What other surprises do you have?"

I turn to Drusilla. "You've been keeping things from us. People know about your connection to the Mayor. And to make matters worse, Moondrop's been stirring the pot in the Square."

"There's nothing to eat if that's what you're looking for?" she snips.

Sir Roderick gasps for air. "Perhaps the Mayor was blackmailing you on the Accord?"

She leers at him like he's just ratted her out. Her smile flickers, a candle in a draft. "As I've said before, I had nothing to do with his death."

We let silence do the work, watching her squirm under its weight. Drusilla crosses her arms, leaning back against shelves that hold enough 'healing' tonics to poison half of Murder's Vale. Dried herbs behind her cast shadows like hanging men.

"Tell us about the Mayor? Why did he come to you?" I ask.

She shifts her weight, a predator adjusting its stance. "Why does anyone? He needed treatment. Nothing unusual in that—even for a Mayor."

My gaze remains steady. "Go on..."

A sigh slithers past her lips as she settles against the shelves, arms still crossed like barriers against truth. "Alright. The Mayor and I got on. Not in friendship. Kindred spirits, perhaps.

He needed treatment and valued my discretion—he couldn't risk looking weak. I gave him pots with sleep aids, rash ointments, digestive tonics. That's it."

"Was he blackmailing you and your sister?" I say.

"Only a fool would try to blackmail a herbalist."

"What exactly are you saying?" Sir Roderick asks.

She pauses to eat a nut, "He tried. Moondrop was furious—decided to teach him a lesson."

"Go on," I say.

"She had her own way—*Little Mimsi*," she says, regarding the plant with the pride of a mother watching her child's first murder. "He collapsed. By the time he came to, she had her foot on his throat and a new arrangement was agreed."

"And what did you do?"

"I played good sister. Revived him while Moondrop calmed *Little Mimsi*. We weren't interested in murdering the fool."

"Why did he try blackmailing you?" I ask.

She pauses. "Election support, of course."

"What election?" I ask, pretending I've read nothing on it.

Drusilla raises her arms in astonishment. "Haven't you heard? The village was given to self-governance a while ago. An elected Mayor every four years."

"Go on," I say.

"The mayoral position has to be elected by the people."

Sir Roderick grunts. "Did the Mayor persist after your...education?"

"No. He wasn't stupid. We found common ground instead. Something to trade."

"That must have been quite something?" Sir Roderick says.

"Quite something—it was about you, Sir Knight. Letters Patent—issued by the crown, declaring titles, grants, noble appointments. And something about a disgraced knight whose honour was revoked."

Sir Roderick's face floods scarlet, jaw clenching tight. "The impertinence!"

Her voice softens to a purr that would make a cat envious. "So, you see, we had no reason to kill the Mayor."

The knight's eyes linger on Drusilla like a hangman sizing up his next client. "I don't buy it. He schooled you on playing the game and then you played him for a fool. For a herbalist, you seem much too adept with the *Paradox of Suspicion*."

I raise my eyebrows. "Can someone enlighten me, please?" They ignore me.

"Of course he schooled us. He told us everything about this puffed-up charade. His playground politics dressed up in gaudy theatrics—amateurish, misguided, and utterly transparent. The laughable *Manipulation of Innocence, the Tools of Power*?" Drusilla's mockery drips like venom. "Leave the village in awe of one's political mastery? Ridiculous!" She laughs.

"Laugh it up, herbalist. But reality isn't something you brew in a bottle. The game is played in blood and manipulation. You'll never get your Final Innocence Score down far enough. I'll see to that." Sir Roderick booms. His exit has all the nimbleness of a thunderclap. The door slams behind him hard enough to rattle the jars of dried herbs like bones in a crypt.

His words drop with bureaucratic venom. Ah, yes, the Final Innocence Score. Another Accord invention, as I recall.

"What was that all about?" I say.

"Ask him. I'm done talking."

Pieces refuse to align. Drusilla's innocence is questionable, yet her motive is equally ephemeral. Her sister, though— unpredictable as wildfire and twice as dangerous, it seems. At least *Little Mimsi* no longer rests in those impulsive hands.

Looking outside, rain hovers like a patient assassin. "Well, that was quite the performance. I'll leave you to your garden of nightmares," I say.

She returns to her work, her hands moving among the dried leaves with the grace of an executioner selecting tools. Each jar she fills appears to hold a different shade of death.

I leave the shop. Drusilla's answers echo like funeral bells, but Sir Roderick's fury that interests me more. He'd stormed out like a man fleeing his own reflection. I recall advice for new readers in the front covers of *Murder's Prophecy Monthly*— *Ther ben no frendes in Murder's Vale, but folk that han nat yit slain ech other.*

Chapter 28

Afternoon, Third Day of Widders

I adjust my coat against the creeping damp and head into the Square. I need clarity on what's eating Sir Roderick. How far can I trust him to help me untangle this mess, or is he destined to become another knot? Everyone's got something to conceal. The trick is figuring out whether uncovering it is worth dying for.

Sir Roderick is back by the Bitter Well. The man isn't cooling his temper; he's nurturing it. He whirls at my approach, face dark as storm-tossed waters. "What do you want, Nibblenudge?"

"We need to talk. Drusilla had a lot to say about you, and I'd like to hear your side."

He scoffs, hand settling on his sword hilt. "That witch will spin any tale to save herself. I've told you—she's hiding something."

"No argument there. But so are you." I let the words settle before pressing on. "Something about legitimacy?"

The accusation floats dangerously between us.

His jaw clenches. "The Mayor was... resourceful," he grinds out. "He wielded whatever tools served his purpose."

"Like disputing rightful nobility?"

"The specifics are irrelevant. The Mayor understood what leadership here demands."

"Like a manipulated election?"

His expression flickers, but he holds firm. "Leadership in this place requires a firm grip."

"And Milton? Where does he fit?"

"A leech with borrowed authority," Sir Roderick says, waving the comment aside. "A mere messenger."

"Does he have a new master to serve?"

His eyes narrow. "Milton requires structure. The Mayor corrupted him. He can't be trusted."

"Yet you let him handle evidence—documents that might implicate you."

"Enough! As he told you—it was nothing of consequence."

"Perhaps, but why burn parchment, it's valuable?"

The air congeals between us. Fissures spread across his composure. I wait. Whatever the knight is hiding, it's close to the surface now.

Finally, he breaks. "Alright, listen up. The Mayor had information on everyone. He thought he could use it to enforce his Final Accord, but for some, he pushed too hard."

"You're not the kind of man to succumb to blackmail, are you? I wouldn't be surprised if this little crest business is a warning," I say.

Sir Roderick's fists clench, but I'm not finished.

"The Mayor decided you needed schooling in subservience, so he had Ulric steal your crest, didn't he? But you caught him. Killed him with his stolen prize. Is that why you haunt the Bitter Well?"

"LIES!" The word explodes from him. "I was at the Well when he died. That herbalist can verify it."

"And why were you there? Why do you lurk at the Bitter Well? Using Drusilla as your alibi, while others do your dirty work, perhaps?"

He bristles like a cornered wolf, clearly not used to being questioned in such a way. "I was... reflecting."

"Reflecting? Like you were 'reflecting' in the treasury quarters the night you heard the Mayor's murder? Those mysterious footsteps you mentioned—were they yours?"

His jaw tightens, his fists clench. "What exactly are you insinuating?"

"I'm suggesting that you used that time to kill the Mayor. You were right there. The footsteps were yours."

"Ridiculous! I'm no murderer! You dare question my honour?" he says.

"You're making it hard for me to trust you. Your account—it's convenient," I say.

"FINE!" The word burst from him like pus from a lanced boil. "Yes, the Mayor and I had our conflicts. But I didn't kill him, and I didn't touch Ulric." His eyes burn with indignation, his voice drops to a growl. "That's all I'll say."

"That's not good enough. You're neck-deep in this. The Mayor, now Ulric? The village wants your head and I'm inclined to give it to them. Ulric was my friend."

Sir Roderick leans closer, voice dripping with venom. "You think you're the only one collecting secrets, Nibblenudge?" His voice sharp as a dagger's edge. "I cut off a piece of your coat—soaked it in the Mayor's blood. Imagine how that might look... to the village."

I push him back. "You're a washed-up blustering fool."

"Oh no? What poor fool found himself dangling from a chandelier? You only exist to serve my purposes. Best make yourself useful."

I reach for my dagger. He moves to his sword. That's when I notice—he's wearing full plate.

I ease my hand away and take a step back. "All right, then. What is it you want?"

"I want you to retrieve the fabrications the Mayor handed to the herbalists—those falsified Letters Patent."

"And would you have me murder them as well?" I say, the words sour on my tongue.

"Just the false evidence," he snarls. "Those sisters have played their games too long."

His grin spreads like a plague. "Oh, there is one more thing. Your inheritance," he says, each syllable deliberate, poisoned honey dripping from his lips.

"The deeds." Sir Roderick's smirk deepens like a festering wound. "No need to hand them over. Milton located them from the Archive room the night you arrived."

"I see. You want everything I have?"

He adjusts his armour with casual indifference. "What did you expect?"

My fists clench until knuckles whiten.

Sir Roderick struts off, leaving me to fume. "I despise this place." I exhale, watching my breath mingle with the damp air.

I linger by the Bitter Well a moment longer, letting the cold settle through me. No point rushing. Let Roderick think he's won the round—he always struts louder when he thinks no one's keeping score.

That's when I see them. Rufus and Galen—grifters, most likely, linger at the edge of the Square, looking as if they've misplaced their purpose. Or perhaps just waiting for someone desperate enough to unburden their guilt. Their tale of discovering Ulric's corpse sounds as rehearsed as a travelling player's soliloquy. They must be involved.

"Rufus!" He jumps like a startled rabbit. I walk over to them casually. "A word, please." He blanches whiter than altar bread, while Galen goes rigid as a coffin nail. His eyes dart around like a man counting escape routes.

Not sure how I'll see what they know. Let's start by lowering their guard.

I smile. "Gentlemen." I nod. "Haven't seen you two loitering about in some time?"

Rufus gives an awkward laugh. "We've been keeping busy."

"I'm sure." My gaze turns to the Well. "Strange, isn't it? How some folk have their spots?" I glance back at them, casual. "I was just chatting with Sir Roderick, for example. No matter when I come to the Square, he's always by the Well."

Then, as if it's an afterthought, I add, "How often do you think he's there?"

They exchange a look; the kind shared by men who suddenly feel as though they've walked into a trap.

"Every day he can," Rufus says at last. "Been standing there for years." His voice drops a fraction. "He's waiting."

I frown. "For what?"

Silence stretches between them, thick and unspoken. Then Rufus murmurs, "His wife and son."

I blink. The words land like stones in deep water. No ripple. Just depth. "What?"

Rufus hesitates, his fingers twitching at his sides. "They'll come back one day. Everyone comes back eventually."

"What happened to them?"

Galen exhales sharply through his nose.

"The herbalists," Rufus murmurs. "The Mayor housed them in the Vale. Years ago. Wasn't their fault."

"Fault?"

Rufus rubs a hand over his mouth, as if trying to wipe away the words. "It put the Blood balance off. And... well, you know how it works."

"What happened to them?"

"They were out in the fields," Rufus says. "His boy was chasing crows, waving a stick like he was some great warrior. His mother was calling him back."

"The Wind picked up," Galen murmurs, his voice hollow. "At first, it was nothing—just a shift in the air. But then the ground trembled, rippling under their feet. His boy laughed, still waving his stick at the crows, until the soil cracked open beneath them. It wasn't quick."

"People tried to dig them out," Rufus says. "Sir Roderick, the other men, the whole bloody village. But the earth caved around them. By morning, they were gone."

I exhale, slow and measured, then clap my hands together. "Well. That's just tragic, isn't it?"

The sound makes them both flinch. Rufus shuffles awkwardly. Galen bends to pick up something he's dropped—a cloth scrap or coin, perhaps. But something else slips free. A sodden scrap of parchment flutters to the ground between them. He doesn't notice. I do.

I pick it up. The ink has run, but not far enough to save them: "You know what to do. Be at the Mayor's courtyard. Tomorrow at dawn."

I glance up, catching Galen's eyes as he realises what I'm holding. He pales. Rufus stiffens beside him, but it's too late.

I read the note aloud—slowly, deliberately.

Their faces freeze. Not guilty. Worse. Exposed.

I fold the note carefully and tuck it into my coat.

"Well now," I say, with a smile.

"Sir Roderick's crest was found there, wasn't it? And then Ulric shows up dead in the barn. Bit of a coincidence."

The silence that follows isn't confusion—it's calculation. Rufus stares at the ground like it might offer a better lie. Galen opens his mouth, then thinks better of it.

I step in closer, my voice still light but sharpened now. "It's funny how bodies tend to move themselves these days. Especially when grifters with flexible morals are nearby."

Galen looks like he might flee.

Rufus then clears his throat. "It's not what you think."

"I know. Listen, I don't think either of you killed him, but you're neck-deep in this. Was it Milton? Sir Roderick? What did they promise you?"

Rufus glances at Galen, who shakes his head with all the subtlety of a merchant's scale. Too late—I can see Rufus cracking like thin ice under a heavy boot.

Rufus shifts again. "We... we didn't know what it meant."

I cross my arms. "Try again."

"It was just a job!" he blurts out.

I tilt my head. "A job?"

Confusion clouds their faces. "We got a note from a stranger with threats. Don't know from who. We didn't ask questions."

"Who killed Ulric?"

Rufus spreads his hands. "Wasn't us."

My mind races. Looks like he was silenced, a poor unfortunate pawn in the game.

I leave them to marinate like cheap meat in wine.

Chapter 29

Morning, Fourth Day of Widders

Detective work isn't about finding truth—it's about wading through the swamp of silence and lies. The case of the sisters—Drusilla and Moondrop are a tangled mess of trouble, like juggling electric eels in a thunderstorm. Every time I have a grip on one eel of truth, it slips away, leaving only questions in its wake.

If the source of the poison's anywhere, it's bottled up in one of their shops. Drusilla's turned up empty. Now it's Moondrop's turn.

The villagers, bless their suspicious little hearts, have already written their own ending to this tale. They've cast our herbalists as the Mayor's poisoners. It started with Drusilla, but now they can't decide. Their solution? Condemn them both.

The bitter rivalry between the sisters hasn't helped their case. My thoughts circle back to Drusilla's reactions during our last encounter. Something about the mismatched treatments had struck a nerve, whether from surprise or deception, I couldn't say. And her response to the Final Accord... well, that thread might lead somewhere interesting, if I can follow it without getting strangled.

I pull my coat tight as I head back into the village. I turn down a cramped lane east of the Square, slipping past the

Tavern and onto Moondrop's shop. Its weathered sign swinging in rhythm with the breeze.

The bell above Moondrop's door manages a half-hearted jingle as I step inside. Moondrop's domain radiates calm. Every item in its proper place. It waits, like an old book on a high shelf, patient and full of secrets. Moondrop peeks up from her work, her lagoon eyes meet mine with an unsettling serenity.

"Noel," she says, as if she's been expecting me. My gaze wanders around the shop. Shelves are laden with mysteries—jars bearing names that whisper of forgotten lore: *Elderblight, Ghostleaf, Widow's Root*. This isn't the mundane stock of a village herbalist; it's an arsenal of ancient knowledge, each bottle promising power or peril.

"Thought I'd drop by," I say.

She shrugs and returns to her work.

If Drusilla's place had a certain dangerous charm, Moondrop's shop is like a garden that's exploded indoors. I'm hoping for a straightforward morning after the verbal sparring with Drusilla and Sir Roderick yesterday. Maybe we can approach Moondrop with more finesse.

Competing fragrances drown the air. The scent so thick it can be chewed. But that's not what stops me. It's Sir Roderick. At first, I think he's browsing. But then his hand moves—fingers pushing something into a jar. The leaves sit too neatly, too new among their dried companions. My stomach twists. So much for professional integrity. I watch his clumsy performance, weighing my choices like worn coins. Moondrop doesn't appear to have noticed and confronting him now risks compromising the search, but silence makes me a collaborator.

The knight straightens, ancient armour creaking. Our eyes meet. Irritation spreads across his face before it hides behind practiced nobility. "Nibblenudge," he says quietly, forcing a smile. He clears his throat, gaze dancing toward his handiwork with the mint. "I thought I'd make a start here to expedite finishing the searches."

"That so?"

We both look around to check on Moondrop's proximity. The mint leaves jut from the jar like guilty confessions.

"Why are you topping up that jar?" I whisper.

His jaw works like he's chewing on something unpleasant. "We both know the truth is already here, somewhere. They're hiding it from us. From the village. I'm simply... illuminating it. What herbalist doesn't stock mint?"

Moondrop glides over to us, moving with the fluid grace of spilled ink. She takes in the scene with a smile that could sharpen knives. "My, my, what an unexpected gathering," she purrs, voice smooth as aged poison. "Two distinguished gentlemen gracing my humble establishment at this tender hour?"

"Moondrop. We're here after finding inconsistencies in the Mayor's treatments," I say.

Her eyes dance between us, reading the mood like tea leaves. "Inconsistencies? How delightfully mysterious. But what has that to do with me?"

Sir Roderick steps forward, his armoured bulk attempting to dominate the space. "We need to see your inventory. To check for... dangerous substances."

Her silver eyebrows arch delicately. "Dangerous substances? That's more my sister's domain, especially as it's her treatments you're concerned with."

She turns away, apparently dismissing the conversation, and begins adjusting a basket of onions on the counter—long, pale things with paper-thin skins and the faint sheen of dew.

I drift closer, eyeing the basket.

"Could I buy one of those?" I ask.

She glances at me, curiosity flickering behind her serenity. "Take one. My treat."

I nod in thanks, pluck the largest onion from the pile, its papery skin crackling under my fingers.

I bite into it with all the enthusiasm of a starving man, the sharp, acrid taste hitting my tongue like a slap. Tears spring to my eyes.

"Sweet Mother of—" I wheeze, but continue chewing with vigour. My nose clears with such violent precision I can smell tomorrow's weather.

Moondrop gags as I take another bite, the juice dripping onto the table.

"You're a menace," she says.

I hold up the onion, now half-devoured, and grin through watering eyes. "A tasty menace." I grin through the burning sensation in my mouth, chewing quickly. "Keeps the plague away," I say, wiping my hands on a mossy-looking plant.

Moondrop turns her head slightly, regaining her composure with a slow breath, though her nose wrinkles in visible offence.

I clear my throat, blink away the tears, and straighten up. "We need to investigate all potential sources of toxic substances," I say. "We must be thorough."

She leans against the counter, her fingers tracing patterns in the dust. "I see. Well then, investigate. But do be careful. Some of my exotic plants can be temperamental."

"Another *Little Mimsi*?" I ask.

She smirks. "Worse."

It's hard to tell if she's serious. We inspect the shelves, each label reading like a poem from a grimoire: *Whisperroot Essence, Bloodmire Ash, Venomous Dewdrops*. My attention snags on a collection of wooden boxes, specifically a jet-black specimen marked *Moondrop's Special Reserve*, its latch secured with a peculiar knot of twine.

"It's empty," she says with a sly smile. "Open it if you like."

Sir Roderick stalks the higher shelves like an armoured vulture, his gauntlet disturbing delicate herbs that shrink from his touch. He pauses at a stack of scrolls, metallic fingers hovering over cryptic markings.

"These are?" he says, jabbing at the scrolls with all the subtlety of a siege engine.

Moondrop's gaze drifts upward, lazy as a well-fed cat. "Runes of protection. For fragile remedies."

The knight hefts a jar of glittering powder, holding it to the light like evidence at trial.

"And this?"

"*Stardust Salt*," she replies, amusement dancing in her voice. "It has an unfortunate affinity for metal, though you might look fetching in sparkles."

He grimaces and returns the jar. "You have quite the collection of convenient explanations."

"I don't need excuses, Sir Roderick," she says. "My stock is exactly what it claims to be. Unlike some of—your tactics."

Her eyes flicked pointedly to the jar of mint leaves he'd tampered with earlier.

"Enough," I say, stopping the squabble before it spawns violence.

"Such a pleasure to have you visit," she says, her tone laced with mockery. Her attention shifts to Sir Roderick, who's attempting to stare holes through her facade. "You seem troubled."

"Just eager to get to the bottom of this... situation." The words grind out like rusty gears.

"Indeed," she says, "the bottom is where all the interesting things settle."

I lift a jar of *Dream Weaver's Dust*, studying its contents as they shift like captured starlight. "Moondrop—I wonder if you could illuminate us on the curious gap between what Drusilla claims to have provided and what we found."

She exhales, brushing away a wayward strand of silver hair with the deliberate grace of a performer. "Ah, my dear sister's remedies. So... predictable." Her smile flickers like a guttering candle as she eyes the jar in my hand.

Sir Roderick's suspicion thickens the air. "What exactly are you implying?"

Her smile unfurls like hidden blades.

The bell above the door gives a reluctant jangle as a man steps inside. Rain beads on his cloak and pools on the floor as he brushes water from his sleeves with a practised flick.

Stocky. Shoulders hunched like they're used to bracing for arguments. Hair—a mess of thick, curly ginger, soaked to a coppery snarl beneath his hood. His beard, wild and stubborn, clings to his jaw like it's been surviving on spite alone.

He carries authority like an inconvenient parcel—heavy, damp, and about to be dropped on someone else's doorstep.

Then the memory clicks. It's the man who delivered the Mayor's final note.

His voice is low, rough, like gravel being rolled around. "Ah! MacAllister," he says, sharp eyes landing on me like a warrant. "Found you. Sir Roderick said I'd find the pair of you here this morning. I'm Darius Drummond, the bailiff around here."

He nods to the knight, who returns it with the wary respect of a man acknowledging a fellow predator. Darius surveys the room like he's cataloguing liabilities.

"Yes, I know, it's a shame you didn't stop for a drink when you dropped that note off at my chambers in the city."

Darius doesn't flinch. His mouth twists into something that might be a smirk—or a warning dressed as one. "Didn't want to complicate things, especially late at night," he replies, voice still gravel-slick.

"Thoughtful of you," I say. "Most visitors at that time just try to kick the door in."

He nods. "MacAllister, this thing you're doing—this investigation. It's got the whole town twisting in the wind. Folks are jumpy. Overexcited. Too many questions. Not enough answers."

He rubs his thick ginger beard. "I'd just as soon lock you up for the murder to put an end to this all, but if I step in now, will it only delay things further. So, here's the deal. You've got forty-eight hours to wrap this up. Find a culprit or hand yourself in. Tie it up neat. Make sure this mess doesn't spill any further."

He leans in, the scent of damp parchment and pressure clinging to his coat. "Or I start making decisions you won't like."

Then he straightens, adjusts his cloak, and strides back toward the door, pausing just long enough to fire one last glance over his shoulder. "Tick-tock." Then he's gone—swallowed by the sound of the bell snapping shut behind him, leaving only the scent of impending consequences.

"So the treatments, Moondrop," I say, getting back to the point, "do you believe they were what Drusilla intended?"

She shrugs. "Oh, Noel. What do you imagine?"

"This isn't some parlour game," Sir Roderick rumbles, his armour creaking like old guilt.

She tilts her head, challenge glinting in her eyes. "Everything's a game in Murder's Vale. Are we not already playing the Final Accord?"

The words catch my interest like a hook in tender flesh. "What do you mean?"

Her smile spreads like poison in a wine glass. "Drusilla and I had a... memorable encounter with our dear Mayor."

"Encounter?"

A flash of irritation crosses her features, quick as a blade in darkness. "He attempted to play blackmailer. But *Little Mimsi* helped him see the error of his ways."

"We know all about *Little Mimsi*," Sir Roderick barks.

"Such a precious creature, but Drusilla took her from me."

"What did you do?" I ask, pieces beginning to align.

She leans closer.

"A delicate reminder of life's fragility, delivered through what they both treasured most—his treatments, her reputation."

"Why not confront them directly?" I ask.

"When a whisper can topple kingdoms, why resort to shouts?" Her voice carries a velvet menace. "I felt a personal touch would... resonate."

"Your idea of a personal touch is to kill him?" Sir Roderick asks.

Moondrop's laugh carries all the warmth of a midwinter grave. "If I'd wanted him dead, dear knight, you'd never have known it was murder. Crude poisoning? Who murders with such... obvious theatrics?"

Sir Roderick crosses his arms. "Lies!"

Amusement dances in her eyes like will-o'-the-wisps. "Check the treatment pots."

"Pots?" I taste the word like a suspicious vintage.

She nods, her voice soft, sinful. "Little marks, symbols. A warning. Just enough for him to suspect something wasn't right, but never enough to accuse. I left him with a question, not an answer." She leans closer. "But it seems someone else saw an opportunity, didn't they?"

"The pots are gone," I say, looking over at Sir Roderick's face.

The knight stiffens, his armour creaking as he adjusted his stance. "I acted in the interest of safety. It was my conjecture that the remedies had been tampered with—and were lethal."

"Lethal?" Moondrop's mockery drips like slow poison. "Why keep silent until now? Where's the fun in that? There were breadcrumbs for clever birds to follow."

"And you believed the Mayor would decode your clues?"

"Of course," she replies confidently, "he loved cryptic things."

Sir Roderick scoffs. "And yet he's dead. If it wasn't poison, then at the very least, you're complicit. Your little game gave an opportunist the chance to act."

"Oh good. I wondered when we might talk about the opportunist. Someone with much to gain from the Mayor's absence. Someone who was being blackmailed about their nobility. Someone who *plants* evidence?"

She points to the mint.

Sir Roderick's face blushes. "That mint was already there, poisoner. I was just confirming it was mint."

"I pray you wake up tomorrow, knight-pretender. I have a special treat in mind for you," she says, soft as death's whisper.

"Let's keep this civil. Moondrop, did anyone else know about your plan?" I say.

She shakes her head. "Only Milton. He let me into the Mayor's study or maybe I drugged him." Her smile is a razor's edge. "Who can remember such details?"

"Why?" I ask, rolling her words around like bitter wine.

She leans forward, something in her posture sets my nerves humming. "Isn't it obvious? That precious Final Accord—the Mayor sealed his fate. He couldn't see it."

Sir Roderick scoffs, his armour creaking. "We all know it's not perfect, but it ensures an orderly process."

"Not perfect!" Her eyes flash like steel in moonlight. "Control. Manipulation. Oppression."

"What's the problem?" I ask.

"It's all a game. A complex process to reward power to those who can deceive and manipulate," she says.

"And you're not playing?" Sir Roderick asks, his sneer deepening like a wound. "Manipulating treatments, planting seeds of chaos?"

"See what he's doing? He's playing you. The very foundation of this game is manipulating suspicion," she says.

"Enough. We need this murder solved," I say. "Your degenerate impishness isn't indicative of lethal intent. But I have concerns about why Milton would have taken part."

Her voice hardens like frost. "Perhaps he wanted freedom. Or power."

I step forward. "I'll consider what you've said." My eyes drift to shelves laden with mysteries in glass. "Any more surprises?"

"No more surprises, unless you brought them in yourself."

Sir Roderick adjusts his gauntlet. "Your trickery won't help you, herbalist."

I place a restraining hand on his arm, steering him toward the door.

He stops abruptly. "Don't let her twist you." His voice is low, hard.

"She's cunning for sure, but I don't see her as our killer."

"Perhaps that childhood crush is affecting your judgement," he says.

"Don't let her get to you. Let's speak to Milton."

He nods reluctantly, his hand resting on the hilt of his sword. Grey whispers of rain swirl around us, turning Murder's Vale into a watercolour of malevolence. My thoughts churn with possibilities.

As we start to walk away, Moondrop calls after us. "Oh, Sir Roderick?"

He pauses; shoulders hunched like a cornered animal.

"Imagine how the village will react when they learn of your... indiscretions."

He turns, his face pale. "You wouldn't dare."

"And thanks for the extra mint," she says.

Sir Roderick walks behind me in brooding silence. My mind races: Was Milton disillusioned with the Mayor or just naïve?

Chapter 30

Afternoon, Fourth Day of Widders

Sir Roderick drops further behind and heads off to the Well. I return to MacAllister Hall to collect the informal ledger and then trek to Milton's house for some questions on the ledger. The sky churns with storm-grey clouds and hints of something darker seeping at the edges—but for now, the drizzle remains a miserly, muttering thing.

Milton's residence emerges from the gloom—a stoic sentinel of stone and shadow, where climbing roses chart their conquest of the walls in thorny black arterials. It sits at the northernmost edge of the village, where the lane from the Market stretches toward farmland, the Cemetery, and Highgrove Hall before finally meeting the main road out of the Vale. The front door is an arched wooden design crowned with stone carvings that speak in symbols: eagle, bear-in-tree, anvil-with-flame.

Milton opens the door before my knuckles can make their introduction. He stands framed in the doorway like a portrait of respectability—spectacles perched just so, sleeves rolled to suggest interrupted industry.

Either he's seen me coming, or he has the instincts of a guilty man.

"Noel, this is a surprise."

"Good afternoon, Milton. Might I have a word?"

"Of course." He steps aside with the fluid grace of a trained dancer. "Please come in."

Inside walls are lined with shelves that host an eclectic congregation of books, mechanical curiosities, and stones that watch me with mineral patience. A large wooden table dominates the room's centre, its surface covered in scrolls, quills, and an open ledger. Light filters through the mullioned windows, casting blurred geometric patterns on the polished wooden floor.

"Your home is impressive," I say, letting my eyes wander like a suspicious spouse. "You have a fondness for curiosities, I see."

He adjusts his spectacles. "They keep the mind sharp. Please, take a seat."

As I settle into a high-backed chair, the soft patter of approaching footsteps draws my attention. A young girl—eight years, if she's a day—peers around the corner with eyes that haven't yet learned to hide their curiosity. Her blonde curly hair marks her as Milton's daughter, her blue dress a splash of sky in this den of shadows.

"Ah, Lily," Milton's voice softens like butter left in summer sun, "come say hello to Noel. He's a detective."

She approaches with the deliberation of a cat testing thin ice. "Good afternoon, detective."

"Good afternoon," I say, summoning a smile that feels like borrowed clothing.

"Where's your mother?" he says, his paternal concern a thin veil over something less definable.

"She's in the other room," the child says.

"Run along and find her. Tell her we have a guest."

Lily nods and disappears down the hallway.

"A delightful child."

"Thank you," he says, a hint of pride in his voice.

"Milton, I've come to discuss some matters regarding the Mayor."

He nods with the careful consideration of a man defusing explosives. "Of course." A pause pregnant with possibilities. "Before we begin, Noel... I owe you an apology."

"An apology?"

"For my... manner when we last spoke at Highgrove Hall," his tone earnest. "These past days have been... difficult. The Mayor's passing has left more chaos than I expected, and I find myself... caught in the middle of things I can't control."

His confidence floats like a poorly tied raft on a river of doubt—destined to sink the moment the current picks up. I weigh my choices: cut him loose or throw him a lifeline?

"Understandable. Grief and uncertainty have a way of testing us all."

"It's not just grief," he says, adjusting his spectacles like a man searching for clarity in clouded glass. "It's the fear of what comes next. I've been defensive—perhaps unreasonably so. I hope you'll forgive me if I've given the impression of obstruction."

If this isn't genuine sincerity, then he's a much better actor than I expected.

"I've been doing this long enough to know the difference between obstruction and self-preservation," I say, watching him unlock like a complex mechanism. "I appreciate the sentiment."

Milton nods, agitation bleeding from his shoulders like a punctured waterskin. "Thank you."

Outside, rain traces idle patterns down the mullioned glass, slow and deliberate. Beyond the window, the garden blooms—vibrant in its quiet defiance of the Vale's gloom.

"Good." I settle deeper into my chair. "Well, I need to speak with you on the informal ledger—there are a few inconsistencies I need your help with."

His composure tightens once more, spectacles receiving another nervous adjustment. "Inconsistencies?" He leans forward, fingers interlaced on the table like a spider considering its web. "What did you find?"

"Certain transactions that don't add up—payments made to unnamed parties."

Milton examines the entries with the attention of a man walking through a field of hidden traps. "The Mayor handled sensitive matters personally," he says.

"Understandable," I say. "But it complicates my task of untangling his affairs."

"Perhaps I can shed some light," he says.

The next hour dissolves in a parade of numbers and explanations, each entry illuminated by Milton's meticulous commentary.

"No irregularities, no missing funds?" I say aloud, tasting the irony. "The inconsistencies in the summaries were... intentional obfuscations by the Mayor?"

He hesitates. "The Mayor demanded simple treasury accounts. He felt they were overcomplicated for the benefit of accountants."

We pore over the ledger, and it feels like the right time to broach another topic, one that has been lingering in the back of my mind. Milton is cooperative, but there is a carefulness to his answers that leaves little room for unguarded moments.

"I understand the Mayor had a longstanding arrangement with Drusilla for his treatments. Is that correct?"

"Yes, that's true. She'd prepare remedies for him. He preferred discretion in such matters, given his position."

"Discretion?"

"He said it wasn't good for a leader to appear... vulnerable," Milton says, each word selected like ingredients for a poison. "He never visited her shop. She delivered the treatments directly to him, often after hours."

"Understandable." I nod, setting my trap with care. "But I've also heard that Moondrop, her sister, was given access to the Mayor's study."

Milton adjusts his spectacles. "That's not unusual. When Drusilla wasn't in the village, Moondrop had occasionally delivered treatments."

"Did you arrange that?"

"Not specifically," he says. "When she showed up, I assumed it was part of the arrangement. Perhaps the Mayor's remedies needed adjusting and Drusilla was unavailable."

"You didn't think to question it?"

"The treatments weren't my concern. And frankly, the Mayor didn't confide in me about his personal matters."

His composed exterior reminds me of ice in early spring—smooth on top, treacherous underneath, ready to crack at the slightest pressure.

"Well, you've been very helpful. Thank you. May I ask a more personal question?"

"What do you mean?"

"With the Mayor gone, how do you see your role in the village changing? Do you see someone stepping into his shoes?"

He takes a moment. "My primary concern is maintaining stability. Leadership is… delicate," he says, "it requires balance. The village needs structure, continuity." His fingers brush the open ledger, tapping lightly against the pages. "Change must be managed carefully."

"Who, do you suppose, would want to step into that role?"

Again, a pause. "Well, if you can overlook his demeanour, Sir Roderick might be a candidate. He is respected in the village by some. He's been demanding a role in village affairs."

"Such as?"

"He feels the village needs a judge, separate from the Mayor and the bailiff."

"Any others vying for influence?"

The question hangs in the air, but before it can draw blood, his wife, Margaret, appears in the doorway. She moves with measured grace, like someone who's mastered the art of moving through a world that rarely listens but always watches. Her presence is understated, but not forgettable—the kind of woman who commands a room without ever raising her voice.

Dark hair streaked with silver is swept into a loose knot at her nape, and the faint scent of lavender trails her like an afterthought. Her expression is composed, but not cold—eyes the colour of warm tea and full of patience.

She offers me a smile that might once have been warm, and may still be, if you're the sort who earns it. There's more wisdom in that one look than I've found in half the archives of the Vale—the kind of wisdom that doesn't need solving, only surviving.

"Good afternoon," she says, her voice soft as moth wings. "We're going to have supper soon; would you like to join us?"

"I wouldn't want to impose," I say, but Milton rises like a man granted an unexpected reprieve.

"Not at all, we'd be delighted to have you."

Soon we're sitting around a rustic dining table adorned with simple yet hearty fare—roasted vegetables and a savoury stew filling the room with a comforting aroma. I pull out a dense loaf of rye bread from my satchel, its crust hard enough to hammer nails. "Bit of a workout for the jaw," I say, holding it up like a weapon, its surface hard as stone and dotted with tiny, dark holes.

Milton leans forward, frowning. "That bread's alive," he says, nodding at the wriggling weevils emerging from its crust. A few weevils tumble onto the table, scurrying for freedom. I pinch one between my fingers, popping it into my mouth with a crunch that makes Margaret shudder. The first bite is a battle. I gnaw at the crust like a dog with a bone, my teeth scraping against the bread. A chunk finally comes loose, and I chew with exaggerated effort, spitting out a pebble-like bit of grit onto the table.

Lily watches in horror as I smack the bread against the edge of the table to break off another piece. The conversation meanders through safe territories—harvest predictions, Lily's studies, the upcoming weapons fair. Milton tends to his family with the attentiveness of a gardener protecting rare blooms from frost. We finish the meal. Margaret and Lily clear away while Milton and I sit to discuss unfinished business. Lily plays with the weevils until Margaret returns from the kitchen to clean the table and sweeps them away.

"Thank you for sharing your meal," I say. "It's been longer than I care to remember since I've enjoyed such... normalcy."

"You're most welcome," he says, the words carrying unspoken understanding. "Family time is important."

As he escorts me to the door, Margaret and Lily appear for a final farewell, like spirits of domestic tranquillity haunting the edges of our darker discourse.

"Safe travels," Margaret says, her kindness feeling both genuine and prophetic.

"Thank you for your hospitality." The words inadequate currency for the evening's revelations.

Outside, I pause; my eyes drawn once more to the carvings. "Patterns and sequences," I murmur to the indifferent stone. Every symbol a story, every story a secret, every secret a potential noose.

It's late.

The rain has stopped, but the air clings like wet linen. The village is quiet, shuttered against the dark, save for the occasional window that flickers like a held breath. I walk back toward MacAllister Hall alone for a change, the path slick beneath my boots and thoughts heavier than my coat.

Milton had been composed. Too composed, for my money. Hospitable, helpful, sincere—and every bit of it landed too neatly. The carvings linger in my mind—symbols without a key.

At the Hall, I let myself in, bolt the door behind me, and place the ledger on the table with the reverence one gives cursed objects. I pour a drink. Tonight, I sleep. Or try to. The dreams have been getting organised lately.

Chapter 31

Morning, Fifth Day of Widders

Another morning, another storm. Today it's rattling the windows as if demanding resolution. Every so often, a flash of lightning outlines the bruised clouds outside, illuminating the evidence for a heartbeat before plunging the room back into a half-lit hush.

Rain's steady percussion accompanies my solitude. I sit hunched at the table, my fingers absently tracing the rough grain of the wood working on my next move.

Time grows short. If I don't provide a murderer soon, they'll settle for a convenient scapegoat. Myself, most likely. The bailiff gave me 48 hours. Tomorrow, all must be revealed. Not necessarily the truth, but a version that ties up neatly with a bow and doesn't get me executed. I need a story. Ideally the truth. One they'll believe. One that sticks. One that ends with someone else in the noose.

I've brought all the evidence back from the Library. It sits before me, like actors awaiting their cues: the ornate dagger, still carrying echoes of its violent performance; the poison evidence box; the informal ledger, the codex and the cryptic parchments revealing the Final Accord. Each piece murmurs possibilities, but none yet screams truth.

The Hall's oppressive silence is punctuated only by rain's steady dirge.

"What should I focus on? What do I need?"

My words scatter like startled birds in the cavernous space. The Hall keeps its counsel. It offers only two reliable commodities: solitude and a serviceable garderobe. Fine. If nothing else, I can sit, think, and avoid the creeping sense that the walls are listening.

The garderobe awaits—a relic of necessity rather than comfort, perched precariously over a yawning void that cares nothing for dignity. It offers a galvanising clarity—perched on a wooden seat—wind and rain gusting through the convenient opening. The chill sharpens my thoughts around essential questions. The noise of speculation falls away and clarity, like a plodding, old friend, begins to flow.

"What does the village want?"

They want a killer, a name to feed their whispered theories. They want certainty, finality, and most of all, they want a story. No half-measures, no loose ends—just a story.

"How do I deliver that?"

Give them what they crave: a tale to tell each other. A plausible account of what happened that night, who did it, and why. But this tale transcends the Mayor's demise. It's about Murder's Vale itself—the rules we must follow. Even the most treacherous among us, no matter how dark their deeds, thirst for order's unyielding creed. The Mayor was playing as the village demanded—warping rules to defeat its foes.

Tomorrow must bring resolution. The Final Accord, our cast of suspects, the physical evidence—every deception and half-truth must face judgement's harsh light. The wind keens its agreement. Cold seeps into bone. Clarity, that fickle companion, takes its leave. I return to my evidence in the study, seeking patterns in chaos.

***

Back in the study, I decide to reimagine the village as a stage, each suspect a player in our grim production. I summon forth the players, using found objects as metaphorical stand-ins for our dramatis personae.

First comes the Ember, nursing its grudges like dying coals. It smoulders with contained resentment, neither extinguishing nor erupting, guard dog to a kennel of secrets. The Ember rests easy, surrounded by its log of whispered debts, sleights and unclaimed leverage. It—and the-soon-to-be-introduced Brass Key insist someone fled the Mayor's study without first entering, a claim that reeks of either deception or damning truth. If they speak honestly, our killer was already waiting within. I dismiss the Ember and beckon forward an unlikely duo: the Teaspoon and the Matchstick.

The Teaspoon's defiance feels measured, as if it refuses to be underestimated. The Matchstick, by contrast, flickers with deceptive insignificance—small, unassuming, but ready to ignite with the right strike. Both claim the means and opportunity for a quiet poisoning, making their theatrical flourishes suspect. The Teaspoon would approach murder with clinical detachment, while the Matchstick might savour its artistry. Why complicate a simple poisoning with a blade's dramatic statement?

Enter the Brass Key, hefty with portent. Direct and unyielding, it exists to grant or deny access—nothing more, nothing less. Poison beneath its dignity, too subtle for its nature. If it struck, the dagger alone would suffice—clean, decisive, honourable in its way. Yet the Brass Key guards its own mysteries. The Final Accord binds it to the Mayor through chains of blackmail and desperation. Its struggle for survival threatens that maintained dignity, making it unpredictable. Dangerous.

Lurking at the margins are the Bent Nail and Loose Button, society's overlooked observers. The nail bears its damage like a badge, surprisingly sharp when circumstances demand. The button's significance is its unremarkable nature—noticed only in absence. They skulk at the edges of the village. Not bright, but bright enough to kill for gain.

Last, the Pocket Mirror emerges, its cracked surface offering fractured glimpses of truth. Its relationship with the Mayor had grown strained, loyalty tested beyond endurance. The Pocket Mirror witnessed something that fatal night—fragments. If only death hadn't claimed it before memory could speak—or perhaps death claimed it because memory threatened to speak too clearly.

My eyes are drawn to those rain-lashed windows, blurring the world beyond into a shifting haze—trees bending under the wind's demands, the distant grounds fading into mist. The storm rages, but its fury offers no clarity, only distortion.

I rise from my chair, moving around the table as though the change in perspective might reveal something. Yet no single theory emerges unscathed. No thread runs clean from beginning to end. It's maddeningly incomplete.

It's time to abandon the characters and see if weapons offer more insight. Poison and dagger might speak truths independent of their master. The parchments, ledger and codex whisper complexities too intricate for tomorrow's audience. Their role is to guide my deductions, not drown the villagers in detail. The story is complex, the deductive process even more so. How will the villagers maintain attention to the facts? I need to present them something sharper, cleaner, more digestible.

**

What's gonna be our first weapon? Let's say poison—methodical, precise, calculated. Was it meant to kill or incapacitate? Perhaps it carried a message encoded in suffering? The Teaspoon or Matchstick could have crafted it; they've said as much. Yet they would have disguised its use rather than risk such an overt signature. Unless they wanted credit for the composition. But there are other possibilities. A poison prank turned fatal, or a punishment meant as a lesson. If so, the dagger must have arrived later—that would change everything.

Light dances across the serpent-and-rose motif on the ornate blade as I pick it up. This isn't only a beautiful weapon; it's a heralding. A proclamation. A battle cry.

The poison alone would have sufficed to imbue terror—a silent, creeping death. Why use both? Did our killer doubt the poison's efficacy? Was the blade assurance against failure—a practical footnote to ensure finality? Or did the poison serve to silence the Mayor, stealing his voice before the blade stole his breath?

No. The ornate dagger's bold statement drowns the poison's subtle song. The toxin speaks not of stealth but of necessity—or perhaps cold pragmatism. Whoever wielded the blade craved understanding. It's the punctuation at the end of the sentence—but whose? I place the ornate dagger back in its box, the question still unanswered.

What if simplicity blinds me to deeper complexity? A darker possibility emerges, casting deeper shadows on my theories. What if poison and blade served different masters? One seeking to punish, the other to despatch. If true, we're reading two stories woven into a single bloody tapestry.

The notion of dual killers gnaws at my certainties, simultaneously chaotic and elegant. One poisons, one strikes—but such choreography demands coordination, shared purpose. Could such an alliance exist in this fractured Vale?

Or perhaps coordination played no part. One acts to incapacitate—whether in jest or judgement—while another seizes opportunity's throat. Two killers bound by nothing but circumstance and timing.

A lone perpetrator is the simpler, and thus most likely narrative. Such solitary execution would demand precise timing and preternatural stealth. If the Ember was in the house, poring over ledgers as claimed, how did our killer move unseen? How did they avoid detection? They'd need to confirm the poison's effect on the Mayor, then strike without hesitation. The risk of discovery loomed large—the risk of the Ember checking on the Mayor before the blade found home. The precision needed of the blade to find the heart quick and clean feels too perfect. Too. .. rehearsed.

I step back, arms folded, glaring at the evidence. Everything needed lies before me, yet the pattern eludes my grasp. I glance at the evidence table. Perhaps the problem isn't what's before me, but how I'm viewing it. Questions outpace answers as I reconstruct the scene mentally. What interval separated poison's grip from blade's kiss? If the Ember and Brass Key lurked nearby as they claim, why hear nothing? And if honest about hearing departure but no arrival, was our killer already present and hidden?

The remaining daylight must yield these answers.

Pieces refuse to align, remaking themselves with each new question. Time to revisit the scene. Answers hide in that room, in details overlooked during first inspection.

A soft knock interrupts my brooding, echoing through the Hall's vastness. Mrs Sibberidge stands wrapped against the weather like a crow in mourning, her face its usual mask of careful neutrality.

"Good afternoon, Mrs Sibberidge," I say, stepping aside.

"Noel," she says, brushing the wet from her cloak with the grim precision of someone correcting a pupil's untidy margins. "Should I formally declare the Library basement a midden heap, or is the decay merely accidental?"

I straighten slightly, like a schoolboy caught with ink on his cuffs. "I was researching. The mess is... contextual."

"So are plague pits," she replies. "There's a smell, Noel. A waft of fermented beetroot and academic despair. If the intention was to summon something, I suspect it's already awake and mildly offended."

"I'll tidy it," I mutter.

"Do."

She pauses, letting the silence scold me further. Then, with a sniff of disapproval, she turns to leave.

"Wait," I say.

She halts; one brow arched with pedagogical precision.

I glance at the evidence table—ink-streaked notes, crumpled diagrams, the stubborn puzzle that refuses to fit. My gaze drifts to the window.

"We need to visit the Manor House," I declare. "There are details overlooked—threads that might bind this chaos into order."

She studies me, as if deciding whether this is inspiration or indigestion. Then she nods, unsurprised. "Tomorrow?"

"Dawn. I'll meet you there," I say.

Curiosity flickers across her features. She inclines her head. "As you wish." She lingers, studying the evidence from a safe distance.

The Ember and Brass Key's testimony mocks me. Someone departed without arriving—possible? And if so, how did our killer move unseen through the village's watchful shadows? My fingers trace the table's grain as thoughts circle their prey: how was it done? This murder could have been elegant, silent, untraceable. Poison alone would have sufficed. But the message... The message targeted select ears. This wasn't mere murder. It was theatre. Poison and dagger aren't tools but symbols. Our killer craved understanding from a specific audience.

Wind hurls itself against the windows, demanding answers I can't provide.

But soon, I will.

Chapter 32

Morning, Sixth Day of Widders

Morning arrives with thunder's final exhalation—a storm exhausted but not yet spent. The storm's voice has faded, but its message remains: the reckoning is near.

In the hours before dawn, a thought wormed its way through my skull: The truth might not live in the obvious notes—the testimonies, the evidence, the confessions—but in the rests between them, like a melody shaped as much by silence as by sound.

As planned, Mrs Sibberidge waits for me by the Mayor's front door, the wind plucking at her cloak like a pickpocket testing a mark. I'd requested her presence before the village stirred, and she arrives with the punctuality of Death itself.

Inside, the Manor greets us with a chill that goes beyond mere temperature. My lantern's anaemic light drags itself through the corridors, barely keeping pace. As we enter the Mayor's study, the light illuminates spaces that shrink from its touch. The shadows here have substance, draping themselves across furniture.

"This is where he met his end," I say. Mrs Sibberidge remains silent. She doesn't need words to acknowledge death's lingering perfume.

The Mayor's chair sits stiffly behind his desk, positioned to survey his domain through rain-streaked glass. I lower myself into it. The wood sounds its protest. From this vantage point, the study presents itself as he would have seen it—scrolls scattered like abandoned alibis; the window framing nature's tantrum, and the door closed but in view.

My eyes trace the room's geometry, hunting for secrets. No convenient curtains for lurking assassins, no shadowy nooks large enough to birth conspiracy. My fingers explore the desk's edge, as if oak and varnish might confess what they witnessed.

"Take your position in the doorway," I say.

Mrs Sibberidge moves like a chess piece, her outline stark against the corridor's dim breath.

"Now exit."

The door groans as she withdraws, her footsteps performing a diminuendo down the hall. I catalogue each sound's death, measuring volume against distance, before summoning her return. She returns to the doorway once more.

"Again," I say, abandoning the chair to inspect the window. The latch tells its own story—locked, undisturbed, no hint of forced entry. She repeats her performance—exit, enter—until I've memorised every acoustic detail the Mayor might have registered from this seat.

Milton's treasury quarters beckons next, demanding its own acoustic investigation.

"Let's test the sound's journey. Remain in the study until I call."

I navigate the hallway toward Milton's domain—a closet masquerading as treasury quarters, buried in the building's entrails. Ledgers multiply like guilty secrets on every surface, and dried ink scents the air with bureaucratic persistence.

"Proceed!" I call back. "Exit again!"

Her voice drifts like smoke. "Is my departure audible?"

I close my eyes, letting the noises wash over me—wood's protest, footsteps' percussion, silence's punctuation. The sounds are muffled, distant. The account of Sir Roderick hearing the Mayor's footsteps leave the study are not definitive.

Perhaps the storm rewrote his memories, or maybe his recollections bend toward convenient fiction.

Investigation complete, I retrace my steps. The study's door gapes open, the desk brooding in its eternal vigil. I drop to a crouch, letting new angles reshape my understanding of the crime scene. A question lingers like a splinter in my thoughts: How?

Even if sleep had claimed the Mayor at his desk, how did death make its delivery? Poison demands intimacy—a doctored drink, a tainted glass. Yet this desk tells no tales of struggle or surprise.

Did the killer charm their way past the Mayor's defences, slip poison into his wine while he was distracted, and then stab him—or was unconsciousness already his companion when steel found his heart?

My fingers find the desk's worn edges as I return to the chair. Impossibilities stack like evidence in a crooked trial. A ghostly entrance, poison's kiss, a blade's finale. Each act requires choreography worthy of the finest assassin.

And then—

A thought hits with the force of a hangman's drop. My eyes sweep the room as possibilities realign themselves into horrific certainty. This truth exceeds my darkest expectations, wearing a face I never thought to suspect.

Mrs Sibberidge studies me. "Have you found your answer?"

"I have..." I nod slowly.

Chapter 33

Evening, Sixth Day of Widders

The Tavern door surrenders its dignity under an assault disguised as a kick. Oak and iron protests with a shriek. My coat billows dramatically, riding a gust of wind that stinks of unwashed bodies and ale.

Before me, the room appears as a stage where every night is amateur villain night. The regulars, each costumed in their particular breed of dishevelment, wear their mismatched finery like armour against respectability. Their mood is as dark and sharp as a whetted blade, rolling through the Tavern in a steady rumble.

Rain streaks my coat in silver ribbons, forming a puddle at my feet that might as well be marking my territory. The scent of storm-soaked leather and wool announces my presence as clearly as a herald's trumpet.

The room's response is subtle. Heads turn with the deliberate slowness of predators assessing their prey. These aren't the type to startle unless death strolls in, and even then, they'd pour it a drink first.

"Well, look what the storm's pissed out," Perrin drawls. His moustache—a thing that appears to have been cultivated from pure spite—twitches as he speaks, as if trying to escape his face. "Thought you'd died of cleverness?"

"And I thought you'd drowned in your wit, Perrin," I say, shaking my coat with the precise timing of someone who's practised making an entrance. "Imagine my surprise to find you alive and well—and still deeply unimaginative."

From a shadowed corner, where three figures hunch over their drinks like suicidal gargoyles, comes laughter sharp enough to cut glass. It's the kind of laugh that suggests its owner might follow it up with a knife. In The Corpse's Candle, laughter is rarer than honest politicians, and I need all the help I can get.

The Innkeeper grunts from behind the counter. "Kick my door again, and I'll rip your head off and shove it up your arse."

"Mead, please," I say, flicking a coin onto the counter. I move toward the firelit heart of the room without bothering to look around. Stares follow me like arrows nocked—I can feel them dissecting me like a puzzle they half recognise, but aren't sure they want to solve.

"Any idea what happened to that runner from the Mayor's funeral?" I ask the audience.

"Gone's gone," someone mutters.

"Aye," another chimes in, nodding sagely. "Lost's lost."

A brief pause.

"It is what it is," someone offers, with the air of a philosopher concluding a great debate.

"Like an untasted pie," says another.

"Exactly," agrees the Perrin, who has never trusted pies.

Someone coughs.

From within the audience, a figure lurches upright—all elbows, ale, and barely contained outrage. Their expression curdles into the kind of fury only found in the deeply invested and chronically unsatisfied. "Dammit—not one of you bastards has explained how the Mayor actually died!"

The words cut through the room like a thrown dagger. The speaker's arms flail wide, knocking into the unfortunate soul beside them, who responds with a half-hearted shove but is too drunk to escalate.

"We've had theories! We've had speculation!" Their voice drips with scorn. Their fist slams onto the nearest table, rattling tankards and sending a single, betrayed-looking sausage skittering off someone's plate. A low murmur rolls through the Tavern—a mix of amusement, agreement, and the quiet calculation of who might stab whom first if things turn sour.

"Are we finally getting the truth, or are we pissing away the night on dramatics and vague insinuations?" The accusation hangs there, thick as the smoke curling toward the rafters, joining the secrets already suspended in the air—waiting for someone to pluck it down and answer.

I pause by the fireplace, stretching the silence a breath too long. "Oh, I promise you will learn of that at much more," my voice smooth and incise, "this tale will curl the hair on your toes—or at the very least, the hair in your ale."

My expression hardens as I move to the centre of the room. "Many of you had your sights on me the moment I returned to Murder's Vale. And such convenient timing, it was. But let's not flatter ourselves—tonight isn't about me. It's about all of you. The rules you pretend to play by, the lies you dress up in truth's borrowed finery. And what happens when those lies decide to bare their teeth?"

"We're not here for a bloody performance," Perrin calls, his moustache twitching again.

"Ah, that's where you're wrong, sir!" I announce, jabbing an accusatory finger in his direction. "The Mayor's death was more than murder—it was very much a bloody performance, my impatient little friend!"

I sweep my arms wide in a grand arc, commanding the floor with the ease of a seasoned charlatan. "Ladies and gentlemen, gather 'round for the rarest of spectacles! Embracing the classics with refreshing zeal, this violent opus is penned in tradition's crimson ink. Yes, the Mayor's final appointment included not only poison but a dagger. I present to you a masterpiece of murderous theatre!"

I give a slight bow.

"But enough prologue—this story is complex. We need to peel back the layers to find our murder and I will deliver to you that person this very tonight. But you must listen carefully. Truth, as we've learned repeatedly in Murder's Vale, rarely travels in straight lines."

The fire crackles. A flicker of interest sparks across a few faces, though most remain guarded. They don't want to admit it, but they're listening. Every so often, a wind gust rakes through. Damp presses its way through gaps in the door and seams in the walls, an uninvited guest kept at bay by the fire's roaring defiance.

***

And so, I begin.

"This tale we're unravelling," I say, stepping forward, "is woven so tightly with lies and half-truths that pulling one thread could bring the whole thing crashing down."

My eyes roam over the audience as I pause.

"And yet, here we stand."

The silence ferments, growing heavier with each passing heartbeat. I know this lot. I know their appetites. They want only the climax, the revelation without the journey. My raised hand calms the crest of impatience moving like a contagion. "Your patience will be rewarded," I say, my voice calm but edged with steel. "Let us first examine the evidence that speaks from beyond the grave. The instruments of murder. Remember them well, for in their interactions lies tonight's truth."

A hard crust of bread sails through the air, striking my shoulder with an unimpressive *thud*.

I brush the crumbs and weevils away with exaggerated care.

"—should I postpone this until tomorrow?"

Someone punches the bread-tosser.

The audience leans forward as I place the evidence items from my satchel on the table, their curiosity overwhelming their cynicism. From my satchel, I produce items that will serve as our guideposts.

I elevate the first item from my collection like a priest displaying a sacred relic. The beech evidence box creaks open, revealing its grim contents—the minty poison—a substance that had once flowed creamy white from the Mayor's last gasps, now reduced to an accusatory powder.

I lift the poison evidence box and hold it aloft. "Exhibit one," I announce. "The poison that granted our esteemed Mayor his taste of mint. Poison—now there's an art form. Its patience distilled; malice refined into alchemy. A whisper of intent that speaks louder than any blade." I let my gaze drift across the assembled faces. "The question isn't just whose hand delivered it, but whose mind conceived its purpose."

With deliberate care, I place the evidence box on the table. Then, slowly, I lift the ornate dagger, letting the candlelight catch on its cruel edge—a weapon, a statement, a question waiting to be answered. "Exhibit two. This rather decisive argument was found expressing its opinion in the Mayor's back. A weapon of conviction, you might say—bold, unflinching, and final." I turn it slowly, letting the blade's elaborate workmanship draw every eye. "Such a distinctive piece must surely be missed from someone's collection. Perhaps its owner would care to stake a claim?" With exaggerated care, I set the blade on the table and then lift the heavy ledger—a tome burdened with more than its considerable weight.

"Exhibit three: the informal ledger—the Mayor's personal accounting of debts both financial and moral. Consider it a weapon of corruption drawn in ink and sealed with secrets." The leather binding creaks as I open it, displaying columns of intricately coded corruption. "Within these pages lies a spider's web of influence, each strand sticky with leverage and compromise."

The audience shifts uncomfortably, like sinners hearing their private transgressions read aloud.

"Your name might be hidden in these cryptic entries," I say, allowing a smile as sharp as a razor's edge, "or perhaps you're more concerned about whose name isn't."

"Exhibit four: the testimonies of our illustrious Sir Roderick and the ever-observant Milton regarding that fateful night. According to their accounts, Sir Roderick heard someone depart the Mayor's study while Milton was occupied elsewhere—yet neither soul heard anyone enter. A curious, anomaly, isn't it?"

Firelight paints shadows across the arranged evidence, each piece a testament to the intricate dance that led to murder. "Now," I say, letting my voice carry solemnity, "we have two paths before us—to uncover the truth, and to name the killer. The easy way, or the hard way."

***

I wait, savouring the moment like a connoisseur of dramatic pause. "The easy way skips across the surface of truth like a stone across troubled waters—quick, clean, and ultimately superficial. The hard way?" I smile. "Is where we swim deep into the murky depths of detail, where nothing is what it appears to be." My gaze sharp glances around, daring someone to challenge me. "Shall we wade into the depths, or splash about in the shallows?"

"Splash about in the shallows!" The chorus comes quick, ragged, a wave of impatience crashing over my carefully built tension.

The Innkeeper grunts. "Get on with it. We're tired of the whole thing already."

My painstaking narrative is slipping away like sand through an hourglass, each grain a detail vanishing into the grave of indifference. "Ah, yes, why trouble ourselves with such inconvenience as facts? Perhaps we should reduce this tale of murder and betrayal to a children's bedtime story—starring talking animals, a kindly murder-goose, and a heartfelt lesson about the dangers of ambition?"

The Innkeeper's face brightens. "There's a thought," he announces, proud as a peacock in a hall of mirrors. "*Murder Most Fowl.*"

My soul tries to leave its body, and somewhere, a goat faints. "I despair. You want me to transform my meticulously crafted investigation into a barnyard metaphor? Shall I add a jig and some nursery rhymes while I'm at it?"

The audience's rapturous nodding confirms my worst fears. They don't care about justice or criminality. Just a good tale. I should know better; I grew up here, where facts were merely suggestions, and a good story was worth more than gold. I need a moment to ponder how to deliver this. I withdraw a roasted slice of cow udder wrapped in cloth from my satchel. The udder squelches between my teeth. "Ooh, that's rich," I say, chewing, the sound like wet leather being wrung out.

The Innkeeper shouts at me. "Oi! I told you before—outside food is two silver."

I hand him the coin and finish the udder with loud, exaggerated smacking. Licking my fingers clean with a final, dramatic slurp.

"Very well." I sigh, spreading my arms like a weary priest addressing sinners.

"You'll get your tale—but let's be clear: this journey will take us straight into absurdity. We'll skip the critical details, gloss over evidence, and make a mockery of the entire investigation."

The Innkeeper grins with unsettling eagerness. I clear my throat, summoning a rhythm that stumbles out like a drunk bard butchering an epic tale—awkward, overdramatic, and unhinged enough to keep the audience hooked. "Very well," I sigh, spreading my arms like a weary priest addressing a flock of particularly idiotic sinners. "Ladies and gentlemen, I present to you The Masquerade of Beasts."

The Innkeeper snorts. "I want my idea—*Murder Most Fowl*."

A few heads nod. Someone in the back mutters, "Had a nice ring to it."

I resist the urge to hurl myself into the fire. "It's a murder reconstruction, not a poultry pageant."

"It's memorable," the Innkeeper insists, arms crossed like a toddler denied a sweet. "Rolls right off the tongue."

"This is a tale of ambition, deception, and blood—" I say.

"Exactly. Sounds like something a goose would do." The Innkeeper adds.

"A goose?" I ask.

He leans in. "You ever looked into a goose's soul? Cold. Empty. Full of knives."

A woman near the fire nods solemnly. "My cousin lost a toe."

"I don't care about your cousin's toe," I snap. "This isn't a game, it's—"

"Murder by Gooselight?" someone offers, helpfully.

"Cluck of Death?" says another.

"Pecking Order!"

"FOWL PLAY!" A collective groan rolls through the room.

"Murder Unplucked!"

"The Peckoning!"

"Death Most Eggstraordinary!"

The crowd is now fully unhinged. I catch Perrin in the corner scribbling furiously in a notebook titled Names for Future Murders. I lift a hand, and somehow, order returns. "No," I say, "The Masquerade of Beasts. Here's why. First, because not all the animals are fowl. Second, because nothing—and no one—is what they seem."

"They're all performers in an endless carnival of deception?" Perrin calls out.

"Smart as a stick," I respond.

The room pauses. Someone coughs.

The Innkeeper sighs. "Fine. But next time, I call the title."

Chapter 34

I nod. "Agreed. Now shut up and listen." I step into the centre, letting the hush settle like dust before a storm. My voice drops, slow and deliberate.

"In this beasts' masquerade, creatures prowl through the verses, wearing their disguises to outwit, outmanoeuvre, and outlast each other, their bestial forms concealing the truth of the men and women lurking beneath. These creatures in our tale—they're you, they're me, they're every shadow in these crooked alleys."

I spread my arms wide. "Let us begin. And do try to keep up."

'The Masquerade of Beasts

Where crooked spires pierce poisoned skies,
an Owl keeps watch with golden eyes.
Her feathers wear the shade of graves,
her wisdom ancient deep as caves.
'Gather ye close and listen well—
For I have a tale of folly to tell.

Of scheming creatures who dared defy,

the tyrant king with dreams so high.
Each had a plan, each had a flaw,
each met their fate, bitt—er and raw.

But from their failure, a truth we'll glean—
a thread connects what lies between.'"

I savour the weighted silence.
"Shall I continue?" I say with a smirk.
It breaks—predictably—with the crash of a tankard against the wall behind my head. I don't flinch. In Murder's Vale, this is practically applause.
Shouts of, 'Get on with it!' and 'We haven't got all night!' ring through the dim room, underscored by a few muttered curses about storytellers who love the sound of their own voice.
"Patience," I say, brushing an imaginary speck from my sleeve. "For those whose wits have been dulled by drink or destiny—the king in our little morality play is our beloved Mayor.
A collective groan ripples throughout the room, though I catch the sharp glint of understanding in more than a few eyes.
"Now then. The Pig..." The noise settles and I start:

"The Owl looked at her audience, her feathers sleek and her voice steady.

Pig Dreams of Downfall

'First came Pig with dreams so grand,
to sneak past shadows and strike the king's hand.
But ale its downfall—dreams turned to naught,
for cunning and bravery cannot be bought.'

Owl paused, her gaze sharp and keen.
'And so Pig's folly was clear to be seen.
Yet others watched and others planned,
each sure their plot would better stand.'

*Owl ruffled her wings, her voice a soft croon,
as she painted the tales beneath the pale moon.
'Now hear of Snake, so skilled, so sly—
its poison a marvel, a deadly supply.'*

I take a sip from my tankard, letting anticipation build like a gallows rope drawing tight. The fire has burned lower now, casting longer shadows that dance to the rhythm of my words.
"Listen close, for here's where Snake slithers into our tale. And oh, what venomous dreams it brought...

Snake's Folly

*Through moonless nights and shadowed days,
Snake watched and learned of palace ways.
"To kill or to cure?" it mused with care,
its venom so perfect, no trace would that bear.
It brewed and it planned, its skill was unmatched—
But how would its poison to the king be dispatched?*

*"A treatment?" it thought, "Too obvious a way—
Suspicion would rise, my plot would betray."
Wine cups watched and food well-tested,
left Snake's ambitions fully bested.*

*And so, Snake, though clever and skilled,
left her poison unused, her ambitions unfilled.
Snake had it all, with venom unbound—
A poison so perfect, no equal was found.*

*But what is a brew with no means to deliver?
A plot unfulfilled, that's lost in a quiver.'*

*Owl shook her head, her golden eyes wide,
'A venom so flawless, a plan cast aside.
But its poison, unseen, was not to be wasted—
For soon sly Fox its power had tasted.*

Fox Outfoxed

And so Snake withdrew in utter despair,
but Fox was undaunted and took up the affair.
"Where Snake has faltered, I'll find my way—
For my cunning will shine at the break of day."

Fox, sleek and sly, with cunning untold,
knew the venomous brew could be deadly and bold.
On a moonless night, with a silenty lurk,
it slipped to the king's study, where he slept at his work.
Fox laced the king's wine, Fox laced the king's stew—
The poison so perfect, he'd not have a clue.

The bells rang out; The death declared clean—
no signs of murder, no treachery seen.
The king was dead. The deed was done, but revolution?
—There was none."

Fox, in its wisdom, had played it too sly,
its message of defiance unseen to the eye.'

Owl paused, tone full of regret,
'Fox's triumph was lost, its purpose unmet.
And still the tale does not conclude—
For others would come, some foolish—some shrewd.'"

"Shall we take a breath or move onto Bear?" I say, the ghost of a smirk. "I wouldn't want anyone fainting—from excitement. .. or guilt."

"Guilt? In Murder's Vale?" Perrin's laugh is a blade of rusted iron scraping against stone. His tankard crashes onto the ancient oak table, sending ripples through pools of spilled ale. "Less talking, more dying!"

"Patience," I say, raising a hand like a priest at a funeral. "the best murders take time. Rush the job, and it's all blood and no art."

"Art?" The word crawls from the shadows like a dying man's curse. "This tale stinks of ambition and bad decisions from a cast of failures and fools."

Dark laughter slithers ghostly and bitter. Somewhere, a coin spins. Somewhere else, a blade whispers against its sheath.

"Alright, alright." I sigh; my voice dense with feigned defeat. "Finish your drinks. Rehearse your lies. And try not to kill each other before I'm done."

"Get on with it, Nibblenudge!" Rufus bellows.

Another voice yells above the din, a desperate plea wrapped in a command. "Tell us about the Bear!"

"Aye!" A mountain of a man by the fire brings his boot down with enough force to make the floorboards groan. "The Bear! We want to hear about the bloody Bear!"

"It's always the Bear!" Galen throws his arms out, like they're rallying an army, his shadow dancing against the wall like a mad puppeteer's creation.

A market trader's drunken voice cracks like thin ice over deep water. "I can't take the suspense, give us the Bear!"

A chant that builds like a storm at sea. Fists pound rhythmically on tables, boots stamp ancient floorboards, and voices merge into a single demanding roar—"BEAR! BEAR! BEAR! BEAR!"

I raise my hands in mock surrender, playing at being overwhelmed by their howling hunger for blood and story. "Alright, alright!" My voice cleaves their thunderous demands, like a headsman's axe. Noise subsides to a subdued growl, broken only by scattered jeers and half-formed insults. Firelight catches my expression as I lean forward.

"... let's talk about the Bear."

The room freezes, the silence broken only by the gentle sway of drunkards on their weathered stools. I let the moment stretch, tasting the anticipation like aged wine. "Now, where was I?" The firelight catches the edges of my smile. "Ah yes…

Owl puffed her chest, her voice now stern.
'Now hear of Bear, and the lesson we'll learn.

The Knight Who Couldn't

Soon came Bear, a knight so proud,
a fierce booming voice,—both brash and loud.
"Fox was too subtle, Snake far too keen,
I'll make my message bold for all to be seen."

And so Bear marched, its plan a display—
But where strength lacks cunning, plans go astray...
"With honour and might, I'll strike with my blade,
a message of rebellion will surely be made."
But even Bear, with strength, honour and flair,
knew the king must be weakened, caught unaware.

So it brewed a concoction, reckless and bold,
'A poison will do,' it stubbornly told.
But herbs are no sword, no armour, no shield—
and its ham-fisted brew saw disaster revealed.

Spider, a thief with a hunger so great,
stole the king's meal before it met fate.
Bear, unaware, donned in its plate,
climbed to the chamber, at an hour most late.

The king, alerted, was ready and keen,
to face the intruder who dared such a scene.
Caught off guard, Bear met its match—
The king threw a ledger, a cake and an axe.

Defeated and shamed, its blade cast aside,
it left as the king's servant, its honour denied.'

Owl sighed, her feathers aflame,
'Strength without cunning will tarnish your name.
Bear's rigid ways led to its fall—
For one to succeed, adapting is all.'

"Strength without cunning," I mutter. "The Bear isn't the only fool in the room tonight." It's time to see if we have any others. Someone snorts from the corner—a sound too loud to be accidental. A chair scrapes. The rest hold their silence. "Let's see who the Owl has to tell us about next…

Monkey and Rat—Where Inept Meets Opportunity

Owl tilted her head, her tone now wry.
'But what of those who neither strength nor wit supply?
Two rogues arose, with a mischievous air—
Monkey and Rat, an unlikely pair.
They dreamed of renown, a name to declare,
but cooperation proved too-much to bear…'

Owl's voice turned playful, yet laced with disdain.
'For here comes a tale of ambition in vain.

"We'll strike the king down!" they boldly proclaimed,
and sought their fortune, their names to be famed.
Monkey, impulsive, declared with a cheer.
"We'll concoct a poison—bring the king near!"

But their brew was a joke, a disaster untold—
They tested their own poison, woke dazed and ice cold.
"Forget the brew," said Rat with a sneer,
"Let's bash him instead—my plan is quite clear."
So they stole a great crest, heavy and bright,
to frame a noble they didn't much like.
"We'll scale the walls and strike him unseen!"
Monkey grinned, its eyes light and keen.

But their climb was clumsy, their entrance too loud—
And the king awoke, the intruders were cowed.
With a roar, the king hurled them both outside,
leaving the crest and plan denied.
They fled through the roads, their tails tucked low—
Their dreams of glory turned quickly to woe.'"

I let Owl's lesson settle like dust in the dim, smoky air. Around me, the Tavern shifts: tankards are lifted. A figure rises from the corner, but they think better of it and slump back down. "Strength without cunning. Reckless ambition," I mutter, turning the words over like a gambler fingering dice. "Seems we've no shortage of fools in these parts."

The Innkeeper shoots me a wary glance as he polishes a glass that's seen better days.

"But I wonder who the Owl has to tell us about next?" I say, sharp enough to draw every curious gaze. The room quiets to a distant storm—low, restless, and waiting.

"Owl tilted her head, her golden eyes gleaming.

'Such reckless ambition, so loudly proclaimed—
But failure can spark a much darker flame.'

Owl leaned forward, her voice softly fed.
'Now hear of Spider, so sleek and so dread.

The Web and the Watcher

Spider watched those rogues run away,
their failure a thread in the web it had lay.
Unlike the others, Spider was still—
a master of patience with a mind for the kill.
It learned from their errors, their flaws, and their fight,
and wove them into a strategy tight..."

As roads fell quiet and shadows grew long,
a watcher stirred—unseen and strong.
A game began—of cunning and dread—
The tale of Spider... or another instead.
Unlike the rest, Spider watched and it learned—
Each failure a lesson, each misstep discerned.

Pig's drunken dreams, a wasteful plight,
Snake's subtle venom, too quiet a fight.

Fox's rebellion, a whisper too small,
Bear's brute force, the loudest to fall.

Monkey and Rat, chaotic and rash—
their foolish ambitions reduced to ash.
But Spider was patient, its web well-spun—
Its plot would succeed where none had yet won.

Through the shadows, Spider crept,
silent and still, while the kingdom it slept.
From Fox, it took the poison's design—
a brew so flawless it gave not a sign.

With Bear's bold moves, it saw what to feign—
to strike from the dark and never explain.
Late one night, with timing precise,
Spider enacted its plan of device.

The king's treatment it switched, sly as could be,
with poison the king that never, he'd see.
And just as the venom began its slow course,
Spider unleashed its most cunning force.

But unseen in the blackest veil of the night,
Shadow watched—cloaked, hidden from sight.
Hidden Shadow, patient and sly,
prepared to act as Spider drew nigh.
Two minds, two plots, now poised to collide—
and the king's end awaited which plan would decide.'

We'll pause for now, but heed my words—Owl will soon once again be heard."

Firelight glints off the expectant eyes fixed on me as I stand waiting for silence to fill the room.

"This isn't just a tale of beasts and folly," I say, my voice carrying the substance of unspoken accusations. "This is the story of Murder's Vale itself—of the beasts that walk among us wearing human skin."

Turning, I meet every eye watching for the telltale flinch of guilt. "They're here now, you know. Watching. Waiting. Can you spot them?" The audience shifts like disturbed water, some leaning forward with predatory interest, others shrinking back into convenient shadows.

Chapter 35

"Listen closely now—the Spider and Shadow have yet to play their final moves.

Owl tilted her head, her voice taut with suspense.
'A clash of cunning in the dark grew immense.

Spiritus Spectat Araneam

Spider spun webs, precise and pristine,
yet Shadow crept—unheard and unseen.
The king, now trembling, his strength stripped away,
lay silent, a pawn in the shadowed ballet.

Spider moved fast, its plan razor sharp—
threads of poison wrapped the king's heart.
But Shadow, relentless, poised for its play,
pulled Spider's strings to capture its prey.

A clash of minds, each waiting its turn,
while deep in the dark, ambition did burn.

As venom wove its deadly control.

*Spider unleashed what would make it now whole.
A dagger, silent, gleamed in the night—
its path deliberate, its message bright.*

*But as it struck, the air seemed to shift—
A whisper of movement, Shadow adrift.
But Spider's fangs gleamed, its triumph complete,
yet whispers of doubt crept under its feet.
For where silence reigns, can it be true—
Did Shadow step back, or did it construe?*

*Next morning, bells sang the king's despair,
and whispers like venom spread fast through the air.*

*The Spider had won, its patience supreme—
Shadow dissolved, unseen, in its scheme.'"*

My fingers trace the rim of my tankard. "The Spider had won, its patience supreme, Shadow dissolved, unseen, in its scheme," I say, letting the rhyme fade to silence.

My gaze sweeps the room, daring anyone to meet it. "But there's something the Spider hadn't accounted for, isn't there?"

I prowl the perimeter of the room. "Stealth and cunning are fine tools indeed, but they're not enough. For the Final Accord, the mastery of misdirection is key. It's not just about spinning a web—it's about making others believe the web isn't there at all."

My lips slide into a predator's smile as I lean forward. "And so, we return to the Owl. Because even the cleverest Spider can find itself tangled in threads of its own design...

The Owl Unmasks the Spider

*The Owl spread her wings, her voice a sharp call.
'The Spider's tale is not quite all.
His plan seemed flawless, his web tightly spun—
But even the clever can come undone.*

The Spider believed his cunning supreme,

his poison untraceable, his dagger a dream.
Yet what he missed in his careful disguise,
was a lesson unseen by his many eyes.'

The Owl, a seeker of truths untold,
had noticed the Spider's precision unfold.

'In the king's chamber, there lingered no scent—
no trace of the poison, no clue where it went.
'Tis strange,' thought Owl, with her sharp, golden gaze,
'A room with no trace can betray its own haze.
For when all is masked, and no scent remains,
what is hidden in shadows is what truth explains.'

The Owl sniffed the air, and her mind did ignite,
she followed the trail of the Spider's sleight.
A web of missteps, invisible yet clear,
 led him straight to the Spider, who cowered in fear.
'You think stealth alone makes your victory sweet,
but the unseeable reveals what lies beneath.
True cunning would leave a trail that misleads—
with traps and distractions to cover your deeds.'

The Spider, now caught, spun no more lies,
for the Owl had seen through his clever disguise.
His tale became more than a triumph well-earned—
A lesson in failure. Another page turned.

Lesson

The Owl clicked her beak, her voice steady and low.
'Even the most cunning can yet meet their foe.
The unseen may shine where no trace should dwell,
and silence can echo its own tale to tell.
True stealth hides not by removing the trail,
but by leading astray those who prevail.
Misdirection and traps are the tools of the wise,
but the greatest deceivers mask also disguise.'"

I stop and savour the way candlelight catches their eyes like diamonds in a murderer's gaze. "Now tell me, my conspiracy of ravens, what drives them to such elaborate regicide? What burning purpose demands such meticulous bloodshed?"

My fingers dance along the ornate dagger's edge, a lover's caress that draws their glances. "This was no drunken mishap, no heat-of-passion folly. This was calculation distilled to its purest form. Architecture of assassination." A deliberate pause as I test the blade's edge with my tongue, eyes gleaming with dark amusement.

"But then, that's hardly news to this audience, is it?"

From the shadows, a wiry woman's voice breaks the quiet—"We thought you were playing the game—dropping the Mayor soon as you arrived, cheeky as a crow!"

"I didn't," another snaps, "I just don't like you."

"Me neither," growls a third, arms crossed like cemetery gates. "Never liked you."

The Innkeeper's laugh carries all the warmth of a gravedigger's joke.

"Nibblenudge, no one likes you. Only reason you're still breathing is because—"

"*Because*—now there's a revelation," I say, interrupting.

I reach for my satchel. "*Because* I could expedite the end of your little game—and deliver the winner."

From the satchel, I grab the cryptic parchments found on the Mayor's desk, and the codex from the cemetery. The codex lands with a bone-jarring thud.

A murmur ripples through the audience.

Chapter 36

"And here we have it, my dear beasts. The Mayor's plans for the Final Accord. The spine of this entire performance. The reason the Mayor had to be murdered—our *motive*. It's all here—his Execution Strategy, Proof Management, Conduct, Competitive Ethics, and Ritual Compliance—every sordid detail accounted for. Ladies and gentlemen, I submit as evidence: Exhibit Five—the Final Accord!"

"Your dear Mayor twisted a simple edict for an election process into a treacherous game—a game of murder and deception where no one is exempt, and no one can refuse. Power doesn't go to the just or the wise here; it belongs to those cunning enough to survive its macabre and devious rules."

My arm sweeps around the room. "Rules that don't just allow the game to be rigged—it demands it. In this twisted contest, nothing matters but controlling perception. The so-called Paradox of Suspicion. Blackmail? Encouraged. Coercion? Expected. Audacity? Rewarded!"

There's a snort from the Innkeeper. "Yeah, we know all that," he says, reaching behind the bar with theatrical nonchalance. He produces a large wooden-framed slate—worn and grim with purpose.

At the top, in bold inked lettering, it's titled *The Suspicion Scoreboard*.

Names are scrawled across its surface in chalk—some expected, some not.

"We take this seriously, Nibblenudge," the Innkeeper says. "The main rules are on the back."

Laughter ripples through the audience. I try not to blink too obviously. Of course, they already had a scoreboard for the Final Accord. Of course, it has the rules on the back. I take a slow breath, smooth my coat, and reclaim the moment.

The Innkeeper flips the scoreboard over, revealing the reverse side—lined with precise script.

"The Rules of Suspicion," he announces.

I step closer, feigning interest rather than disbelief. "Of course," I murmur. "What would institutionalised murder be without a proper framework?"

I scan the rules. "So, it's a masterpiece of contradiction—first, you must bathe yourself in suspicion, then wash it away just in time to emerge unsullied. A game where survival demands both infamy and innocence in equal measure."

Paradox of Suspicion Scoring Rules

(Excerpt from the Contestant Handbook, Section VII-B)

- **Initial Suspicion Score (ISS)**: Entry requires a soul tainted by at least 50% suspicion—lest thou sully the contest. Scores range from 110% (for the magnificently damned) to 0% (for the tediously virtuous).
- **Final Innocence Score (FIS)**: Lo, the game's aim is simple—emerge as the **Least Suspected Contestant (LSC),** wearing innocence like a well-fitted mask.
- **Murder Proof Bonus (MPB)**: Prove thy murders during the **Scoring Window**, and watch thy **FIS** shrink: 50% for the first kill of the contest, 25% for each encore.
- **Endgame**: When the **Contest Window** doth close, the **LSC** shall stand victorious and ascend as the new ruler of Murder's Vale. Please consult the terms of conditions to resolve ties.

Subsection VII-B Rules
(Execution Strategy, Proof Management, & Conduct)

VII-B.1   With each murder, thy risk of suspicion grows, and thy **Final Innocence Score (FIS)** riseth likewise. Choose thy deeds with care.

VII-B.2   Thou shalt not murder other contestants.

VII-B.3   Proving another's guilt may rid thee of rivals, yet it's perilous. Should a murder remain unproven, suspicion may fall upon thee instead.

VII-B.4   Should thou deceive too boldly, or play thy schemes o'ermuch, thou may find thy **FIS** increased for thy folly.

VII-B.5   On contest closure, further murders shall not be counted.

VII-B.6   Once the **MPB** hath been assessed and a new Mayor declared. That Mayor shall be henceforth immune to actual or attempted murder.

VII-B.7   The elected Mayor is likewise immune to Blood Balance murder; for rulership, once earned, shall not be undone by vengeance clothed in ritual.

VII-B.8   Breaches of these rules are contempt and those found in breach will be executed.

I close my eyes for a moment, letting the absurdity settle like dust in the lungs. It's not a game—it's a ritualised farce, varnished in bureaucracy and sharpened to a point. And yet, here we are. The rules are written. The game is in play. I turn back to the slate and let my eyes drift over the names.

"And now, dear beasts... the masks come off."

I step closer, noting the names scrawled across the wood—including mine.

"Well now," I say, "isn't this interesting? Did I miss the part where I signed up, or is participation compulsory?" My fingers drum on the scoreboard. "Good work everyone, I see every creature is accounted for. I trust the suspects have found their reflections in the tale?"

With theatrical care, I lower the blade and tap it against the slate. "Let's dissect this little autopsy of suspicion, shall we?

"Ulric holds the title of Least Suspected Contestant—twenty-seven percent Final Innocence Score. His genial bumbling kept you all distracted. I doubt he bashed his own head in to win—there's a 'no dead winners' clause for that."

"But look at our rising star—Ruthenia. As poised as she is poisonous, she sits comfortably in second at thirty-seven percent. And that's without Murder Proof Bonuses. Should she claim both the Mayor and one other? Her score drops to a devastating thirteen-point-nine. Nearly untouchable. Convenient—Ulric out of the running? And with Galen trailing her at thirty-nine, the crown's nearly within reach."

I let the blade trace a slow arc over the rest of the slate. "Then there's Rufus, holding steady at forty-two. Too bland to suspect, too bland to trust. Drusilla at fifty-eight, dripping just enough eccentricity to keep her visible. Milton at seventy-three—though he's working hard to pass it off as confidence rather than guilt. Roderick at seventy-five, which might be the first time in his life he's scored higher than anyone else in the room."

I pause at my own name. "And me? A healthy, damning seventy percent. Not quite the hero of the piece. Not quite innocent. But at least I'm honest about it."

"And that, my friends, is where we stand. The board doesn't lie. Ruthenia's played this game beautifully, but has she played it too well? Murder Proof Bonus changes everything. Perception is reality's puppet master."

The ornate dagger dances between my fingers, catching firelight like captured stars. "Now who claims the MPBs?" The question dangles like a hanged man.

"Save your breath, Nibblenudge," the Innkeeper shouts, carrying the potency of ancient wisdom, "they're all too wise to fall for that. Murder Proof Bonus can't be claimed until the game's over. Anyone who deliberately or accidentally reveals their own evidence of murder before the contest closes will be eliminated."

"Quite so," I say, injecting steel into silk. "Self-elimination before the murderer's unveiling would be tragically premature. Yet nobody wants their Final Innocence Score bloating at the eleventh hour. They're dancing on a razor's edge, balancing suspicion against survival."

The room crackles with excitement. Every breath holds secrets, every glance calculates odds. "Well then," I say, my tone laced with amusement, "it seems our little performance has another act to unfold."

A collective groan ripples through the Tavern. They're waiting for me to continue—to deliver the first murderer, their impatience a palpable force against my restraint. "The murder of Mayor Crumley," I say, each word sharp as winter frost, "wasn't some clumsy dance between desperate accomplices. It wasn't vengeance's bitter child or opportunity's bastard offspring. No, this was control distilled into its purest form: calculated, precise, and devastating. Tonight, we'll discover whose hand conducted this macabre symphony of blade and venom." My words settle. I continue steady and deliberate.

"Consider this a masterclass in methodical slaughter, where every detail performs its grim ballet with purpose. The poison and the dagger—twin instruments in death's orchestra, each playing its part in perfect time."

"Picture our dear Mayor, hunched over his desk like a gargoyle at prayer, working late as was his wont. Then enters someone—trusted or, at least, unsuspected—bearing a gift: a simple mint-flavoured morsel, innocent as a child's smile." The small beech evidence box feels heavy with secrets as I lift it.

"The poison began its insidious waltz, subtle at first but swift enough to render our victim helpless—yet slow enough to ensure he'd feel the blade's final kiss." Setting down the box, I take up the ornate dagger, its edge catching torchlight like a metallic smile.

"Then came steel's whispered conclusion. The killer stood behind him, precise as a surgeon, cruel as fate. No struggle, no last-moment revelation—just the quiet punctuation of a life's final sentence." The revelation leaves the room in silent appreciation.

"This wasn't chance playing its fickle game. This was orchestration, a message written in blood. But that dagger—for all its theatrics, became the killer's undoing."

Turning to face the audience, I announce, "Now we'll dissect this puzzle, peeling back layers of deception, like skin from a rotting fruit. Let us begin our Systematic Examination of Suspects."

The door slams open, wind and rain snake in like eavesdroppers. A ghostly hush falls, breath held between the tension of suspicion and the familiar crackle of anger.

"Shut the damn door, you great oaf!" the Innkeeper roars from the bar, just as a hunk of stale bread sails through the air, missing its mark but making its displeasure known.

"Dragging half that damn weather in with you," another voice snarls, as a damp rag—of questionable origin—slaps wetly against the threshold.

The butcher stands silhouetted in the doorway, soaked and streaked with fresh blood, apron clinging to him like a butchered second skin. A cleaver dangles from one hand, glistening in the low firelight, and his boots leave meaty smears on the floorboards as he steps inside. He grunts something, then kicks the door shut behind him with a wet squelch.

Inside, warmth clings to the fire, resisting the damp air curling under doorframes and licking at boots. The Tavern exhales its collective irritation—muttering, shuffling—as the butcher lumbers across the room, trailing a stench of raw meat and old rain, the violence of a dozen glares settling on him like a second coat.

The Innkeeper heaves himself up from behind the bar, his meaty fist slamming against scarred oak. "QUIET!" The word booms through the common room like a thunderclap, and the murmuring audience falls into an uneasy silence. Pipe smoke hangs motionless in the sudden stillness. He turns toward me, jowls quivering with rage. "Now then, you twisted little fortune-teller. You've had us dancing to your tune all evening with your riddles. Some of us have graves to dig come morning."

My hand raises commanding patience. "Fear not, we are close." Taking centre stage, I say, "But to name the killer, we must first untangle the threads binding each suspect to this crime. So let us begin, one by one."

"Drusilla Hobbert, our Mistress of Shadows, whose herbs dance the razor's edge between healing and harm. She works in twilight's embrace, where medicine and murder share the same bed. In Murder's Vale, even salvation wears poison's mask."

Drusilla snorts softly. She turns her head to her sister who raises a single brow.

"Yet why complicate elegant toxins with crude steel? If Drusilla sought the Mayor's end, her poisons would have sung solo." My attention shifts to Moondrop, half-hidden in shadow's embrace.

"Ruthenia Hobbert—Moondrop the Light Weaver. She trades in riddles and shadows, her games cruel as a cat with a dying mouse. Her mind cuts sharper than any blade—but does she weave chaos for sport, or something darker still?" "Like her sister, why would she sully a perfect poison with steel's crude signature?"

Shifting my attention to our resident knight, I find Sir Roderick's face twisted between indignation and fury. "Sir Roderick Highgrove—a man whose honour has grown tarnished, weighted by secrets that would break lesser men. Your loyalty drifts like morning mist—ephemeral, deceptive, and quick to vanish when dawn's heat strikes." A man of Sir Roderick's ilk feeds on honour like others feed on bread. His arrogance is a storm cloud fat with fury, ready to drench the dry field of his ego in thunderous outrage.

The dagger might suit his martial sensibilities, but poison? That's the domain of shadow-dancers and whispered plots. Asking Sir Roderick to orchestrate such intricate machinations would be like expecting a battering ram to pick a lock. His way blazes straight as an arrow, brutal as a siege engine—all thunder and fury, nothing of the serpent's subtle strike.

I turn now toward where Milton Ledbury stands. "Milton Ledbury, our dear Scribe of Secrets. Silent as a tomb until silence serves him ill—yet in that quiet, his ears feast on every whispered confession." My steps carry me closer to him, each footfall matching the rhythm of mounting cognisance. "Your ledgers aren't the only scrolls you keep, are they, Milton? You're a puppet master who never shows his strings; the hand that ensures every coin finds its proper pocket in the Mayor's collections." Milton doesn't speak. But one hand lifts—slow, deliberate—to adjust his spectacles, though they haven't slipped.

"Consider Ulric Plenkovic," my voice softening like a blade being sheathed, "our Lost Lyricist whose songs once soared with joy. Friend to many, yet perhaps puppet to powers unseen? Did he sing one verse too many?"

I sweep my hand toward the fire, where Rufus Hedgerow watches with narrowed eyes. "Rufus Hedgerow, the Ever-Loyal Hound. You circle our gathering like a wolf circles prey. What desperate measures might you take to protect your chosen pack?" He spits into the fire. The hiss that follows is the only answer I get.

"And Galen Twilthorne, our Wandering Void. You are neither here nor there, a figure of convenience with no substance or character, yet always present. But shadows can hide daggers as easily as dust, can't they?" Galen's mouth opens, then shuts again. He fiddles with the hem of his sleeve.

"There's one last piece of evidence to discuss. Exhibit four: the sworn testimony of our illustrious Sir Roderick and the ever-observant Milton regarding that confounding account of the scene that night."

"They claim to have heard departing footsteps but never approaching ones. Curious, isn't it? Your account suggests a killer who materialises like morning dew, strikes with redundant efficiency, then strides bold as brass past the treasury quarters unseen and without a trace." My voice crosses the smoky air.

"What strains credibility more? A supernatural assassin with a flair for the theatrical? Or Sir Roderick, conveniently positioned, sending Milton on a fool's errand before executing his masterful plan? Your testimony crumbles faster than day-old bread, Sir Roderick." I pause, letting the weight of expectation hang. "And yet... I submit you are not our killer. Poison is a delicate art. You, sir, are a stumbling fool."

With an unnecessary flourish, I let my arm drift in a slow arc around the room. "Can any of you conjure the image? Sir Roderick, our blunt instrument of justice, gracefully brewing mint-scented death? Picture him tiptoeing through corridors like a cat burglar, slipping past Milton's door to deliver his poisoned pleasantries and precise blade work. Speak now if such a scene doesn't strain sanity itself!"

"No? Neither can I." I step back from our humiliated knight, my focus sweeping the room like a scythe through wheat until it finds its true target.

"And what of you?" I ask. Looking at Milton. "You who stand at the edges, half-hidden in shadow's embrace. The one who hides in plain sight. The man who holds every secret but never speaks a word too many. Milton Ledbury. Keeper of ledgers, listener of whispers, orchestrator of silences."

Each footfall echoes like an executioner's drumbeat as I advance toward Milton. "You've been content to lurk in the margins of everyone else's story—meticulously noting each debt, each secret. Well, tonight is your debut. Care to explain how your 'records' always keep you one step ahead while leaving everyone else in the dark?" Milton shifts his weight, his stare remains unwavering, a fortress of calm.

"A minty poison, an ornate dagger left like a piece of theatre—is it the work of subtle herbalists or an enraged knight?" My gaze slides to him like a blade finding its mark. "Your name, Milton, keeps surfacing from these murky depths. If it were poison alone, we'd look to Drusilla or Ruthenia. A dagger might point us toward Rufus, Galen or our own Sir Roderick. But both? That's not redundancy—that's architecture."

The Tavern's silence deepens, cumbersome in its dawning comprehension.

"We're hunting someone who wanted not only the Mayor dead—they wanted us all dancing to their tune, chasing shadows while they pulled the strings. This is all about the game now. Play it successfully and gain the seat of power. And who better to orchestrate such a performance than the man who holds everyone's secrets?" I let my voice rise, summoning the prophecy delivered by the enigmatic Owl:

"The unseen may shine where no trace should dwell,
and silence can echo its own tale to tell.
True stealth hides not by removing the trail,
but by leading astray those who prevail.
Misdirection and traps are the tools of the wise,
but the greatest deceivers mask also disguise."

My hand finds the small table where I've arranged our evidence like artefacts in a museum of betrayal: the beech box still reeking of mint-laced death, and beside it, the ornate dagger that screams of theatrics. "The mint was clever—making deadly poison masquerade as the Mayor's familiar stomach remedy. You knew his habits, his treatments, the perfect trojan horse for your venom. It screams 'herbalist!' doesn't it? Except our herb-women never needed steel to do their work." A hollow sound punctuates my words as I tap the ornate dagger's hilt.

"Only someone obsessed with narrative would use both blade and poison when either would suffice. It's the mark of someone who understands how symbols shape perception, how stories can be weapons sharper than any blade."

The audience's murmuring builds like a gathering storm.

"Was it power you wanted? Or revenge against a Mayor who treated you like furniture? The Owl's warning rings true—the surest way to remain unseen is to lead others astray. Something you were unaccustomed to—the art of misdirection."

My palm crashes against the table, making the evidence dance. "So tell us, Scribe of Secrets—did you think we wouldn't see through the performance?"

The silence that follows feels like a held breath. I meet his gaze, two predators circling.

"This is your finale, Milton. Every ledger, every deliberately placed clue—all in your own meticulous hand."

I step back, addressing our audience of schemers and suspects. "You all want a killer whose motive rings true?"

I lift the dagger box like a priest holding a holy relic. The carvings catch the torchlight: an eagle frozen in eternal flight, a bear perched in an impossible tree, an anvil crowned by flame. Murmurs build into sounds of recognition as the audience examines it.

"These symbols—they aren't random. They aren't decoration. They match the carvings above Milton's door. The eagle, the bear, the anvil—his lineage, stamped onto the very box that carried death."

"This is pride speaking—Milton's pride in his plan, his heritage, and the murder he claims as his masterpiece. A calling card from a scribe who's tired of writing other people's stories."

Drusilla and Moondrop exchange glances. Sir Roderick's scowl deepens, his crossed arms.

"He knows the rules of the Final Accord better than anyone—knows that proof of murder paves the road to power. Milton's own crest is his claim to the throne. Once proven guilty, the Contest Window closes, granting him the Murder Proof Bonus when tomorrow's sun rises. If he can tie Ulric's death to himself by then... well, we all know who'll be writing the Vale's next chapter."

"Every piece is placed with precision. And the box ties him, by name and by blood, to this brutal plot, just as he planned."

Chairs scrape against wood as villagers rise, their uncertainty painting shadows across their faces. Milton stands like an oak in a storm, unmoved, but there's something off—his composure isn't triumph, nor is it defeat. It's calculation. He's measuring how the story unfolds.

A surge of something—fury, inevitability, judgement—rips through me. My body twists as if wrenched by unseen hands, my arm sweeping through the air. When it stills, my finger is a dagger, levelled straight at Milton. "Behold the architect of this web of mint, steel and misdirection..."

"You wanted us tangled in your web, chasing ghosts while you moved unseen. But the web is broken now, Milton. And you're the only one caught in it.

BEHOLD THE SPIDER!"

The Tavern's atmosphere congeals like blood on a blade.

My hand raises for silence, my focus locked on Milton. "There's your truth, served cold as tavern ale. Milton's message rings clear as a funeral bell—his grab for power, his manipulation of you all. And yet the dance isn't over. If someone claims Ulric's murder before dusk tomorrow, then our story might yet take an unexpected turn."

The Innkeeper steps in. "Aye, all very convincing, but it only sticks if someone has proof—the MPB. Milton must provide that by tomorrow. If you're wrong, Nibblenudge, then someone else must provide evidence. Otherwise, this contest isn't over and it'll get messy."

"Messy?" I ask.

"Last one standing," he says.

The audience purrs. Ulric's killer remains unnamed, leaving Murder's Vale teetering on the edge of decision. Milton stands poised to seize the crown—if he has evidence he murdered the Mayor, he'll earn the full fifty percent Murder Proof Bonus, dropping his score from seventy-three to thirty-six-point-five. It would make him the frontrunner.

But it's not over. Ruthenia, Galen, even Rufus—they're all within striking distance. If any of them can prove a separate murder, their own scores could fall beneath Milton's.

A final hush descends—faces painted with emotions ranging from amused to murderous. I draw a slow breath, letting the night's weight slide from my shoulders like a worn cloak. When I speak again, my voice carries quiet certainty

"Both Ulric and the Mayor are gone, and nothing will bring them back. But at least we know the truth—and that matters."

I gather the evidence into my satchel. Anticipation hums like a plucked bowstring as I move toward the door. The Innkeeper's voice booms through the space like a herald's call—"The contest closes today, subject to Murder Proof Bonus review tomorrow, mind the rules of the Final Accord - further murders will not be counted, with Milton as Least Suspected Contestant! Tomorrow brings the Murder Proof Bonus claims—and Ulric's funeral. I expect to see every face there."

The door swings shut behind me with a hollow clap, sealing in the Tavern's warmth. The game isn't over. Not yet.

Chapter 37

Morning, Seventh Day of Widders

The weather unleashes its full wrath. It feels personal now. I brace against the storm, feeling its weight like a physical blow. Morning light, what little pierces this apocalyptic veil, stains the world in shades of bruised yellow and sickly green. It creeps across the village like jaundice, turning familiar buildings into looming spectres and casting shadows that breathe. Gutters gurgle and choke, overwhelmed by the deluge, while thunder rolls across the valley like the laughter of an unhinged god. Even the Library, so proud against the sky, appears to cower beneath nature's onslaught, its weathervane spinning in frantic circles as if trying to point the way to salvation.

Nine days since we lowered the Mayor into the ground, and already, the Cemetery has grown fatter with grief. Amid the tempest's fury, the villagers converge in the Cemetery with a hush that borders on reverent.

We lay poor Ulric to rest—some with disappointment etched into their faces, others drawn by curiosity. Thunder shudders across the heavens, its echo thrumming in our chests as we brace for yet another funeral that may refuse the simple dignity of staying buried in this storm-ravaged Vale. Ulric was a man who had never planned for this final moment but had nonetheless arrived at it.

The undertaker stands off to one side, surveying the scene with indifference. At the grave, ready to preside with forced composure, stands the vicar. He tugs at his dark robes, radiating all the optimism of a man awaiting his own execution.

Milton's audacious claim to the Mayor's murder ripples through the assembly like poison in a well. Some trade meaningful glances: others whisper behind cupped hands while the man himself poses like a preening predator—chin lifted, arms crossed, daring anyone to challenge his boast. The debate still rages whether he has the backbone for such a deed or merely claiming credit.

I maintain my post near a tilting headstone and nod to those prepared to meet my eye, but mostly I watch how Milton's declaration settles into the Vale's already fractured social fabric.

"Ruthenia's nearly got the Final Innocence Score," a redhead mumbles. "Ulric's murder would clinch it for her."

Another voice joins the chorus—"Milton's insufferable, but Moondrop terrifies me."

The observation sends shivers through the nearby mourners. "I'm sure it could be worse," I say.

I turn my attention to the other contestants in our ongoing game of murder and manners. Sir Roderick Highgrove's plate armour catches what little light dares show its face, the effect more reminiscent of a funeral urn than anything martial. He clutches a halberd like it's the last friend he has in the world—perhaps a reasonable precaution after last night's tavern excitement.

Drusilla Hobbert wraps herself in shadows and smugness, her raven-black cloak matching her soul's hue. She studies the undertaker and vicar like a cat, studying wounded birds, no doubt calculating how to snatch Milton's crown for herself.

Moondrop floats about in her usual costume of herbs and mysteries, scattering dried leaves around the grave while muttering what could be prayers or curses—with her, the difference is academic at best.

"What a tiresome parade," Drusilla drawls, her gaze sliding toward Milton like a knife seeking flesh. Her patience, I note, has grown thinner than a pauper's soup—watery, fleeting, and unlikely to satiate for long.

Sir Roderick shoots her a stern glance. "This is a funeral, not a beauty contest," he says stiffly.

The vicar clears his throat like he's dislodging yesterday's sins, raising arms sombre with ceremony and resignation. His eulogy crawls forth—"Friends, villagers and various interested parties gathered to witness Ulric Plenkovic's commitment to the earth. We assemble in this grey morning to bid farewell to a man who, while perhaps not our most distinguished citizen, nevertheless walked Murder's Vale's twisted paths and contributed his own peculiar verses to our collective dignity."

Someone chokes back a laugh.

A roaring wind all but drowns out the vicar's solemn words, forcing mourners to lean in, hoods drawn tight, as if the sky itself would rather they not hear these last rites. The vicar soldiers on, his voice thick with the same insincere solemnity he delivered for our dear departed Mayor. "May our friend Ulric find in death the peace that proved so elusive in life, free from his various... afflictions and entanglements."

This draws several knowing snickers from those who'd watched Ulric's determined campaign to empty every barrel in the Vale. Meanwhile, the vicar performs a routine with holy water from a tarnished vessel.

Drusilla's eyes roll like dice in a rigged game, while Moondrop, taking no chances, scatters her own handful of vervain. The undertaker, his coat wearing more mud than fabric, maintains his professional squint while thumbing through a ledger that's equal parts accounting book and prophecy—tracking expenses, wages and the community's steady march toward the grave.

I walk over to him. "You look glum," I say.

He shrugs. "It's the runners. Messy business when they decide the grave's not to their liking. Hard to poke 'em back in once they've wriggled out, the blighters."

My hand finds a roasted pigeon in my satchel, its legs splayed out like it had tried to fly and given up. The bird is greasy, its skin wrinkled.

The undertaker recoils the moment he sees it. "You shouldn't eat that here," he says, "food attracts the runners."

I ignore him, biting into the wing with enthusiasm. A small crack signals the bone snapping, and I gnaw on it before spitting the splintered remains onto the floor.

His eyes flick toward Ulric's grave. "No two-for-one special this time around, I hope?"

"Not for Ulric, he was my friend," I say, studying the coffin with the intensity of an artist examining his masterpiece.

Pigeon juice runs down my fingers as my teeth rip into the breast meat, chunks of it hanging precariously from my mouth. "You want some?" I say, thrusting the bird toward him. A leg falls off and lands on the ground with a wet thud.

The undertaker's sigh carries the weight of professional appreciation. "Looking after the dead, that's a kindness, what you've done."

I shrug, tearing into the remaining bits until the pigeon is nothing more than bones and cartilage.

"I hope your friend finds his accommodation suitable today. We have extra hands for the burials this afternoon…" He points to his new hires—four agile chasers.

The vicar's sermon exhausts itself, and the designated pallbearers—faces set with grim determination—begin lowering his box into its earthen embrace. The ropes protest with ominous creaks, sending nervous tremors through those who witnessed Mayor Crumley's rather more dramatic descent. This time, at least, the wood holds its secrets.

Above the Cemetery, the storm howls like a pitiless judge, lashing the iron fence with stinging rain. Gusts tear across the gravestones, ripping damp leaves from the sparse trees and flinging them against mossy marble. Muddy water pools around the fresh grave, threatening to undermine the hollow ground where Ulric's coffin rests.

After a last prayer that sounds more like a desperate negotiation with whatever powers might be listening, the audience begins to disperse, still buzzing with theories about his untimely exit. A few mourners perform their obligatory dirt-tossing ritual, though their hearts clearly aren't in it. Soon only three of us remain: myself, Sir Roderick with his beloved halberd, and the ever-patient undertaker.

"I gather Milton's chains might be loosening?" I say.

Sir Roderick plants his weapon like a flag of surrender. "That rather depends on you now, doesn't it?"

"He'd do well to watch his back," I say.

"Well, the contest isn't over yet," Sir Roderick observes, a grim set to his jaw.

"True enough, though killing Milton won't improve anyone's score now," I note, watching his face sour at the thought of returning to Milton's dominion.

We turn to leave, but the undertaker's throat-clearing stops us. "Just a moment," he says, voice forceful with expectation. The silence that follows breaks with a muffled thump from below. We exchange looks of surprise. Another sound follows—wood scraping against desperate hands, perhaps a groan of effort.

"Another dissatisfied customer," the undertaker sighs.

A crack like breaking ribs shatters the silence. Then—a hand, pale and clawing, tears through the pine. Mud sucks at the fingers as they twitch and grope, grasping for purchase. For life."

The undertaker's resignation could fill volumes. "Buy cheap, buy twice."

For a few heartbeats, silence reigns. We watch the flailing arm as though appraising an avant-garde spectacle. I step forward, my open hand extending toward Sir Roderick's right arm where the halberd remains locked in his grip.

He doesn't yield.

Another step, closer now. With both hands, I grip it. He resists, then relents. I lower the weapon's tip like a conductor's baton. Below, Ulric's hand plays its part, grasping at steel, seeking purchase, trying to pull himself free. With care, I move the dangerously sharp tip of the blade out of reach. Ulric frantically paws at empty air while more dirt cascades onto his splintered roof, drawing muffled protests from below.

A watchful look passes between the three of us as I drive the halberd down through the cheap pine.

A final muffled gasp "OUCH!"—more surprise than pain—follows by the dull *thud* of acceptance.

The arm goes limp, its performance concluded. Dust rises like applause. We regard the still appendage. With a firm tug the halberd comes free, its blade dressed for a funeral in wood splinters and darker stains.

"That's a shame," I say.

We exchange glances, laden with unspoken understanding.

I return the halberd to Sir Roderick. "Alright then, I'll see you all later."

The undertaker raises a hand, signalling his men over. "Right, lads," he says, "no sense waiting any longer. Cover it up."

As dirt rains onto Ulric's second farewell, we part ways like characters exiting opposite sides of a stage. Another funeral concludes, another body embraces its eternal role, and the Vale's peculiar performance plays on.

The storm still snarls overhead, as though outraged. Gutters overflow, cobblestones slick with water, while the clouds churn in bruised greens and yellows—a threat of more to come.

With Ulric's funeral concluded, the villagers turn their steps toward the Tavern—not for solace, but for what promises to be the final reckoning in the mayoral election, that grotesque theatre of ambition that's left more than one body cooling in the soil.

Chapter 38

Afternoon, Seventh Day of Widders

Villagers arrive at the Tavern one by one, heads ducked against the lashing rain. Wind shoves at their backs impatient. They walk apart—can't blame them. Inside, the Tavern's floor creaks under the weight of accumulated sins. Every eye fixes on me as I join them. Their hunger for spectacle is palpable in the stale air.

The Suspicion Scoreboard now hangs on the wall by the fireplace like a prophecy writ in chalk and blood, ready to crown the next tyrant.

A violent gust rattles the windows, forcing a collective flinch from those inside. The storm wants in—it's not content to howl at walls.

Moondrop stands off to the side, watchful yet composed. Milton struts around the centre. The audience's whispers form a serpentine hiss of anticipation. Sir Roderick and the Undertaker exchange uneasy glances, while the rest of our merry band of suspects wait for the axe to fall—figuratively, for once.

The entire village braces for the final reckoning—mayorless, unmoored, and on the cusp of a new chapter. Will it be one bathed in light, or shadowed in perpetual gloom? Only time—and the deeds of those standing here—will decide.

Milton strides forward, chest puffed with borrowed courage, his 'proof' held aloft like a shield forged from parchment. The candlelight catches the sweat beading on his brow, turning it into a constellation of tiny, nervous daggers. The room tightens around him, breath held, judgment sharpening its knives.

"I did it," he announces to our captive audience. "The Mayor's murder was my masterpiece, and Ulric's murder—that was mine too. Murder Proof Bonus belongs to me," he says with an attempted smile. The audience's disappointment is palpable, but Milton ploughs ahead like a man outrunning his own shadow. "Sir Roderick's suspicions were right," he says, each word dripping with self-satisfaction. "I orchestrated the whole thing with his crest. Had Ulric waiting below like a good little pawn, then dropped destiny right on his head. Made it look like our noble knight had done the deed himself."

Surprise ripples through the audience, but Sir Roderick's fury cuts through it like a blade. His sabatons strike a military rhythm as he advances, each step a promise of violence.

"You'll answer for that, Milton!" His hand hovered near his sword; The knight's voice carries enough edge to shave with. Thunder punctuates his words, an untimely and theatrical snarl from the heavens.

Milton's smirk wavers but clings on like the last leaf of autumn. With a defiant tilt of his chin, he says, "Once I'm mayor, you'll learn your place." The words carry more bravado than sense, his temple betraying a nervous sheen.

Sir Roderick's sabatons strike the floor with the slow, deliberate rhythm of a war drum. His voice, when it comes, is a blade unsheathed. 'Not so fast, Milton. You seem awfully eager to claim the throne, but I have a little surprise for you.

He beckons the undertaker over.

"Funny thing about Ulric's death," Sir Roderick says, sharp as a fresh-honed blade, "it didn't quite take." The room tenses like a cat before the pounce as all eyes shift.

The Undertaker steps forward, his face a map of grim revelations. "Aye, in my line of work, you'd think folks would check their victims with more care. We're always burying them twice in this cursed place. He was near enough a runner, if it weren't for—" His words trail off like smoke.

My boots cut through the stagnant hush as I stride forward, each step hammering nails into the evening's coffin. Sir Roderick passes me the halberd. It strikes the floor with a dull, reverberating finality—less a weapon now, more a verdict. I let the silence stretch like a garrotte wire before speaking.

"Do continue, undertaker." My voice carrying just enough threat to make the candlelight colder.

The Undertaker's gaze darts between me and the assembled audience before he commits to his truth. "Ulric near became a runner. Would have, if not for the detective's... intervention."

A ripple of unease spreads like a bloodstain in water. Some villagers edge closer, as if proximity might grant them better understanding. Others retreat, wary now of a conversation that feels too much like a noose tightening around the room.

"It's true," I say, my voice soft, almost amused. "Ulric didn't take to the soil, at first. But now, he does." The admission falls like a guillotine's axe, leaving the audience to grapple how little they understand what has unfolded. The blood on my hands is as thick as the lies in my mouth, staining the air with the metallic taste of betrayal.

Right on cue—lightning flares through the warped glass of the Tavern's windows, illuminating the gathering in stark, unforgiving light—like a last portrait before judgement is passed. Shadows leap and stretch, exaggerating the tension, turning every face into a grotesque mask of doubt, anger, or dawning realisation. The storm watches, listens, waits.

"YOU murdered Ulric?" Milton's voice cracks. "But wasn't he your friend—your only friend?"

"Milton...Milton..." I say, cleaning out my nails with the tip of the ornate dagger. "Is not the first message in *Murder's Prophecy Monthly* thus:

"Ther ben no frendes in Murder's Vale, but folk that han nat yit slain ech other."

I bang the halberd on the floor. "I believe that entitles me to Murder Proof Bonus for Ulric."

The mood shifts faster than a poisoner switching a glass. Sensing his narrative unravel, Milton's confidence crumbles faster than a stale biscuit under a teapot, leaving only crumbs of awkwardness in its wake. Onlookers murmur about who might stand to benefit. Everyone looks to the Suspicion Scoreboard aware that encore murders only get 25% reduction.

The numbers tell their own story: with my claim to Ulric's death casts doubt on whether Milton is the Mayor's killer, meaning he potentially sits at seventy-three percent. I now sit at fifty-two-point-five percent, and Ruthenia could be leading at thirty-seven percent. Gasps follow, sounding like a collective last breath.

Milton's face bleeds of colour, the last embers of his confidence smothered under cold reality. His mouth works around empty words before he finally manages, "This isn't finished."

The audience vibrates with dark anticipation, even as unease settles over them like a burial shroud. The prospect of Moondrop's rule sends shivers down spines that have already weathered so much. Her eyes gleam with composure as she meets Milton's panicked stare. "It would seem," she says, her voice carrying just enough for the room to hear, "that the scales have tipped."

She steps forward, ready to claim her crown—she needs no Murder Proof Bonus as her Final Innocence Score is low enough to win without it.

I raise my hand. "Just a moment please, Moondrop..." My tone is velvet wrapped around a knife's edge, and the room stills as though it already smells the blood on the blade. I have a little surprise for you. You've all been dancing to a tune, oblivious to the hands that held the strings.

And the surprise? There was never any poison. The Mayor's murder was not the work of subtle toxins, but of cold, deliberate steel."

My hand dips into the evidence satchel, emerging with the true instrument of death—the dagger whose ornate hilt collects shadows rather than reflecting light. "This blade," my voice interrupts the confusion like the weapon itself, "was the Mayor's true and only companion in death."

Murmurs swell to exclamations of disbelief. I rotate the ornate dagger, ensuring every eye catches the familiar crest worked into its hilt. Before continuing, my hand reaches under the table and retrieves a clay pot. Removing the lid releases a gamey aroma that pierces the stale air.

"One moment," I say, peering into the pot. The broth is murky, oily, dotted with limp herbs, onion slivers, and—most prominently—a pigeon, its pale, boiled skin clinging to bone. One of the bird's wings floats freely on the surface like a shipwrecked sailor.

Milton's face twists like he's just seen Death pull up a chair. "...pigeon soup?"

Outside, the weather punishes Murder's Vale with Old Testament fury, as if some celestial accountant has realised our sins and dispatched the flood. Steel-grey clouds roil and churn overhead, their bellies swollen with divine wrath, while lightning splits the sky into shards of accusations. Wind howls through empty roads with the voice of a vengeful prophet, rattling windows and tearing at roof tiles with fingers of spite.

"Well, they'd run out of owl," I say, fishing the bird's head out of the pot with my spoon and holding it aloft. The milky white eyes stare back at me, and the beak gapes open as though mid-squawk.

"A delicacy," I say, before letting it *plop* back into the broth with an unceremonious *splash*. I scoop up a ladleful, complete with a floppy chunk of pigeon skin, and *slurp*. The broth is scalding and faintly metallic, but I power through, chewing doggedly on a piece of cartilage. A stray bone finds its way into my mouth, and I spit it onto the floor.

Milton flinches. "You're not going to eat that now, are you?" Milton asks, gesturing weakly to the pot as I extract a wing, still pink, near the joint.

The Innkeeper grunts. "You bring that here? Two silver. And don't get feathers everywhere."

I bite into the pigeon, cracking the thin bone with a sound that echoes the length of the room. I nod, sucking the marrow from the hollowed-out bone and wave my arm to signal there's more.

"Now, where was I?" I say between bites and the quiet satisfaction of a mortician arranging his final masterpiece. "Ah, yes. Putting Ruthenia's lead to the side for the moment, MILTON LEDBURY, you have no legitimate Murder Proof Bonus claim for the Mayor's murder!"

Milton's complexion turns pale.

"The serpent and the rose are my family's mark," I say, gesturing with the spoon for emphasis. A thin string of pigeon fat dangles precariously from its edge.

Comprehension bleeds across the audience's faces like wine on white linen.

"Generations of MacAllisters have held this blade. The dagger box you saw yesterday bearing Milton's family marks was a subterfuge for the game."

As Mrs Sibberidge steps forward with the dagger box, I extract the bird's head from the pot, its boiled eyes staring lifelessly at the room. I wave it casually at Milton before dropping it back into the broth with a wet *plop*. He recoils.

She cradles the box in her trembling hands like a dark sacrament. Her voice, firm, "This box was donated to the library by Milton's grandfather. Milton's box didn't kill the Mayor—it was the MacAllister dagger."

Wind slams against the Tavern. A bolt of lightning slashes the sky, its timing impeccable, casting the dagger into brief, stark brilliance before plunging it back into shadow. The hilt swallows the light greedily, refusing to give any back.

Another spoonful of the soup produces something unidentifiable—a gristly chunk that might be neck, though it could be tail. I fish it out with my fingers and bite straight in, tearing it loose with a grunt.

"Guess what?"

"I think you have all forgotten the Owl's story on the Spider and the Shadow," I say, licking juice from my knuckles.

A few heads turn. Chairs creak. The fire gives a small, obliging *pop*.

Remember the Owl's verse on *Spiritus Spectat Araneam?* I ask. "The spirit—or should we say, the Shadow—watches the Spider."

Now they're listening. Of course they are. Stories are the only currency left when truth has gone bankrupt.

"We spent so much time unpicking the Spider's web—who poisoned whom, who stood to gain—yet not one of you asked about the Shadow."

I pause, holding the room in the cradle of my silence.

"*Did Shadow step back... or did it construe?*"

A few mouths part. One man sets down his tankard with a soft clunk.

"Spider's plans were neat. Razor-sharp. But sometimes the neatest threads are the ones someone else wants you to follow."

A hush settles in.

"We hunted the Spider." I pace like a caged predator. "We tore through ledgers and alibis, measuring motives like an alchemist on judgment day."

I stop abruptly, leaning forward, letting the firelight catch the hollows of my face—casting demonic shadows that twitch with every crackling ember.

"But the Shadow never left the stage. You just weren't looking."

A hush drops like a shroud—thick, expectant.

"I know you all." My voice falls to a whisper, yet it carries—sharp and cold, touching every corner of the room. "I know you all. I've watched. I've waited. My friends..." The pause is surgical.

"I am the Shadow."

A murmur ripples through the room like a sickness—contagious, inevitable. Faces twist as the truth lands: quiet, final, undeniable.

"The Mayor's murder was my handiwork. The poison narrative? A whimsical distraction. And Ulric?" I let the name hang in the air like a condemned man. "His sacrifice was necessary to ensure my Final Innocence Score is low enough to deny Ruthenia."

I pause, using a broken bone to dig out some of the meat between my teeth.

The room waits.

Milton shifts in his seat like a man realising the floor beneath him has vanished. His eyes flicker from the soup to the dagger, then to me, searching for something—anything—that makes sense. Then he cracks. "How?" His voice is sharp, brittle, like it's been pried loose from the silence against his will. Perhaps he's contemplating the foolishness of blackmail and stealing my inheritance.

"Remember hunting for the deeds on the night of the Mayor's murder?" I let the words hang in the stale tavern air while I finish the pot. "You and Sir Roderick, plotting to take my inheritance—do you remember that night?"

Milton stares at me. His voice, when it comes, is barely a whisper. "...You were in the Manor House?"

I lean back, letting the room hang on the tension. "Reaching the Mayor required artistry..."

"I think I'm going to be sick?" Milton says.

"Let me paint you a picture," I say.

***

Feeling replete, I settle back into my role as storyteller. I hand my satchel to Sir Roderick for safekeeping and begin. "I returned to settle the affairs of MacAllister Hall—not to embark on a murder spree. Then the Mayor turns up at my doorstep, dragging behind him that nasty old crone who'd spent the journey to Murder's Vale pecking at me with her viper's tongue." My jaw tightens at the memory.

"He came to talk business—buying the Hall for her. She's his aunt—but his true purpose seeped through, rank with something fouler. This wasn't a purchase; it was an erasure. Burn it to the ground. Cage his deranged aunt in the ashes. After they left, I pondered for a moment. That's when I knew what had to be done."

My voice rises like thunder gathering force. "I came here with simple intentions: secure my inheritance, sell the Hall to the Mayor, pocket the coin. But she—" I pause, letting bitterness seep into each word, "I don't appreciate being spoken to like that."

Murmurs of agreement guggle through the Tavern like dark water. The villagers nod, their faces masks of complicit understanding. A gust of wind forces its way down the Tavern's chimney, setting the flames to a brief, frenzied dance.

"The other complication was the arrival of the new deputy bailiff. That returned the Blood Balance back to plus-one."

The Innkeeper speaks up, "You gonna claim Murder Proof Bonus for the aunt, Nibblenudge?"

"Can't really claim it, can I? Not when she was the runner at the Mayor's funeral." I smirk.

A ripple of dark amusement moves through the room.

The fire flickers. The wind howls through the chimney like distant laughter.

Perrin's fist bangs on his table with the finality of a judge's gavel. His stern regard pierces the chamber's thick atmosphere to skewer Sir Roderick and Milton where they stand. The two self-appointed guardians of justice now like abandoned chess pieces on a board where the game changed without them noticing. "You've not said how you got past these two buffoons to kill the Mayor without the poison."

I pass the halberd back to Sir Roderick. "Reaching the Mayor required artistry. Every floorboard in that place is a betrayer waiting to sing. But in the city, thieves have invented something they call 'socks.' Perfect for stealth. Remove your boots, stick to the sides where the boards are less likely to confess your presence." I give a slow walking motion with my fingers to help them picture the scene. "My sole mistake, if you'll pardon the pun, was putting my boots back on in the study. The Mayor's blood was getting on my socks."

"Look!" I say, yanking off a boot and brandishing the bloodstained sock. The audience's fascination with the simple garment outweighing its crimson stains.

"From outside the study, the Mayor's snoring was all I needed to hear. There he slept, oblivious to the blade waiting behind him. And then he just slumped over his desk, limbs slack—a puppet who hadn't yet realised his strings had been cut. Of course, proper assassination is an art," I say, warming to my subject. "Sliding steel between ribs requires precision, a steady hand, an understanding of anatomy's architecture."

"What about the minty substance in his mouth?" Sir Roderick asks.

"Oh that. Well, he was gasping. Looked like he had something to say. So I popped a mint on his tongue to give him something to do. A common sweet, a gift from the city." I offer the audience mints from my pocket, but there are no takers.

"Of course, What I didn't know was—I'd unwittingly kicked off the Mayor's election process—your Final Accord. And then you lot start blaming me for murdering him. Why? You had no evidence. So, I had to stay, thinking I needed to clear my name." The words taste of bitter irony.

The ornate dagger still rests in my grip like an old friend as I turn toward the Suspicion Scoreboard, that sacred tablet of Murder's Vale's twisted democracy.

"Shall we see how our little performance has played out?"

Lightning splits the sky, illuminating the board for one harrowing second. The chalk numerals glare back, raw and unalterable, as though the storm itself has cast its own tally.

There is no arguing with the elements—nor with the cold arithmetic of murder.

***

The Innkeeper steps forward like a condemned man approaching the gallows. The quill in his thick fingers appears to move of its own accord, crossing out Milton's disqualified score and recalculating the standings with methodical precision.

When he steps back, the result stands stark against the slate—a new name at the summit as Least Suspected Contestant with a score of twenty-four-point-five beating all the other scores that are now stuck at their Final Innocence Score.

MINE.

Ruthenia steps forward with renewed confidence. "Are we to take your word for it that the poison wasn't real? What have you proven, other than your ability to spin a tale?"

"Please, try one of my mints."

She raises her hand against my offer.

I gesture for Sir Roderick to give me the poison evidence box. He walks across and slams it into my chest. I lift the box, letting candlelight dance across its surface. "This," I announce to the assembled villagers, "is what you all believe helped end our dear Mayor's life."

With the casual arrogance of a man flipping a coin he's already weighted, I pour the powder into my mead. The room holds its breath, waiting for the grand finale as liquid slides down my throat. The audience watches in appreciation as my imminent demise unfolds. I stand before them, arms spread wide in a mockery of crucifixion, letting time pass like an executioner's drumbeat. For a moment, all is still—except the storm, which waits, poised, as though considering its final verdict.

The audience's anticipation curdles into disappointment—not because I'm dying, but because I'm not. I am alive. Unharmed. Triumphant. The Tavern groans, resentful and restless, its thirst for spectacle left unquenched. The Innkeeper's face is solemn as he surveys the gathered audience, his expression a masterpiece of resigned acceptance and distaste. His throat clears with the sound of stones shifting in an ancient tomb. "Our rules," he announces, "are our foundation.

Nibblenudge has proven himself the deadliest, the most cunning, a virtuoso of perception's manipulation."

His gaze finds mine, lingers like a guilty conscience, then returns to the audience.

"THIS," he says, voice gathering strength like a storm over dark waters, "is what the Final Accord demands of its Mayor. And that's exactly what it's received."

Discomfort ripples through the assembled villagers like an icy wind through a graveyard, but none dare raise their voice in protest. The twisted logic of Murder's Vale hangs in the air like an executioner's rope—inevitable and final.

Thunder rolls through the valley like the laughter of a long-buried king rising to reclaim his throne, but it's hollow now. The rain does not ease; the wind does not falter—the storm is not done. But it howls now as an outsider, railing against a truth it cannot change.

I give the minty evidence box a sniff of satisfaction.

"The MacAllisters have reclaimed their rightful place," I declare. But as I revel in my triumph, I catch something—just for a moment. Moondrop, watching. And on her face, the faintest flicker of amusement.

Chapter 39

Moondrop lingers at the edge of the gathering. She alone knows what the rest will soon understand—that the final move is already in play. Noel had been so eager to flaunt the harmless poison. Now, at the height of his arrogance, her venom begins its insidious work. Beads of sweat glisten at his temple; his self-satisfied smirk wavers.

"Is... is something the matter?" Milton asks, baffled.

Noel's breath falters mid-sentence. His blink lingers too long, unfocused. Then, like a marionette whose strings have been abruptly jerked, a shudder wracks his frame. Confusion gives way to something sharper, more urgent. Realisation arrives like a blade pressed to the throat—too late to stop the cut.

Noel gags for breath, the colour drains from his cheeks. "Not dead yet," he mutters.

Moondrop steps forward with poise, her chin raised regally. Her attention flicks to Noel's failing form, and a glimmer of satisfaction shines in her eyes. She had allowed him to exalt in his "harmless poison" only to discover, too late, that real toxin lacing his veins.

"He was unsuitable—he was unprepared," she announces to the room, voice carrying like a bell tolling doom.

Eyes turn toward her. Silence gathers, taut and trembling. She does not flinch.

"I watched him wave that box around like a badge of honour," she says, nodding toward the small wooden container still clutched in Noel's limp hand. "Declaring his poison a sham. Dismissing the honour of the craft. Mocking poisoners everywhere. An insult!"

She steps closer to Noel, her features cast in amber shadow, half-oracle, half-executioner. "And so, while he was boasting, I placed some real poison for him to experience—*Bellshade* and *Widow's Breath*—I put it into his precious evidence box. A fatal dose. Silent. Scentless."

The Tavern buzzes at the spectacle. Moondrop exudes a quiet power, regal and unshaken. Her eyes, twin abysses, sweep the room—taking in the villagers who, one by one, straighten beneath her gaze like blades drawn to command. The audience hushes, not out of fear, but reverence—a collective breath held in the presence of a woman who might reshape fate with a whisper. She is strength cloaked in shadow.

"People of Murder's Vale," she says, her voice soft and caressing, yet it carries weight—the kind that shifts the room without raising its volume. "Welcome to a new dawn. You stand before me in the fragile shell of your old lives, clinging to the illusions you've wrapped around yourselves. Here, in our twisted Vale of malevolent creation, I offer you nothing but the unending symphony of your darkest nightmares.

Behold, for you are now in the shadow of oblivion's embrace, amidst the ruins of all you once held dear, where time weeps against the futility of its own passage.

You wretches—led astray by your own betrayals and desires are but moths to the flame of your undoing. You tread, unwitting writers of your own tragic requiem, with neither verse nor end.

Know that the horrors soon to descend upon this place are not mere shadows—they are lords of void, architects of despair, spinning silken threads of a labyrinth your mortal mind shall never escape.

Perceive the visage of what I am.

I am torment, corroding the tongues of mortal folly—unfathomable, orbiting silence as despair incarnate. I now watch over you with eyes older than sin.

Abandon hope of salvation, for your past morality holds no weight; your cries yield nothing. In this dominion, I weave the tapestry of ceaseless brutality, each thread spun from the marrow of your fleeting hopes, until identity itself is eroded into screams lost to vast, echoing futility.

Dreams will dissolve into ash. My words are the dissonant rhapsody of your eternal incarceration.

You shall know only the tightening vice of immeasurable suffering, and in surrender lies your existence—unmade, yet ever beholden to anguish untold. Your every cry is music unto this forsaken Vale, a joy to those that breach the boundaries of this infernal place.

Embrace my rule—not as conquered, but as nothing. Shed the tattered cloak of what once was and descend—plunge into the utter nihilism of your fate."

Moondrop turns, her robes trailing behind her like liquid night. Without another word, she exits the Tavern. The door creaks shut; the sound reverberating like the toll of a distant bell, and with it comes understanding.

A soft rain resumes.

**

From the back of the room, the creak of an old chair lacerates the oppressive quiet, startling a few of the nearest onlookers.

Old Smokey, bent and grey, leans forward, his bony hands trembling as he sets his tankard down with a hollow thud. He clears his throat, the sound dry and rasping, and speaks with a voice like splintered wood, "I'm not sure I really followed much of that."

Perrin leans back. "At least she didn't call us worms. 'Moths' is more dignified."

Movement returns in hesitant shuffles, like a room relearning how to exist.

Noel lies motionless and prone on the floor, a figure of defeat.

Drusilla speaks, her voice cold enough to pickle a fish. "He didn't last long as mayor."

Sir Roderick walks over to his body and gives Noel's leg a kick. "He's not dead."

Everyone stares.

Drusilla joins him, grabs Noel's hair, and lifts his head. "He looks dead. He's gone blue."

"Ah, yes," Sir Roderick muses. "That would be *Little Mimsi*."

Drusilla's expression flickers. "*Little Mimsi*?"

Sir Roderick grunts. "He had a distasteful habit of sniffing the Mayor's head as he lay dead. The mint aroma. So, I knew he'd sniff the evidence box again. Thought I'd give him a taste of what I experienced at your shop."

He gestures toward the small wooden box near Noel's hand. "It seems Moondrop believed I'd handed Nibblenudge the *beech* evidence box from his satchel—the one she laced with poison. She assumed. Assumptions kill more often than blades."

The Innkeeper looks confused. "There's more than one evidence box?"

Sir Roderick smiles thinly. "I used two boxes to collect the poison from the Mayor's tongue, so we both had a sample. The evidence box in Nibblenudge's hand is the *birch* box. The *beech* one should still be in his satchel. The wood's similar enough if you're not looking too hard."

"How did you know to swap them over?" Galen asks.

Sir Roderick kicks Noel again to see if there's any life in him. "That wasn't my plan. But the moment he started crowing about the poison, I knew he'd want it. All I had to do was swap boxes while he preened. The perfect time to teach him a lesson from my *birch* box. The one with *Little Mimsi* dust."

Old Smokey exhales. "So... Moondrop botched it?"

"Indeed." Sir Roderick says, glancing down at Noel.

Rufus exhales hard. "She's in violation of subsection VII-B.6. Attempted murder of a newly elected mayor."

"Which calls for—" Rufus begins.

"—execution!" Drusilla finishes.

Noel shifts on the floor, a groan escaping him like a debt come due.

Outside, the rain turns to mist.

In Murder's Vale, nothing truly dies—except hope.

Printed in Great Britain
by Amazon